Love

Mary Felix

The erotic adventures
of an Edwardian government agent.

Volume One

Published by The Claverham Press Ltd. London.

ISBN 9798839355460

Dedicated to the valiant women
who served in the early years
of the British secret service.

Their country called them,
and they came.
Often repeatedly.

Author's Note

I remember Mary Felix well.

In the 1950s I grew up in a large Victorian villa in a well-to-do area of Exmouth, on the south coast of Devon, England. The house was one of a pair and Mary lived next door, having arrived from London after the war ended in 1945. I think she inherited the property from her parents.

She became friendly with my mother, who had lost her husband, my father, in the late stages of the war and just had me at home. I remember her being an extraordinarily charismatic and beautiful woman, even though she must have been into her sixties by then. She kept a staff of two: a pretty girl called Amy and a strappingly built driver and general factotum called David, both of whom had come from London with her, according to my mother.

I used to enjoy the visits we made to her house very much, and we became firm friends. She was wealthy and exuberant and exuded a level of exotic sophistication and worldly experience which burned brightly in drab post-war Exmouth. I was powerfully drawn to her as I grew older. She had a busy social life, and my mother and I were unashamedly intrigued by the succession of glamorous visitors she entertained. In the evenings her driveway was often occupied by a Bentley or a Rolls Royce and on many occasions it was still there the following morning.

On the morning of my sixteenth birthday, whilst preparations were underway at home for a party in the garden, a note arrived from next door asking me to come around, as Miss Felix wished to give me a present.

When Amy showed me into the expensively furnished salon at the back of the house, Mary was sitting on a settee wearing a dark blue and red Chinese silk robe and looking wonderfully elegant and poised. She smiled and beckoned me over, indicating that I was to sit next to her. I remember the rose-scented perfume she was wearing to this day and occasionally still smell it at parties. It always makes me smile.

She wished me a happy birthday and talked about how I was a young man on the verge of adulthood and a fine handsome fellow and lucky to have my whole life ahead of me, whilst bemoaning her own declining years. I hastened to tell her that both my mother and I thought she was very beautiful. Which was true.

She smiled at this and thanked me before picking up a large envelope.

'Can you keep a secret?' she asked, looking at me with an intensity to her wonderful green eyes that made my heart pound. I assured her very earnestly that I could, and she added that what she was about to give me was to be strictly between ourselves and never to be discussed with anyone else. She put her hand on my thigh whilst saying this, and the pressure of her fingers was very distracting.

‘Have a look,’ she said, smiling, and handed the envelope to me.

I opened it and removed a single black-and-white photograph some six inches by four. I remember both my furious embarrassment and instant arousal as the image of a naked and utterly captivating young woman appeared before me. It was the first time I had seen anything of the kind.

She was standing smiling at the camera, with a double bed and a big wall mirror in the background. Her high, full breasts and large dark nipples caught my eye immediately, but as I stared I realised that a tattoo of some kind of serpent was wrapped around her perfect, lush body, its mouth open and a forked tongue stretching down towards her hairless groin.

‘I wasn’t always old and wrinkled.’

Her quiet voice broke the silence as I stared, transfixed. It was her, of course. Even as she said it, I had realised who I was looking at. ‘Stand up,’ she said, and I complied, my heart beating wildly. ‘This is my present to you. May it be the first of many.’ Sitting forward, she unbuttoned my trousers and gently released me.

‘My word, look at this.’ She laughed delightedly as her hands stroked my achingly hard shaft. ‘I’m going to put it in my mouth now. You can come inside me. Don’t worry, just let it go.’ With that, she took me into her mouth and sucked me off, her hand pumping firmly as I stared down at her bobbing head.

The sensations were exquisite, and I came within half a minute of course, crying out loud as my knees trembled with the intensity of it. But instead of releasing me, she moaned and continued to suck and stroke for some time. Then she leant back onto the settee and pulled her robe open with one hand, and I saw that she was naked underneath. Smiling wickedly, she opened her legs and drew me forward.

With a gasp, I slid into her and, following her whispered instructions, soon established a delicious rhythm. She climaxed quickly with a loud cry, and as she bucked and thrust upwards onto me, I followed suit.

Afterwards we lay together on the settee kissing and talking quietly until she stirred and told me it was time to go home. At the front door, she took my hand and kissed me again before opening it.

'That was the only time, my darling. You are a man now, so remember to keep our secret and go out and find yourself a naughty, pretty girl who will do that with you.' I followed her advice and have adored women ever since.

When Mary died in the mid-1960s she left my mother a large cabin trunk. I think she must have looked inside once and realising the contents, left them well alone. So in due course the chest came to me undisturbed when she herself passed.

The contents were a revelation.

Mary had kept a detailed journal from an early age, and this was supplemented by letters, press cuttings, society invitations, and a mass of other scribbled notes and jottings that, taken together, formed a picture of her extraordinary journey from innkeeper's daughter to skilled secret agent and friend of the highest society in the land.

From these resources she had written a rough and remarkably frank draft of her memoirs. It was complete in some places but with amendments on other pages, and it included various notes about events that had occurred when she was not present.

Even more surprising were the contents of three battered photograph albums at the bottom of the chest. They contained a collection of images, some merely erotic, others pornographic, featuring Mary, the woman I came to know as Georgina, Jimmy, and many others. I counted over two hundred photographs in total, in many of which the participants are labelled.

Finally, packed to one side of the chest was a finely made but worn briefcase that contained a collection of beautifully tooled implements for the delivery of pain and pleasure.

This is Mary Felix's story. I have sometimes updated the language and added or rewritten some pieces to help link the narrative, but the voice is Mary's own, and the events she describes are faithfully reproduced without embellishment.

What a story. What a woman.

F.P.

Somerset, England, 1980

Prologue

Bancroft Hall, Dorsetshire, England.
September 1902.

In the late afternoon of the second day after her arrival at Bancroft, the countess returned from a ride and found me in her sunlit bedroom tidying up, as befits a lady's maid. I noticed she was moving stiffly and enquired as to the problem.

'I almost fell off my horse in the woods on the far side of the lake,' she answered, her slight German accent noticeable in the quiet room. 'He stumbled and I have strained the bottom of my back. It is quite painful.'

'Perhaps a warm bath might soothe it, my lady?' I suggested.

'A bath? Yes, perhaps. Very well, Mary, you may run me a bath,' she replied.

I made another suggestion. 'My previous mistress suffered from back pain and taught me to how use Swiss massage to alleviate it. After your bath I would be happy to treat your back if you like, my lady. It may help to ease the discomfort.' She looked at me as if the implications were running through her mind. I met her eye and smiled innocently.

Finally, she nodded. 'Very well, Mary Felix, do your worst.'

Heart beating faster, I went into the adjoining bathroom and turned on the taps, pouring lavender salts into the water as it started to steam.

When the bath was ready, I walked back into the bedroom to find the countess wearing a beautiful pale blue silk dressing gown. She was standing barefoot at the window looking out over the grounds. Her glorious deep red hair had loosened a little and lay in soft curls over her slim white neck, and the sunlight picked out the curves of her body under the fine fabric in a most delightful way. I had been told she was aged forty, but her extraordinary beauty showed no signs of fading.

She turned and smiled at me, her haughty authority lost for a moment. 'Ready?' she asked.

'Yes, my lady. Would you like me to assist you in the bathroom?'

'No.'

'Then I will go and get the massage oil from my room and return directly.'

She nodded and walked into the bathroom, leaving the door open a foot or so. Seconds later I heard a rustle of silk as the gown fell away, followed by delicate splashing and a muted gasp of pleasure as the hot water engulfed her.

Climbing the stairs to my room on the top floor, my mind was fizzing with excitement. The thought of laying hands on the countess was intoxicating, and I resolved to please her to the best of my abilities. I was also very aware of how such sessions with Georgina sometimes ended, and, although I doubted that she would permit such liberties, the thought sent delicious sensations through my body.

'I'm back, my lady,' I said quietly as I returned with the dark brown bottle in my hand.

There was no reply from the bathroom. I put the bottle on the window ledge to warm in the sun and glanced towards the bathroom door. Through the gap I had a brief glimpse of the countess. She appeared to be dozing, her eyes closed and head leaning back on the rim of the bathtub, but my gaze was held by the sight of her delicious pink nipples protruding from the water. My head swam for a moment, then the vision was gone.

I removed a bath towel from the wardrobe and spread it out on the bed. As I did so, a gentle splashing signalled movement from next door and I heard her say, 'You may come in and dry me.'

I entered the room as she stood up, the water cascading off her like falling diamonds in the late afternoon sunlight. Try as I might, I could not muffle a gasp. Truly, she was a goddess. Lustrous red hair framed her blue-eyed, fine-boned face, and her alabaster-white body was beyond perfection. For a maid, my exclamation was inexcusable, but thankfully she seemed to treat it as a compliment.

'We've no secrets now, Mary,' she said in a low voice.

I did not trust myself to speak but gently towelled her dry, helped her into the dressing gown and then waited as she led the way into the bedroom.

I picked up the bottle of oil.

'If you'd like to lie face down on the towel, my lady,' I said. With her back to me, she silently shrugged off the gown. It slid down her back and crumpled around her feet. I went to pick it up, and when I looked again, she was on the towel, both arms folded upwards and crossed under her face, which was turned away from me. 'I'll start at the top of your back,' I said quietly, standing next to the bed.

Pouring the sun-warmed, rose-scented oil into my cupped palms, I set to work, massaging the base of her neck and shoulders. In the silence, I slowly worked down her spine, taking my time and feeling her tension ease. She gave a couple of quiet sighs and I saw her legs visibly relax and roll slightly further apart as she gave herself in to the soothing sensations.

'Is this helping, my lady? Shall I continue?' I murmured as my hands worked on the base of her spine. Taking her silence as acquiescence, I started to gently knead her buttocks, working with quiet concentration and occasionally easing my fingers into the crack where a dribble of oil lingered. Her legs imperceptibly parted as I continued, so that more and more of her pretty secrets were revealed to me.

Greatly daring, I let some oil dribble down past her rosebud bum. As I slid my fingers down to collect it, she gave the faintest of sighs.

'Will you turn over, my lady?' I whispered, my voice barely audible in the silent room.

She did so with no hesitation and lay there with her eyes closed, looking utterly glorious, one arm crooked behind her head and the other thrown out towards the middle of the bed. I worked the oil through her delicious russet-coloured tuft, letting dribbles run downwards and gently rubbing them in. The oil was not really needed, as she was most luxuriously wet. Clearly intimacy with another woman was not something that held any fears for her, and I reflected, not for the first time, that ladies' secret lives really are a closed book to most gentlemen.

I stroked her sweet upstanding clitty with my thumb and she stirred and sighed again, her legs parting. Then, as her sighs turned to moans and her legs slowly bent at the knee and raised, I firmly slid two fingers from my other hand into her. She gasped as I pressed upwards, feeling for that patch of slightly rougher skin that resides just an inch or two inside. A place of great wonder and pleasure to the initiated.

For a full five minutes I pleasured her with my fingers and thumb. Her groans became deeper and more urgent as her arousal grew. Looking up, I saw her throat and blue-veined breasts were flushed red and she was pulling on her nipples, twisting them between her fingers in a way that must have been deliciously painful.

Not long now. Feeling distinctly aroused myself, I drove her onwards until, with a single plaintive cry of surrender, she spent, her hips jerking upwards and her body held rigid as wave after wave of pleasure broke over her.

Slowly the shuddering spasms quietened until at last she relaxed with a low moan, panting for breath as though she had been running. I looked down on her as the after-tremors ran through her body and wished for all the world that she would ask me to lie naked beside her. But her eyes remained resolutely shut.

I gently drew the coverlet from the far side of the bed over her and moved away, thinking that I would leave her to sleep. But she stirred and opened her eyes.

'Did you enjoy that, Mary? Did you like serving me?' She looked at me with a lazy smile. A sheen of perspiration had dampened her face and a curl stuck to her forehead, but her look was direct and there was challenge in her voice.

'Yes,' I answered simply, meeting her eyes.

My affection must have been apparent, because both her expression and voice softened. 'And you are very good at it too, I must say. Do you favour both men and women?'

'I do, my lady.'

She nodded acceptance at this before continuing. 'As do I. And now, as you have seen me at my most vulnerable, I would like to watch you pleasure yourself, Mary. Remove your clothing and show me.'

'You want to watch me spend, my lady?' I whispered.

She smiled, a delicious combination of authority and desire in her eyes. 'I do, yes. Do it now. On the chaise longue.'

As she sat up and gathered the coverlet around herself, I pulled the seat away from the wall and positioned it parallel to the bed, about six feet away. Standing next to it, I started to unbutton the front of my dark blue uniform dress, turning my back on her as the deep valley of my breasts became obvious. Mirroring her earlier actions with the dressing gown, I shrugged the dress off and let it fall to the floor. The warm weather made underclothes superfluous for servants, so I was left naked but for my neat black laced brogues.

I turned my head and caught a side view of myself framed in a long freestanding mirror. Even now, all those years later, I can still see that image in my mind and can still describe the girl I once was.

I have no time for false modesty. The reflection showed a strikingly beautiful green-eyed girl of medium height, with very pale olive-brown skin. Her hair was glossy and black, with a slight wave and cut unfashionably short, with a fringe and exposed neck. Her figure was curvy but perfectly proportioned, with full, firm breasts and large dark-brown nipples, rounded buttocks, and slim thighs and calves.

In the mirror I could see the narrow coloured band of a snake tattoo an inch wide running horizontally across my ribs at elbow height. The tail commenced just below my left nipple and then slipped under my armpit and across my back. Reappearing under my right arm, it prescribed a bold loop around my tummy button before ending deep on my belly. From its head a long, forked tongue flickered downwards, ending an inch or so above my clitty. For this reason, and because Georgina insisted on it, I shaved myself bare down there.

'Well, well, Mary Felix, what do we have here? A tattoo?' The countess's question interrupted my reverie.

'It is Shesha, my serpent, my lady,' I said over my shoulder.

'I see. Then you had better show the rest of Shesha to me.' There was a delicious authority in her voice, and I shivered with arousal, slowly turning until I stood naked in front of her, my body fully exposed to her gaze. She inhaled deeply and looked for a long moment before breaking the silence in a quiet voice.

'You were not put on this earth to labour in the fields, were you, Mary?'

'I don't think I was, my lady, no.'

‘And Shesha is a consequence of your previous employment, perhaps?’

‘Yes, my lady.’

‘And the shaving?’ She gestured at my groin.

‘The same. A habit I got into.’

She nodded at this. ‘Proceed.’

I eased lengthways onto the chaise longue, leant back on the armrest, and parted my legs, so my nakedness was fully displayed to the countess. She leaned forward, smiling and licked her lips.

Giving involuntary gasps of pleasure, I pulled and stroked my fat nipples until they stood proud. My hand traced a gentle pattern over my curved belly before I reached down with my fingers and stroked my slit. The countess inhaled deeply as my large clitty was revealed to her.

‘This is my palace guard, my lady,’ I whispered as I gently rubbed it. ‘A soldier wearing a bearskin hat, an old friend used to say.’

‘Indeed so.’ She seemed incapable of further speech at that moment.

Head back and legs spread, I let my hand go to work in earnest and watched the countess watching me. For some minutes there was silence in the room apart from my involuntary and increasing loud moans of pleasure. Then she spoke.

‘What are you thinking about, Mary?’

‘I’m thinking about watching you spend, my lady,’ I whispered, for it was the honest truth.

She smiled knowingly. ‘Would you like me to do that to you? Touch you until you come?’

‘Oh yes. Yes, I would.’

‘Perhaps even suck your pretty palace guard into my mouth?’

‘Oh, my lady, yes,’ I gasped breathlessly. My hand was moving fast now, my hips thrusting and open. I closed my eyes and waited for the wave to break.

‘STOP. Stop it, Mary. Put both your hands behind your head.’ Her powerful voice cut across my pleasure. Stunned, I jerked my eyes open and stared at her.

‘Stop?’

‘Yes. Stop pleasuring yourself and put your hands behind your head. Leave your legs spread.’

Moaning in frustration, I did as she had instructed and met her eyes pleadingly, but her expression was imperious. For a long ten seconds neither of us spoke, then she quietly said, ‘You may resume.’

I reached down and continued, but she again interrupted at the last moment, a cruelly lascivious smile on her face.

‘Please, my lady …’ I begged.

She eyed me speculatively before answering. ‘Very well. You have my permission to spend this time. Look at me while you are doing it. Do not close your eyes.’

‘Thank you, my lady.’ My climax followed almost immediately as the countess leaned forward and drank in the sight of me in the throes of the greatest pleasure, hips thrusting upwards. As the peak passed and the sensations slowly faded, she slid out of the bed and stood naked and unashamed in front of me, supremely confident of her own power and beauty.

I looked up at her, passive and compliant, my breath still heavy. ‘Thank you,’ I whispered.

Her expression was serious as she spoke. 'Do you wish to be my maid permanently, Mary?'

'Yes, more than anything.'

'There are three things I require from a maid. Honesty, discretion and complete obedience. Do you accept my terms? Think well, Mary, because to transgress is to invite punishment and pain.'

But I did not need to think, indeed, could not. Such was my captivation that, in that moment, the prospect of serving the countess every day made my head swim with wild excitement, and I answered without hesitation. 'I accept your terms, my lady. I will be your maid.'

'Very well. From now on, your pleasure is mine to give. And mine alone. You will not spend, save with my permission. Absolutely not. Do you understand?' She smiled at me with a bewitching combination of tenderness and authority.

'I understand,' I replied. In that moment I would have gladly kissed her feet, had she asked.

'Then you are my creature now, Mary, and we shall face the world together.'

Much later, as I walked down the corridor, two things occurred to me. Firstly, that Sir Hector and Captain Ransome would be delighted, as I had been successful in my mission to become the countess's permanent lady's maid.

And secondly, that in so doing, I had also been most expertly seduced.

Chapter One

My early life in Devon.
Lucy and Ben introduce me to intimacy.

I was a foundling baby, left on the steps of Exeter Cathedral on Christmas Eve 1882 and taken in by my adoptive parents Henry and Elsie Connors, who had not been blessed with children of their own.

My father owned the Royal Oak inn on the high road between Plymouth and Exeter. It was a successful establishment which he had bought with prize money from his time in the Royal Navy. My mother had worked for him for a few years before they were married. They called me Mary because that had been my father's mother's name, and so Mary Connors it was, at least until my new and eventful life in London began.

I remember my years at the Royal Oak being happy ones. My parents were hard-working and kind, and I went to school in the mornings and worked in the inn in the afternoons and evenings. It was a Georgian building over three storeys on the edge of a village called Handley.

My own small bedroom in the attic overlooked the sizeable coachyard and I became used to the bustle and noise of coaches and travellers on horseback coming and going at all hours. Before bed I would often rest my elbows on the window ledge and dreamily imagine I was inside one of the coaches clattering out onto the high road and bound for London, a mysterious lady on her way to a secret assignation.

I had no idea how close to a description of my adult life that would become.

Through my early teenage years, I was something of an ugly duckling, a quiet bookish child with glossy black hair, which I habitually wore in a French plait, green eyes, and a faint natural tan to my skin.

'Our Spanish girl,' my mother would say affectionately. One evening she found me in my room looking in the mirror. She laughed at my anxious expression and said, 'Don't worry, Mary, you will be a beauty soon enough. We can all see that.' Then she sat on my bed and held my hand and talked about growing older and what that meant for me. About how men were and the attention I should expect. I remember finding it all rather interesting and exciting.

I learned a great deal by watching Lucy, one of the serving girls, as she moved around the crowded bars, laughing with the men she liked and being civil to the ones she did not. She was three or four years older than me, an attractive curvy girl with an easy manner, and we became good friends, often chatting and giggling about the guests that had caught our eye when we finished work.

As I grew up, I realised that my mother's prediction was to be proved right. When people of either sex saw me, they often looked twice, and I sometimes overheard people speaking to my parents about their 'beautiful daughter'.

'You're becoming famous, Mary, and good for business,' my father would joke. 'People come in just to have a look at you.'

For my part, I was also very aware of some of the more handsome regulars in the inn and often wondered what it would be like to be courted and even kissed by them.

So it was that, late one evening, as the inn quietened for the night, I was in my accustomed position, leaning on the window ledge and looking down into the shadowy moonlit yard. There was a two-storey barn on the left-hand side, with a double door halfway down. As I watched, Lucy appeared below me and walked briskly and quietly up to the barn door. With a quick glance round, she opened it a crack and slipped inside, pulling it shut behind her. I wondered what errand had taken her there at that time of the night but did not think much more of it. Not until I saw her do it again three nights later, and again the following week.

Finally my curiosity got the better of me, and one evening when we were talking in my room before bed, I came right out and asked her.

She looked at me for a moment and then grinned. 'I'm meeting Ben Williams, the apprentice blacksmith from Torton. We go in there to be together in private,' she added. Then she leaned forward and put her mouth to my ear and whispered, 'I let him fuck me, Mary. We're to be married next year, but no one knows yet.'

I was aghast, thrilled at the rudeness of her language and intrigued in equal measure, and, once I had congratulated her and sworn secrecy, she told me all about their trysts.

'He's a fine strong man and very good at it.' She giggled again. 'He isn't my first, but he's certainly the best, and when he gets going, oh my word, Mary, I'm worried someone might hear me sometimes.' She went on in some detail. Lucy was a very pretty girl, and I found her candid descriptions of their lovemaking fascinating and thrilling and her secret-sharing intimacy delightful.

Without thinking about it, I said, 'I wish I could watch,' at which she burst out laughing and smacked me playfully on the arm.

'Naughty, naughty, Mary. What are you thinking!' she whispered in mock horror, but I noticed behind her eyes there was a speculation that sent little tingles of excitement through me.

Nothing more was said until one lunchtime a couple of weeks later, when she met me on the stairs. She smiled and put her hand on my arm to stop me before leaning in and whispering, 'Make sure you're in the barn by half past ten this evening. Hide in the upstairs gallery where the flour sacks are stored. I'm meeting Ben at eleven. I'll keep him down on the hay bales.' She raised her eyebrows and grinned at me before putting a finger over my lips. 'Watch and learn, Mary. Not a word.'

And with a swing of her hips she was gone, leaving me with the memory of her soft Devon voice in my ear and her breath on my neck.

To say I spent the rest of the day in frenzied anticipation would be an understatement. Indeed, my mother admonished me in the kitchen for being 'so distracted', leading Lucy to glance up from her work and secretly smile at me. The evening seemed to go on forever, but at last I was able to announce I was going to bed before quietly slipping across the yard and into the barn. It was a warm night in midsummer, and some of the hay bales lay in a single layer on the ground floor with the remainder stacked behind. A three-quarter moon shone through an upper window directly onto them but left the gallery in deep shadow. I climbed the ladder and made myself comfortable, heart beating in anticipation.

Shortly afterwards the door opened, and Ben appeared. Safely out of sight, I had a long look at him and could see why he had caught Lucy's eye. A good six feet tall, with broad shoulders and dark curly hair, he was a fine figure of a man, aged in his early twenties, I suppose. As I watched, he reached onto a shelf and grabbed a blanket, which he spread over the bales, then pulled his shirt over his head and hung it on a hook.

I was vaguely aware of my own intake of breath as his muscular torso was revealed, then the door opened and Lucy entered. Did her eyes momentarily flicker upwards towards the gallery? It was hard to tell, and anyway, Ben quickly crossed to the door and silently swept her up into his arms. Indeed, not a word was spoken, not even a greeting, before they kissed passionately. Lucy ran her hands all over his shoulders and back whilst he grasped her buttocks and pulled at her dress, their bodies in full contact from shoulder to hip.

Groans of desire filled the quiet space below me as I watched, fascinated, intensely aware of my own awakening emotions. Lucy finally pushed him back a little and, breathing heavily, quickly unbuttoned the front of her dress, pulling it open and then down so she was naked from the waist up. Her fine white breasts looked beautiful in the pale moonlight, and with a moan, Ben ducked his head to her nipples, licking and sucking each one in turn while she gasped and stroked his neck. At last, with an expression on her face which I had never seen before, she put her hand on Ben's crotch.

'Let me see it, then, Ben,' she said.

He grinned and sat down on the blanket, pulling off his boots and trousers in fast order before standing up again stark naked. His lean muscled body looked quite magnificent to my eyes. Even now, all these years later, I still think fondly of my first view of a big cock standing proud and ready for battle.

Lucy went over to him, her hand grasping the shaft as she raised her mouth to his for another long kiss. I watched as she slowly moved her hand up and down, seeing his thigh muscles tense. At length he broke away from her and spoke for the first time, his voice thick with passion.

'You know what I want. Give me a sucking, Lucy.'

'You always want that, Ben.'

She laughed briefly, then knelt before him and took the swollen head of his cock into her mouth. I fear I spluttered with amazement at this point, but they were so distracted it went unnoticed. Cupping his balls with one hand and pumping his shaft with the other, she nodded her head rhythmically as he gasped and shivered. I noticed she varied the pace quite considerably at times before she finally leaned back and squeezed him firmly with her thumb and forefinger at the base.

'Not yet, Ben, my darling,' she said quietly. Then she wriggled out of her dress, revealing that she was naked underneath. Ben picked her up and placed her gently down on the blanket. She parted her legs to reveal her thick dark bush.

'That's what you want, Ben. Isn't it?

'Oh God, yes.'

His eyes were fixed on her cunny, as indeed were mine. The next second his face was between her legs, and he was licking her with an intense hunger. She groaned and reached down, holding his head in place as his mouth and tongue went to work.

I watched, fascinated by the passion washing over her face. Her moans grew louder as her hips moved up onto his mouth until suddenly she spasmed, her expression contorted and hips working frantically. Then she froze for a long moment before subsiding as her expression relaxed.

But she was to be allowed no respite, as Ben knelt up between her legs, his cock straining towards her.

'Go on, then, Ben, give your Lucy a good fucking,' she gasped, parting her legs wide as she reached for his cock. He thrust onwards as she guided him in, the muscles in his shoulders and buttocks working as he balanced on his arms and settled into a regular rhythm. From time to time he would shift position and I was treated to the delicious sight of his thick white cock driving into Lucy's dark-haired cunny. His naked back glistened with sweat as he steadily built up the speed and power of his thrusts while Lucy moaned and pushed upwards, hands clinging to him, her mouth on his neck.

As I watched, she raised her legs and linked her ankles over his buttocks, pulling him harder and deeper into her as she spent again. Then, with a loud cry, he came powerfully, kissed her deeply and rolled off to lie panting on his back. His cock was still hard and jerking. Lucy stroked it and whispering in his ear. Whatever she said, it made him smile and open his eyes in surprise. They both looked up at the gallery where I was concealed and Lucy spoke, her voice shockingly loud in the silence of the shadowy barn.

'Come down here, Mary.'

Mortified, I gasped in horror and peered over the edge of the platform.

'Come on,' she repeated, beckoning with her finger. 'Ben wants to meet you.'

There was nothing for it but to climb down the ladder, which I did and stood there scarlet with embarrassment. Lucy came over, her breasts swaying beautifully, took my hand, and led me back to where Ben was still lying stretched out on the bales, smiling and fully erect. I could not take my eyes off him. Lucy stood right behind me, her breath on my neck, her low voice in my ear.

'Do you want to touch it, Mary? You can if you want to. I'll give you permission just this once.'

Well, horrified I might have been, but I needed no encouragement and reached forward with my right hand and grasped him. It felt as though my heart would beat itself out of my chest as I worked my hand up and down, feeling its power and watching his smile as the pleasure reached his eyes. I slowly stroked the shaft and balls, using both hands in tandem as Lucy gave me some instruction on the best methods to employ. Ben said nothing, just smiled his handsome smile, opened his legs a little, and arched his hips in sympathy with my hands.

'Best get naked, I think, Mary. You must be very wet by now.' Lucy's voice was in my ear again, then, before I could reply, her hands were at my dress buttons and within seconds she was pulling it off my shoulders and down over my hips. I only wore a thin shift underneath, which rapidly went the same way. Still behind me, she reached round and gently lifted my full breasts, squeezing the long brown nipples between her thumbs and forefingers.

'What about these beauties, then, Ben? Do they deserve a little suck, do you think?'

With a grunt of approval he sat up on the bale and, as Lucy cupped and raised them, he sucked each of my nipples into his mouth in turn. It was electrifying. I moaned and put my head back, only vaguely aware that Lucy was kissing my neck from behind, her tongue busy below my ear and her soft breasts pressing against my back. As Ben continued, her hands started to stroke downwards, sliding across my ribs, then the rise of my belly until they encountered my dark thatch.

'Shall we see if you're ready for Ben's big cock, Mary?' she murmured as her hand slipped down and into my wet slit.

Unable to speak, I parted my legs a little and let her gentle fingers explore me. As Ben sucked and worked my nipples and her sweet voice whispered what it was like to feel his big cockhead sliding inside, my hips suddenly started to thrust involuntarily and I spent, crying and moaning, my arms tightly grasping Ben's shoulders, sandwiched between their hot naked bodies.

I felt him pick me up and lay me down on the blanket. Lucy knelt beside my face as he loomed over me, then slid inside. There was no pain, just ecstasy as he worked me, driving deeper and deeper.

'That's it, Mary, let him give you a fucking now. You know you deserve it, you naughty girl. Hiding in the gallery and watching us like that. A good hard comeuppance for a peeping Tom. That's what you need.'

I could hear the excitement in Lucy's voice and realised her hand was busy on herself as she carried on talking, encouraging Ben to greater heights and asking how tight and wet I was. Then she suddenly leaned over and kissed me full on the lips, her tongue like quicksilver. I responded willingly, opening my mouth to her, and then came again, waves of pleasure coursing through me as Lucy's agile tongue licked my mouth and nipples in equal measure.

I think the sight of us kissing must have sent Ben over the edge, because he moaned, and his thrusting rapidly sped up.

'Not inside her, Ben,' said Lucy, moving down towards my hips.

Panting but obedient, he pushed backwards, kneeling upright between my outstretched thighs. Lucy was onto his straining cock in a moment, her hand pulling it mercilessly whilst he moaned and gasped. Finally, with a strangled cry he came, three powerful spurts splattering across my belly and breasts in the moonlight.

Eyes gleaming, Lucy licked it up with obvious enjoyment before suddenly her mouth was on mine again, sharing his juices with me. She kissed me for a long time before easing back, and the three of us relaxed on the blanket, breathless and sated.

Finally Lucy turned her head to me and said, 'Well, what do you think of all that, Mary?' I saw handsome Ben raise his head and look at me, smiling warmly and clearly curious.

'Wonderful, just wonderful,' I whispered, unable to say more as my emotions overcame me and I started to sob a little. Lucy laughed gently.

'Hey, hey, no need for that. You get off to bed now and we'll talk tomorrow.' It was clearly time for me to go, so I did, having first kissed Lucy goodnight. I went to kiss Ben too, but she put her hand on my arm. 'No, Mary, no kissing Ben,' she said quietly.

I nodded in instinctive understanding and left them to it.

The following day was a very busy one in the inn, and Lucy and I did not have a chance to talk until bedtime. Indeed, it was later than that, as I had retired and was in bed when I heard a creak in the corridor outside and my bedroom door opened.

Lucy stood there in the moonlight in her nightgown, her light brown hair freshly brushed and nipples visible through the thin cotton fabric. She crossed the room and sat down on the bed as I sat up, pushing the pillow against the headboard at my back.

'What a busy day, Mary, but anyway, I think it's better we talk now when we won't be disturbed, don't you?' I nodded before she picked up my hand and continued. 'Last night was a singular occasion in many ways. I was just thinking to let you watch and learn, and in truth I liked the idea of you watching us. But something made me beckon you down. I hope you're not distressed by what happened?'

'No, no,' I said. 'It was wonderful. All wonderful.' I pressed her hand tightly as I said this, for it was true. My congress with muscular and handsome Ben had been a revelation, but I also could not forget Lucy's passionate kisses and her knowing hands. Hands that had given me my first climax as her man worshipped my breasts and nipples.

I met her eye and her expression changed. She suddenly looked unsure of herself.

'What we did, woman to woman. It's not the first time for me, Mary, but some people – most people – think it's unnatural. I wanted to make sure you were not …' she paused and searched for the right word, then shrugged her shoulders, 'overwhelmed. With Ben and all, I mean?'

I leant in and kissed her gently on the lips, smiling. 'I've no regrets, Lucy. None at all. I loved it with you, and I loved it with Ben. It was quite an unusual introduction to such matters, I do acknowledge, but I survived – nay, deeply enjoyed it.'

But her serious expression remained, and she spoke again.

'About Ben. He's my man and I love him. You won't take him off me, will you, Mary? That's why I didn't want you to kiss him. I am so worried that he will only want you and not me anymore.' She carried on, the words spilling out of her. 'I know you are a great beauty, everyone does, but when I saw you naked, when I kissed you, I realised that you can have any man you want, Mary, and probably any woman too. You can captivate people, and I worry that in letting Ben fuck you I have made a terrible mistake.'

I shook my head urgently. 'No, no, I will never ever step between you and Ben. To do so would be to betray you in a way I would never countenance. Be assured of that.' I saw her eyes were moist with tears and felt myself welling up in response. 'Honestly, I would never do it. I will find my own man, I promise.'

We continued talking for some time, and her anxiety passed as she realised I meant what I said. Indeed, before long we were giggling away as normal, especially when I enquired whether, as Ben's cock was my first, I should expect those following to be of similar size. Her reply was informative and, as I subsequently found out, accurate.

At some point there was a lull in our conversation, and I impulsively leant forward and kissed her softly on the lips. In the still night, her breath, her earthy scent, her simple nearness were suddenly intoxicating, and as we paused, then kissed again, I felt her hands gently stroke my breasts.

'Perhaps we don't need Ben here this evening, Mary,' she whispered.

As I smiled in agreement she stood and pulled her nightdress over her head, and for the second time in two days I saw the curves of her wonderful naked body in the moonlight. Desire surged through me. Grasping my own nightie, I pulled upwards as, laughing quietly, Lucy helped to lift it over my head. She flicked the sheet back and stood over me for a second, looking at my naked form lying on the mattress, then we were lying side by side sharing a long and passionate kiss that left my head swimming.

The next half hour passed quite delightfully as we stimulated and adored each other. I came twice, once through her skilful fingers and a second time, quite overwhelmingly, when she ducked her head between my legs and sucked and licked me until I quietly begged for mercy. I willingly reciprocated, delighting in the rush of her sweet juices as she came, hips thrusting joyously upwards, her hands firmly holding my head in place.

Later, as we lay together in that direct way she had, she told me I had a very large clitty. 'Like a grenadier in a bearskin, guarding the royal palace.' I had no idea at the time, but experience since then has told me she was right. We talked some more before, with another lingering kiss, she slipped out of the bed and back to her room.

Chapter Two

And so to London.

Without further ado, I set about the business of choosing a man. And I must admit I felt a certain urgency. Now that Ben had given me a taste of what a strong young fellow could do, I wanted more of it and saw no reason to wait.

After discreetly trying a number of possibilities, I settled on The Honourable Julian Chambers, son of Lord Pemberton, if you please. As Lucy observed approvingly, 'Money and class, Mary. There is no reason for you to go with a village lad when you can trade up to the gentry'.

Jules and I settled into a steady relationship for which he paid me a guinea a week. I was surprised when he proposed the arrangement, but could see no reason to refuse the money, especially as I earned no wages from the inn. Also, there was no denying that I found the fact he was paying for me rather stimulating, and I was happy to play the part of the available and compliant mistress.

We became completely engrossed in each other, fucking like rabbits through that autumn and winter. He would collect me in the phaeton around nine o'clock and we would take the twenty-minute drive back to

Pemberton, often running through the hall in our urgency to get up to his room.

Time passed by. Lucy and Ben married the next summer. She had a noticeable bulge in her belly as she walked down the aisle with a big grin on her face. In villages like ours, that was considered a good thing, confirming that the marriage would be blessed with children.

Jules and I celebrated our second year together, but I noticed he became increasingly preoccupied. One evening as we were sitting in bed he came out with it.

'Father says I should marry. Says I need to find a nice girl from our set and settle down here at the hall. Start a family and all that.' He looked at me, so miserable. I was upset, of course, but something in me was a little relieved as well. In truth I had started to wonder what the world held next for me and was not at all ready to settle down. I took his hand.

'You were always going to be tied to the estate and need a wife that is born to this life. What we have had has been wonderful, but it couldn't go on for ever, my love. And it may well take you a few months to choose a suitable girl, so we needn't say our goodbyes yet.'

As I finished my sentence, I peeled the blanket back and reached down for his cock. Ever willing, it responded most enthusiastically to my hand, and he said firmly, 'On your knees, mistress. Show me your bum,' It was a command, and I shivered with delight and licked his ear.

'Yes, my lord. You're paying.' I knelt down with my buttocks up in the air, knees apart, my face sideways on the pillow. I had a brief glimpse of his lithe muscled body, hard cock in hand as I acted up the hungry tart and wiggled and pushed backwards, trying to capture him. 'Oh yes please, my lord, let me have it. Give your Mary a good hard fucking.'

And he did, driving in mercilessly all the way to his balls in one long thrust. I cried out and splayed my hips, pulling and twisting my swollen nipples until we spent. As we lay panting and entwined on his big bed he turned to me.

'My God, Mary, if my new wife, whoever she may be, serves me half as well as you have done, then I will be a lucky man indeed. You are quite exquisite, and I am sure I will always love you. What will you do without me, my darling?'

I looked at him with a smile. 'Why, seek my fortune in London of course.'

*

The train from Exeter to Southampton was fifteen minutes late and I arrived on the London express's platform in something of a rush and with less than two minutes before it was due to depart.

'This way, madam,' the ancient, knobbly-kneed porter called over his shoulder, heading for a first-class carriage, which was an indulgence I had allowed myself, intending to arrive at the Empire's capital in style. He pulled open the door of a compartment and peered in. 'Room for one more, sir?' he wheezed breathlessly.

'If you must, damn you,' came the reply from within. It was a man's voice, cultured but with a faint colonial accent.

'Wait and see, sir,' the porter muttered in reply. He swung my case into the carriage and stepped back to allow me to enter. I handed him a tip and placed my foot on the step.

My appearance in the door frame created a pleasing impact. The compartment ran crossways across the carriage with doors on either side of the train but no corridor, and its solitary occupant was slumped next to the door at the far end. A quick glance was all I needed to take him in. He was a tall man in a well-cut travel-stained brown suit, a soft-collared blue shirt, and a red tie. Regimental, I think. Aged around thirty-five, I guessed, and sandy haired with a tanned face and strong jawline. He looked lean, capable, and confident, and his hazel eyes took me in with a long direct stare.

A smile slowly replaced the scowl he had been wearing seconds earlier.

'Everything all right, madam?' the porter asked.

'Thank you, yes,' I replied.

'Indeed it is,' the stranger added – rather impertinently, as the question had clearly not been addressed to him. As the porter slammed the door, he stood up and held out his hand. 'Good afternoon, Miss. Gabriel Chandos, at your service.'

'Mary Connors, Mr Chandos. I'm sorry to have disturbed your solitude, but rest assured you will hardly notice me sitting here.'

'Miss Connors, I cannot imagine any red-blooded male not noticing you. If you will forgive the presumption.'

I looked at him coolly. His eyes had flecks of gold in them, I noticed, and his cheekbones were quite pronounced. 'Hmmm, Mr Chandos. That may or may not be the case, but I hope that either way, you will be a gentleman during our time together.' I sat down by the door, as far from his seating position as possible, and looked out of the window, a poised and interested expression on my face. In the window's reflection I could see him still standing in the middle of the compartment, looking at me.

'Please don't remain standing for the entire journey on my account, Mr Chandos,' I remarked, continuing to observe the comings and goings outside as the train pulled away. I waited until he had resumed his seat before adding, 'But perhaps you'd be kind enough to put my suitcase on the rack.' He rose again, did so, and then sat down again, an amused smile on his face.

He made a pass at me fifteen minutes later, of course.

They all want to. Some do, some do not, but Mr Gabriel Chandos was most definitely a doer, and I must admit I set the tone by permitting a little flirting. He was very pleasant company, and as we rattled through the dark November evening, the atmosphere in the warm, dimly lit carriage became increasingly intimate.

'It's funny, isn't it, the way one meets people when travelling,' he observed. 'So many of them are bores, wrapped up in their own affairs. Yet meeting you, I feel I could talk to you for many hours without getting tired of your company at all. In fact, just sitting looking at you would be reward enough, so to find you are also an intelligent and pleasant young woman is a happy coincidence indeed.'

'You are not entirely without charm yourself, Mr Chandos. Indeed, I think that with hard work and application you may find a woman in London who will consider marriage to you to be tolerably acceptable,' I replied primly.

He roared with laughter at that. 'Marriage? That is not on my agenda, Miss Connors. Not at all. Although thank you for the compliment.' He nodded at me, still smiling.

'Then what is on your agenda, I wonder?' I asked, smiling back. Which was apparently all the encouragement he needed, as he briskly moved to sit next to me.

I raised my eyebrows at him and awaited developments.

'If I wasn't a gentleman, I should be attempting to seduce you and to pass the remaining,' he glanced briefly at his wristwatch, 'hour and ten minutes in delightful congress.'

I let him see me shiver slightly and licked my lips before answering. 'But you are a gentleman, aren't you, Mr Chandos?'

'Up to a point.' He smiled rakishly at me. 'But even a gentleman might attempt to steal a kiss from a woman as beautiful as you.' He leaned towards me, his face close. A delicious masculine aroma of sandalwood and tobacco reached me, and I felt the unmistakable stirrings of arousal.

Knowing where it would lead, I raised my face to his, and the next moment his lips were on mine. My hand reached up and held his cheek as I opened my mouth to him and we kissed long and hard.

'This is warm work, Mr Chandos,' I said at length, gently pushing him away. 'I think I will remove my hat and coat.' Standing up, I did so, and he leaped to his feet and placed them on the opposite seat. Quickly moving behind me, he kissed my neck in exactly the place that makes a girl tremble. And I should know.

I gasped and bent my head to the side as his hands encircled me, his own arousal only too apparent as he closed with me. I moved my buttocks gently, pressing backwards as his hands reached upwards towards the top button of my dress and flicked it undone. There were five in total, I recalled.

I opened my eyes and saw he was looking at me in the window's reflection. 'I hope I am not going to disappoint you, Mr Chandos,' I said, breathing rather heavily.

'Gabriel, please,' he muttered, returning to his delicious work on my neck for a moment before continuing. 'And you are not disappointing me, Miss Connors. Not at all.' He smiled at me in the window.

'It's just that there are four more buttons, and they are a guinea each,' I said.

His stunned reaction was a delight to behold, and I must admit bringing him down a peg or two held a certain satisfaction.

'Four guineas to have me, Gabriel, and I will endeavour to give complete satisfaction.' I wriggled my bum again, pressing back against his hard cock.

'Well, I'm damned,' he eventually managed to say after a range of emotions from anger to confusion and finally wry amusement passed over his face.

I turned to face him and kissed him long and hard again before reaching down and gently closing my hand over his cock through his trousers. 'Well, someone's keen. What say you, then? Do we have an accord?'

This time it was my turn to kiss his neck. Reaching up, I let my lips and breath run over the area below his ear and felt him shudder. His scent was intoxicating.

‘What’s it to be, Gabriel?’ I whispered, my hand squeezing away down below.

‘My God, yes, Mary.’ he replied, his voice thick with emotion.

‘In advance, my darling,’ I breathed into his ear.

Two minutes later, the funds were safely ensconced in my handbag and Gabriel was sitting in the middle of the seat taking off his shirt. He had a fine strong body, a chest lightly covered with sandy-coloured hair, broad shoulders, and well-muscled arms. Most acceptable, I thought.

‘Sit back and enjoy what you’ve paid for, Gabriel,’ I said, feeling as though electricity was running through my veins. I reached for the remaining buttons on my dress and popped them one by one, before letting the dress drop to the floor and doing a slow turn for my admirer, who was making approving noises and showing signs of advancing on me.

‘Do you like what you see?’ I asked innocently, well aware of the passion my thin lacy shift and tight drawers had generated in dear Jules on many occasions. ‘I worry that my nipples show through, especially when they are standing proud like this.’

I turned back to the window and struck a pose in the reflection. I was right; they did show quite clearly. In a second Gabriel was behind me again, his hands moving forcefully to bare my breasts by pulling the shift upwards. They were momentarily lifted by the material, then bounced free. He cupped them and groaned with pleasure before I turned and gave myself to him, my hands at his belt, my mouth open.

In spite of my head spinning with lust, I managed to remain in control of the situation enough to push him back to where he'd been sitting, and, kneeling down, I removed his lower garments to reveal a very hard, good-sized cock.

'I think this needs a sucking, don't you, Gabriel?' I said without further ado and leant over to lick the head of it.

'Go on, then, Mary, earn your guineas,' he said, then gasped as my warm mouth engulfed him. I felt his hand reach under my arm and caress my breast, as the other wrapped itself into my hair, guiding my mouth, and I obediently followed his direction as we continued in this delightful fashion for some minutes.

'I want you naked now, Mary,' he said.

I pushed back off him and stood up. Raising the shift over my head, I turned away a little and pulled my drawers down, pushing my backside out as the cheeks were exposed before stepping out of them. I turned to face him, letting him have his first view of my cunny, dark haired and nestling between my legs.

'You can leave your footwear on, Mary.' He smiled and nodded at my neatly laced ankle boots. 'Now come here.' Leaning back on the seat, he stretched his long legs out across the compartment and held his cock upright.

His intentions were clear, so without a word I straddled him and slowly slid on. We moaned in unison as he sank deep inside me, and his hands gripped my buttocks. I reached past his head and slipped my own hands over the top of the seatback, where a handy gap provided excellent purchase.

Well braced, I began to ride him, my knees splayed wide, cunny pressed down as far as it would go into his lap. We got into an excellent rhythm as I leaned forwards, licked his neck and whispered what a fine stiff cock he had and how much he was pleasing me with it, before his moaning and increasingly frantic mauling of my breasts indicated he was about to explode.

'Let it go, my darling, fill me up with it,' I gasped as my hips bucked powerfully and my own climax approached. He came with a loud cry and I followed suit, waves of exquisite pleasure flooding through me. It lasted a long time for both of us, fused together as we were, and I ground down onto him, extracting the last shuddering sensations of pleasure before leaning forward and burying my neck in his shoulder. We did not speak for some time, but I realised he was still hard; indeed, his orgasm seemed to have had no effect on his cock whatsoever. I squeezed him gently and moved experimentally.

'Another, Mr Chandos?' I enquired sweetly.

'Is it included in the price?' he said, his voice muffled.

'Given your excellent performance on the first occasion, a second fuck would be appropriate, my darling.' I looked round the compartment and, seeing no inspiration, added, 'I suggest like this again, as we have no bed.'

'More work for you, then,' he replied, his hands moving to my bum as I started to slide backwards and forwards again. We fucked again joyfully, and as we approached the climax I realised that the train had halted. Glancing through the window I saw our compartment had stopped next to a narrow gap in the thickly wooded embankment. A lighted and un-curtained bay window was clearly visible, and a woman was standing in it staring down at us. She was only twenty feet away at most, perhaps aged forty-five with a handsome, refined face, red lips, and dark hair piled high, dressed in crimson evening wear and pearls.

I turned a little to her so she could see my breasts bouncing as I rode Gabriel, head back and panting. Our eyes met and I held her gaze as I came, highly excited by the sensation of being watched by an anonymous observer. She quickly glanced behind her before unbuttoning the front of her gown and exposing her white breasts to me, pulling and stroking the nipples, her face expressionless. Gabriel had not noticed as, eyes shut, he concentrated on the job in hand.

'Change of plan, my darling,' I said, sliding gently off him and kneeling down on the opposite side to the window. Grasping his cock firmly, I pulled it upright and began to wank the shaft with my hand. I looked up at the window again. She was still there, eyes fixed on his member, one hand on her exposed breasts, the other now out of sight below the window frame as her elbow moved rhythmically. I saw her head go back a little and her mouth open as she watched me working his cock.

'Are you going to show me how much you can come, Gabriel? Let me see what a big spend you can give me.'

'My God, you're a filthy bitch, aren't you, Mary?' he snarled, his feet braced against the base of the seat opposite.

'I want to see it spurting right up onto your chest, as much as you can, darling. Then I'm going to lick it all up.' That seemed to do the trick. He groaned and his body stiffened and rose clear off the seat as my hand worked its way up to full speed, squeezing his slick cockhead with every stroke.

'Yes. Now. It's coming,' he panted.

'Look out of the window. See the woman in the house. She's touching herself while she watches you coming. Meet her eyes, Gabriel. Keep watching her as you come.'

'Jesus Christ!' His cock started to spasm and pump repeatedly as, face contorted with his orgasm, he stared open-mouthed at the older woman, now clearly masturbating in the window. As I watched, her face slackened and her body juddered as her elbow worked frantically. Leaning forward, I licked his chest and nipples, swallowing it all before taking him into my mouth again. 'She's still watching you,' he whispered, head turned towards her.

With a clank, the train suddenly jerked forward and slowly gathered pace. Our last sight of the woman was as she slipped her breasts back into her dress and raised a hand in salutation. Her face remained expressionless as she watched us until we were out of sight.

'You might say she saw us come and go, Mr Chandos,' I said as I curled up into Gabriel's lap.

Chapter Three

I meet Mrs Georgina Beaufort.

At half past six on a Friday evening, Waterloo station was a cacophony of noise, steam and excitement, all brightly lit by the electric lights recently installed at great expense by the London and Southern Railway.

Gabriel was clearly keen to continue our association, to the point of asking for my hotel address in London and suggesting that he accompany me there in a cab before adding, 'Miss Connors, it would be the greatest pleasure to see you again in a day or two once you are settled in your hotel. Perhaps for dinner and er, so on.'

I smiled prettily at him. 'So it would Mr Chandos, but do you have another four guineas? And would you be prepared to disburse them? These are the questions we must ask ourselves I think.'

He fell silent and looked a little sulky at this, so I took pity on him. 'However you may escort me to the Exeter Hotel on Pall Mall where I will be residing for the next few weeks. 'Go and find a porter and I will keep an eye on the bags. You can't be too careful in a place like this.'

He shouldered off through the crowd one arm raised to gesticulate at a pair of porters standing with their barrows further up the train. As soon as he was out of sight I pulled my case out of the train, set off briskly down the platform, and was soon lost in the crowd.

Mr Gabriel Chandos had been a most stimulating and profitable travelling companion, but I had no desire to burden myself with an admirer so early in my new life.

Outside the station I secured a hansom cab and fifteen minutes later I was being warmly welcomed by my distant cousin Miriam Lancaster, proprietor of the Empire Hotel on The Strand.

The Empire was a smart hotel of some thirty bedrooms and for the first two weeks of my stay, I remember walking in ever-extending circles, exploring the centre of London and the wonders at the very heart of our marvellous empire.

Miriam was full-figured, brown-haired cockney with a ready laugh and an accent that I struggled to pick up sometimes, whilst Andrew was a diminutive Scotsman who had inherited sufficient money from his parents to make a down payment on the hotel some twenty-five years ago. The business had prospered through hard work and luck, meaning the mortgage was now nearly paid off, and soon they would be the proud owners of the property in its entirety. She called him 'the Jock', which I found rather endearing.

Christmas and the New Year came and went, and I chose not to return to Devon for the celebrations, preferring to remain at the hotel in London, which was heavily decorated and alive with social activity as we prepared to set forth into the twentieth century. I fear my parents were disappointed by this, but I wrote at length and promised to visit them before too long in 1901. My father wrote back, announcing to my surprise that they were intending to sell the inn and retire to Exmouth, where they had their eye on a new villa being built with a fine view of the sea.

In the middle of January, the entire empire was thrown into mourning as our great Queen Victoria passed away at Osborne House on the Isle of Wight. We were all expecting it, as the news had not been good for some weeks, but nevertheless her death was a profound shock after so long on the throne. Like many Londoners, Miriam, the Jock, and I paid our respects by joining the throng of people who watched the gun carriage carrying her from Waterloo station to Paddington, from where she was taken to Windsor for her burial.

On the first floor of the Empire there were two private dining rooms where customers could entertain guests away from the general public. I was a guest at the hotel, paying an agreed rate, and so not expected to work, but one evening Miriam asked me to help, as one of the waitresses had gone home early complaining of stomach pains.

'She's been waiting on a couple in the small dining room upstairs. They've finished their meals, I imagine, so can you take up a bottle of port for them.'

Happy to help, I collected the tray and climbed the stairs to the first floor. Turning left, I walked down the pleasant, red-carpeted corridor. At the second door, I paused and slipped one hand under the centre of the tray, then quietly opened it with the other. Concentrating on not dropping the tray, I completely forgot to knock, which was unfortunate, as it is always wise so to do before entering a private dining room later on in the evening.

I came upon a very distracting tableau. The room was nicely furnished, with a small dining table in the bay window on which the remains of a meal lay. Richly coloured Turkey rugs covered the floor, and a deep blue settee was set in front of a brightly burning fire. Warm yellow light from two electric lamps on wall tables illuminated the scene. An older man – well over fifty, I guessed – with thinning hair and a modest paunch was standing by the settee just wearing a white long-tailed shirt unbuttoned and a pair of breeches, which were pulled down to his knees.

Kneeling in front of him, his cock in her mouth and her hands busy, was a very attractive woman aged about thirty. Her blonde hair was piled high on her pretty head as she gently nodded and worked away. He noticed me at once, but she did not, and I should have turned tail and left immediately, of course. But had I done so, my life would have turned out very differently.

As you now know, my first experience of the act of love was decidedly voyeuristic, and the sight of this couple awoke delicious sensations. Placing the port down silently on a convenient table, I simply stood and watched them. He stared at me for a while before reaching down to gently disengage his paramour. The blonde leaned back on her knees and looked up at him, smiling.

'Yes, Sir Anthony?'

He nodded in my direction. 'We are observed.'

She looked over towards me and raised her eyebrows, and I noticed she had curiously compelling brown eyes. She really was delicious, I thought.

‘We are indeed. And by a beauty, no less,’ she said in a low, cultured voice, partly directing the remark at me. I said nothing, but the man spoke again as he eased her head forward again.

‘Carry on, madam.’

She bent to her task with a will, seemingly unconcerned by my presence. The man pulled his shirt back to fully expose himself and smiled at me as his hips moved rhythmically. I reached up and unbuttoned the top of my dress, popping each button slowly,

‘Ah, yes,’ he said. ‘Yes, indeed. Let’s see them, then, my dear,’ he said, not unpleasantly.

Reaching up to my shoulders, I peeled the dress down far enough for my nipples to show through my shift and stroked each one to a fine stiffness through the material. He placed his hand on the back of the woman’s head and started to push her mouth onto his cock, his hips speeding up. She moaned and complied.

‘That’s it. That’s it,’ he said more urgently, although I was not clear to which of us the remark was directed. Then, moments later, he emitted a single short expletive, closed his eyes, and shuddered as he emptied himself in the blonde’s willing mouth. She swallowed it avidly, I noticed. Then, breathing heavily, he opened his eyes and held my gaze for a long moment. I stared back, allowing him a small smile and lift of the eyebrows as I buttoned my dress before reaching for the door and slipping out into the corridor. I had said nothing during the entire encounter.

An hour later, I was tidying the downstairs dining room as the last of the guests were leaving when the woman I had seen upstairs entered. She walked over, her lovely russet-coloured dress swaying gently as she moved, and I found myself looking into the most vibrant and expressive brown eyes I have ever seen. Amusement, curiosity, passion, anxiety, and promise were all there, each one a fleeting moment but together an intoxicating, intriguing cocktail. I realised that she was utterly beautiful, and my heart began to pound as she stood before me.

'What is your name?' she asked.

'Mary Connors, madam,' I replied.

'Please come and see me tomorrow at two o'clock, Miss Connors.' She handed over a card, gave me a look of such ravishing charm that I almost swooned, then turned and left the room.

I heard the man say, 'Ah, there you are, Georgina,' but her reply was lost as they moved away. I looked down at the card.

Mrs Georgina Beaufort,
1 Arundel Court,
Surrey Street,
London, W.C.

There was no doubt I would go. I was looking for adventure, and my every instinct told me that Mrs Georgina Beaufort could provide it.

I discovered that Surrey Street was not far from the hotel. One turned left out of the door and walked east past Aldwych, to where it ran southwards downhill for three hundred yards before meeting the Embankment and the river Thames.

It was a busy road, clearly used as a cut-through, and crowded with carriages, heavily laden carts, and pedestrians. As I set off, I was passed by a splendid open motor car, its uniformed chauffeur negotiating a way through the throng as a warmly dressed couple sat talking in the back. Motor cars were still quite a rare sight even in the capital, and some scruffy boys whooped and waved their caps as it drove past.

I walked down one side of the street and back up the other, passing some newish apartment blocks and older houses, but saw nothing called Arundel Court. Repeating my route and looking more carefully this time, I noticed a roofed and cobbled passage between two houses, not more than five feet wide. High up on the wall, a painted sign and an arrow indicated Arundel Court was to be found within.

After ten yards, the alley turned sharp right, then sharp left, and I glanced behind, a little uneasy at how quickly I had become separated from the bustle and noise of the street. But as I carried on, I suddenly found myself in a paved square some forty feet wide and the same deep. A large tree, leafless in mid-winter, grew from a railed enclosure in its centre, and high brick walls formed three sides. Facing me, the fourth side consisted of a three-storey Georgian town house. A large number One was displayed on the stone column next to a glossy royal blue front door upon which a brass door knocker rested. I mounted the three steps and knocked, hearing the distant bells of St Paul's strike two in the ensuing silence.

The great fork in the road of my life was upon me, had I but known it.

Footsteps sounded behind the door and it swung open to reveal a tall West Indian fellow dressed in open-necked white shirt, neat blue jacket, and grey trousers. Although his attire was casual, he looked very smart and handsome to my eye. It was clear his clothes were expensive, and he filled them very well indeed. I guessed him to be in his late twenties. His head was shaved, and his scalp glistened slightly with some preparation. Together with his delightful smile, he was altogether a striking prospect.

'Miss Connors,' he said, then paused and took me in, his smile if possible becoming even more fulsome. 'Ah yes, Georgina did not lie. Right, indeed.'

He held the door open as I confirmed I was Miss Connors and walked into the airy hallway, which was floored with small black and white tiles. He shut the door and introduced himself, his deep voice rich with the lilt of the Caribbean.

'I am Jimmy. I look after the house for Georgina.' He bowed his head slightly and I smiled back, wondering at the intimate use of her name when he was, it appeared, just a servant.

'A pleasure, Jimmy,' I replied holding out my hand, which almost disappeared as he gently squeezed it. I was charmed as I realised he was being careful. We both turned as a door down the corridor opened, and the next moment Mrs Beaufort was bustling towards us.

'Miss Connors, I thought I heard you in the hall. Do come through into the sitting room. You have met Jimmy, I see. Good. He is a darling man and may be relied upon.'

I thought this both a curious and a reassuring recommendation but did not have time to reflect further as she had taken my elbow and was ushering me along the corridor. Turning to the right, we entered a room some twenty feet square with a large window that faced out onto the square through which I had just passed.

To my left a low fire glowed in an ornate fireplace and a long dark green settee faced it, with a low table in front and an armchair to the right. The carpet was a paler green and the walls a shade of yellow that matched it beautifully. Fine oil paintings covered the walls, except where a large mirror six feet high and four wide was attached to the wall near the fireplace. Several chairs, side tables, and a beautiful walnut sideboard completed the furnishings, and I noticed the room had electric lights fitted to the ceiling. Altogether it was a most pleasing and harmoniously decorated chamber.

'What a delightful room, Mrs Beaufort,' I said.

'It serves, it serves, my dear,' she replied airily as she closed the door and gestured to the settee. 'Do sit down. I'm sure Jimmy will bring us some tea in a minute. If that is all right?' she added, her ever-mobile eyes suddenly worried.

'Yes, thank you.' I nodded.

She sat down opposite me and stared for a long moment. 'You are quite beautiful, my dear. Quite beautiful. But I imagine you have been told that many times already in your young life. You being how old, Mary? May I call you Mary?

I smiled. 'Yes, Mrs Beaufort, of course. And I think I am eighteen years old, although I was a foundling baby, so no record of my birth exists.'

She nodded at this. 'Will you tell me about your life, Mary? I should be most interested to hear about it, and the circumstances that led to you interrupt us with the port last night.' Her eyes gleamed with such outraged humour that I could not help but smile back.

So I told her. The telling took about ten minutes, during which time she did not interrupt once, even when Jimmy appeared with a laden tea tray and placed it on the table between us.

'And so there we have it. A common enough story of a well-brought-up country girl who is curious about London and keen to make her way. Is that a fair summary?' she asked as I concluded my account.

'Yes, Mrs Beaufort,' I replied.

'Except we are missing some pieces of the jigsaw, are we not, Mary?' she continued, directly meeting my eye. 'Those parts that mean a girl not yet out of her teens will not just observe a man being pleasured by a woman but calmly expose her breasts to him whilst he climaxes. That is not at all normal, nor is it respectable. Most girls would have shrieked and closed the door last night. But not you, it seems.' She raised her eyebrows at me in delighted outrage. 'You may speak freely with me, Mary. In particular you may add those elements to your story which concern men, their desires, and their passions. And your own, too.'

Yet again I found myself lost in the extraordinary depth of her eyes. It seemed as though she offered understanding, passion, desire, and empathy in a single glance, and although embarrassed at the idea of revealing such intimate secrets, I found I could offer little resistance to her. Indeed, when she stood and moved across to sit beside me, I was ready to reveal all.

And so I told her in full chapter and verse about my passionate night with Lucy and Ben in the barn, my ongoing liaison with Lucy and my affair with Jules. She smiled in mock horror as I described my encounter with Gabriel Chandos and clapped her hands and cried 'Bravo!' delightedly as a revealed my simple subterfuge regarding the hotels.

When I had finished, she sat thoughtfully for a short while, then asked me a question.

'So, am I right in thinking that you take great enjoyment from the company of men and women and are a woman capable of great passion?'

I nodded. 'Yes, Mrs Beaufort, that is the truth.'

'Forgive me being direct, my dear, but did you not fall pregnant during your time with Jules? You appear to have taken no precautions with him.'

'I did not, Mrs Beaufort. To begin with, I didn't even think about it and I was so besotted with Jules that it seemed not to matter. By the time my mother realised what was happening and spoke to me, we had been together for two months. Jules told me he had got one of the maids at the hall pregnant when he was younger, and that she had been paid off by his father. Because of this, to put it simply, I think I am barren. Which is not something that distresses me greatly, as it does give me the freedom to enjoy a gentleman's attention without worry, and I am not drawn to motherhood.'

Mrs Beaufort looked at me with benign calculation in her eyes. 'I feel that my instincts were correct when I saw you last night. You are not just a natural beauty but also a free spirit, inclined to follow your desires without fear or favour. In that, you are very much like me and very much unlike most of society.' She smiled and took my hand in hers. 'To have strong desires and the beauty and character to act upon them makes us the chosen few, Mary. There is someone I should like you to meet. He is a friend of mine and a good man who serves this country with passion and distinction. He is also the fellow who provides all this.' She repeated her gesture of earlier, encompassing the room.

Well, I am no ingénue when it comes to such matters. Jules's father had kept a mistress, and his son had followed in his footsteps. 'Are you his mistress?' I asked – rather directly, I realised. She laughed.

'In a manner of speaking, Mary. But it is best if you hear it from him.' She glanced at the clock on the mantlepiece, which showed the time to be exactly half past two. 'He's a punctual fellow and I asked him to come now, so …'

A faint knock on the front door interrupted her. She smiled and nodded to me. 'There we are.' Voices in the hall followed, and seconds later the door opened, and Jimmy appeared.

'Mr Hector Wyatt,' he announced.

Chapter Four

I meet Hector Wyatt and observe Georgina at work.

We stood up as a grey-haired, clean-shaven gentleman wearing a formal morning coat entered. I guessed him to be in his late fifties. Of average height and build, he had a refined and intelligent face and an expression that combined authority and wisdom with a faintly world-weary air.

'Hector, how nice to see you. May I present Miss Connors. Mary Connors, in fact.' Mrs Beaufort looked at me, and I looked at him and then did something that I had never done before. I curtseyed. It was instinctive and over before I had even realised I had done it. The thought flashed through my mind that I was a long way from Devon now. He looked at me and smiled a small smile, then glanced back at Mrs Beaufort.

'Ah,' he said.

'Ah indeed,' she replied.

'Miss Connors, it is a great pleasure to meet you.' He stepped forward and took my hand, a distinct twinkle in his eye. Mind you, most men have that, and they are all invariably pleased to meet me.

'And you, Mr Wyatt,' I replied.

We sat down. I perched on the settee and he sat in the armchair, whilst Mrs Beaufort busied herself with pouring more tea for the ladies and a whisky and soda for Mr Wyatt. Whilst this was going on, he just looked at me, smiled gently, and waited. It seemed like a long time. At last, when we were all settled, I plucked my courage up and spoke before he could. My tone was a little cool.

'Well, Mr Wyatt, you've had a good long look. Tell me, what do you see?' He smiled fully at this, and I heard Mrs Beaufort snort quietly with laughter.

'I see that I am in the presence of a great beauty, Miss Connors; one of England's finest, perhaps.' He glanced to his right, where Mrs Beaufort sat. 'With all deference to the lovely Georgina, of course. But perhaps I should ask you the same question?'

I paused and gathered my thoughts before answering. I was being interviewed, firstly by Mrs Beaufort and now Mr Wyatt, that much was clear. But for what task I had no idea. Nevertheless, I felt profoundly that whatever world I was being given a glimpse of, I wanted to see more of it.

'I grew up in an inn on the high road between Exeter and Plymouth, Mr Wyatt,' I answered. 'Innkeeping is a robust profession where one must be a good and speedy judge of character, and my father taught me well. My instincts tell me that I am in the presence of a man who is not just used to exercising power but who is also used to living with the consequences of decisions he has made. Your authority shows in your face and your manner, sir; indeed, the atmosphere in the room changed with your arrival. But what I cannot see is why a man like you would be interested in a girl like me.'

He listened to this little speech, his face expressionless, and then glanced at Mrs Beaufort again.

A look passed between them that suggested an accord of some kind had been reached. Then, turning back to me, he spoke again.

'That was an astute answer, Mary. Tell me, are you a patriot? Do you believe in king and country?'

I nodded and lifted my chin a little. 'I do, Mr Wyatt. My father was in the Royal Navy, and I am proud to be a citizen of the greatest country in the world.'

'I am glad to hear that. And would you be prepared to act in its service? To help protect it, in fact?' He must have seen the question on my face because he quickly continued before I could answer him.

'Oh no, Mary, please do not misunderstand me. We have our army and our navy to protect our interests around the world. Rest assured I am not asking you to don a uniform and carry a weapon. No, the dangers that I am concerned with are of a more subtle nature and generally much closer to home. Even here in London, there are many that wish the empire harm and are working constantly to land heavy blows upon us.'

I nodded carefully at this and looked at Mrs Beaufort. 'Not all battles are visible, Mary,' she remarked before Mr Wyatt continued.

'We sometimes need to deal with people who are a threat to our interests, our institutions, or even to the king himself. Some of them are British citizens, revolutionaries and anarchists, for example, intent on creating trouble for political or social ends. Others are here by invitation, highly intelligent and dangerous men and women working in the embassies of foreign powers whose interests are not compatible with our own. Do you understand what I am saying to you, Mary?'

I did, although my head was whirling a little at this brief introduction to the unseen threats to our country. 'I do, Mr Wyatt, but why are you telling me this?'

He glanced at Mrs Beaufort and gestured gently in her direction before answering my question. 'For some time, Georgina here has been using her particular talents to help me fight the good fight. She works for me on occasions when we need to nullify the activities of individuals intent on harming us. Those who cannot be dealt with by other means and over whom we need to establish a position of power and control.'

Mr Wyatt spoke for another ten minutes, laying out in an unflinching way the exact nature of Mrs Beaufort's service to the nation and the role for which they thought I might also be suitable. To all intents and purposes she was a government courtesan who seduced men, and sometimes women to order, so that the state could blackmail them into obedience.

'I will speak plainly,' he said as he concluded. 'This is vital work for king and country, but it is not honourable, and it is occasionally dangerous. Unlike normal life, you cannot pick your suitors, as I am sure you are used to doing. Put simply, I will tell you who we are interested in, and you will seduce them. We photograph them with you in a compromising situation, show them the photos, and threaten them with exposure. It is highly effective in controlling the individual and even occasionally persuading them to change sides.'

He looked at me calmly for a moment, then continued. 'Georgina and I have developed this operation between us. Because of her looks, her unique skills, and her character, it has been very successful. But our enemies are many, and she is a woman alone. So we are looking for another to join our discreet little band, and Georgina believes you are well suited to the task. That is my invitation to you. Rest assured, you will be well remunerated.'

He finished speaking and there was a silence in the room. I heard the bells of St Paul's cathedral sound through the window and thought about what was being suggested to me. I was not shocked. Life in the inn had given me plenty of examples of the hardness of the world and having seen Mrs Beaufort with Sir Anthony the previous evening, I had guessed that her line of work probably involved something of an intimate nature.

'What do you think, Mary?' she asked.

'How do you obtain the photographs?' I asked back. I heard Hector give a little sigh of satisfaction. Afterwards I realised that he knew that if I was going to reject the idea, it would have been at that moment. Instead I had asked a question about how it was done. It was enough for him.

'I'll show you when Hector has gone,' Mrs Beaufort replied, then she smiled and added, 'In fact, you could watch some being taken tomorrow if you like. A client on whom I have been working for a few weeks is coming to see me in the afternoon. Would you like to do that, perhaps, before making a final decision?'

'Is it Sir Anthony? I asked.

'No; someone else. A lady,' she replied. She raised her eyebrows a little, and her wonderful eyes locked on mine and glowed with a shocked naughtiness that had me smiling back at her before I even realised it. I felt a delicious tingle somewhere down below.

‘Very well,’ I said. I must admit, I was intrigued, and the idea of watching the beautiful Mrs Beaufort in such a situation was not without its charms. Not at all.

‘That is a good idea,’ said Hector and stood up. ‘Time for me to go. Mary, it has been a pleasure to meet you. I am sure you will have many questions which Georgina can answer, so talk to her. I look forward to hearing your decision in a day or two, and I hope it is a positive one. Georgina has been so successful that her work has expanded to cover some other tasks. If you agree to my proposal, I think we can promise you an adventurous and interesting role in the defence of the realm. And I say again, you will be well paid for this work. Remember, your country needs you, Mary.’

With a little bow and a rather charismatic grin that lit up his face, he shook my hand, nodded to Mrs Beaufort, then turned and left the room. I heard him say goodbye to Jimmy in the hall and the front door slam shut.

Mrs Beaufort looked at me, then reached out and put her hand on my arm as an infectious smile suffused her face. ‘How exciting, Mary. It will be simplest to show you, I think. And please call me Georgina from now on. Come with me.’

I followed her out of the sitting room and turned right, going deeper into the house. We entered a well-proportioned corridor with the main stairs rising upwards on our left.

‘The house was extensively remodelled to accommodate our requirements some years ago,’ said Georgina, turning right again into what proved to be a large kitchen. ‘You’ll notice that the doorways are surprisingly deep.’ I looked back and sure enough, rather than a simple door through the wall, there was a short passage some five feet long leading back to the hallway. 'This is why,' she added, leading me to a wooden door to the right of the one through which we had entered. It led into a pantry with shelves of foodstuffs and household items on the right-hand side and plain wood panelling on the left.

She reached out towards it and with a click a panel moved open an inch. Turning, she rolled her eyes at me with excitement. 'No going back now, Mary. These are our secrets.'

Pulling the panel open wider, she ducked inside. Fascinated, I followed her into a dimly lit and narrow passageway. After some twenty feet, she stopped and gestured to the left. Joining her, I found myself looking though a clear glass window into the sitting room that we had left less than a minute earlier.

'This is how we take the photographs without the client being aware, Mary. You are looking through the large mirror you saw when you were in the salon. It is a mirror from that side but a window from this.'

She sat down on a wooden chair, picked up a box brownie camera from a shelf, and held it up for me to see. 'Jimmy sits in here and clicks away whilst I perform with my paramour on the settee. Thanks to Mr Kodak's invention, we can easily take twenty photographs and develop them ourselves here. Then they are passed to Hector, who raises the issue with the client in his own inimitable way.'

I was amazed. It was so simple and so effective. I could easily see how a man or woman, when presented with such photographs, would move heaven and earth to avoid them becoming public.

'And, of course, the more extrovert the performance, the more powerful the persuasion. We have a vested interest in ensuring that clients partake enthusiastically in the most unusual of activities,' she cooed at me, her eyes gleaming. I felt a thrill run through me as she leant forward and whispered in my ear, 'This is a house of great freedom, Mary. Nothing is forbidden. Absolutely nothing.' I felt her breath caress my neck, then she gently stroked my hair back and placed an electrifying soft kiss below my ear that left me shivering inside and outside.

Later that evening, I lay awake in my room in the hotel and thought about the remarkable events of the day. After seeing similar mirrors in Georgina's beautifully appointed boudoir and bedroom on the first floor, we had repaired back down to the sitting room and each had a whisky and soda, which was most welcome. She told me more about the arrangements for the following day and a little about herself.

She had married in her mid-twenties, and when her husband had died of cholera four years later, leaving her with debts, she had had little choice but to place herself under the protection of a wealthy man. This man knew Hector, and she had been asked to perform a single act of seduction which had produced a successful result, and the thing had blossomed from there. She had then added a further brief explanation.

'Like you, Mary, I am barren. My darling husband Ross and I found ourselves with child soon after our honeymoon, but there were problems with the birth and little Alice was stillborn. It was dreadful for both of us, and I was terribly ill for a while, but we picked ourselves up and in due course tried again. But I fear I was damaged beyond repair, and we did not conceive again before dear Ross's death.'

Sleep would not come. I could not get that brief intimate moment behind the mirror out of my head, and, as I imagined what it might have led to, I began to stroke my nipples, pulling and gently twisting them as I pictured Georgina kissing my mouth and undressing me. As if of its own accord, my hand slipped down between my legs, and I eased them apart and let my fingers slowly work over my clitty until it was standing proud. I was wet and spent easily and strongly, my mind busy with thoughts of what I would see tomorrow from behind the mirror.

So it was that at four o'clock the following day, Jimmy and I entered a cupboard on the landing and slipped down a passage to the window that looked out into Georgina's boudoir.

It was a lovely room, smaller than the salon and richly decorated in autumnal colours, with a fine carpet and velvet curtains pulled shut to keep out the gathering darkness and winter chill. A large, soft, and very comfortable-looking settee was placed some twelve feet away, half facing a fine marble hearth in which a bright fire burned. Looking to my left, I could see a pair of double doors that led to a bedroom. A double bed was visible, a dimly lit bedside lamp throwing an intimate light onto the blue silk coverlet.

We sat down on wooden chairs and Jimmy picked up the camera. He held a finger over his lips to indicate the need for silence as voices sounded on the stairs. He was wise to remind me, as the sense of being present in the room rather than watching from outside it was profound. Shortly afterwards the door opened and Georgina entered, looking absolutely divine in a sea-green silk dress, her blonde hair arranged in loose cascading curls.

She was followed by another woman. I fixed my eyes on her, intrigued and excited to see her completely unaware of her observers. Georgina had simply told me her name was Mrs Elena de Haan and she was the wife of a senior diplomat in the Dutch embassy. I gathered that the objective was to reach him through her. Their voices came clearly through a concealed grille in the wall above the mirror.

'I've told my man that he can have the evening off, so we won't be disturbed, my dear,' Georgina was saying. 'Do sit down and I'll get you a drink. Gin? It's Dutch, I believe,' she added and gave a little laugh at this.

'That would be nice,' replied Mrs de Haan, smiling in return, her English fluent. I think she was aged around fifty, a tall, full-breasted woman with dark brown hair piled high. Her eyes were also dark and quite distinctive in her unlined and very pale face. I think she was wearing some powder, as her cheeks showed a lovely pink blush which matched her red lips. Altogether, she was a distinctly attractive woman, and the dark blue dress she wore was well chosen.

When they were both settled on the settee and started to talk, it became clear that this was not her first visit to the house, but it was her first time upstairs in the boudoir. They chatted about the room and this and that for some minutes before Georgina, to my surprise, mentioned me.

'I have just employed a new maid, Elena, a quite beautiful girl named Mary. It is a pity she is not here tonight, or I could have introduced you. After all, with your maid and all, well …' She tailed off and raised her eyebrows with that amused intimacy which she did so well.

Mrs de Haan looked discomfited. 'Georgina, I told you that in great confidence. It is not for further discussion.'

'But it's just the two of us here, Elena, and this room is ideal for sharing intimacies. And secretly watching your maid bathing is unusual, you must admit. Although I have heard some women do have such feelings,' she added casually.

Mrs de Haan shook her head violently. 'No, Georgina, they do not. It was a most unpleasant and sinful thing to do. I really don't know why I did it.'

'But you did enjoy seeing her naked?' Georgina asked, her tone a little harder. The Dutch woman dropped her eyes to the floor and clasped her hands across her lap. She nodded slowly, then answered the question, her voice low.

'I wanted to walk away, but something held me there. I am deeply distressed that such an urge came over me, Georgina. My husband and I are God-fearing people who live by the Bible's laws. He pays me little attention with the demands of his work, and sadly none in the bedroom, but nevertheless, to find myself subject to such feelings … I am truly ashamed.' She shook her head again, and I could see her eyes were filled with tears.

Georgina moved closer to her on the settee and took her hand. Out of the corner of my eye, I saw Jimmy pick up the camera. A quiet click followed as he took the first photograph of the evening.

'I fear you are right to be, Elena. Such feelings must surely be a perversion in God's eyes and a great burden upon your shoulders. Will you accept my assistance? Perhaps we could work together to help you control these unnatural urges.'

She nodded and replied tearfully. 'Yes, please. I would do anything to ease my conscience.'

Georgina stood and walked a little way towards the mirror before turning to address her again. 'Anything, Elena? Are you sure? Because there is a way, but it will require endurance and fortitude on your part.'

'Is there? What is it?' She stood up and crossed over to Georgina. 'Is it a cure?' She dabbed her eyes with her handkerchief.

Georgina reached out and put her hand on the older woman's cheek, then gently stroked it as their eyes met. So often she looked as though she was sharing a delightful joke with you. Not now. Her eyes were radiating a power that was intoxicating from where I was sitting. Heavens alone knew what it was doing to Mrs de Haan.

I watched and listened in fascination as she guided her along a path she clearly already had in her mind.

'It is a treatment, certainly, but it is also a punishment, my dear. For I am sure you understand that to sin in God's eyes requires a penance. A cure may only be sought after that.' She nodded firmly as she finished saying this, and sure enough, Mrs de Haan, still locked into that devastating gaze, nodded back.

'I do deserve punishment. A forfeit must be paid. I see that.'

Georgina crossed to a mahogany chest and slid open the top drawer. She reached in and picked some things up before returning, holding her hands behind her back. 'Elena, you caused God great pain when you betrayed his grace with your perverted behaviour, therefore it is only right that you receive some pain yourself. It is the first step to repentance and redemption.'

As she finished speaking, she held up her right hand. It contained a tawse, a foot-long leather strap about two inches wide with a polished wooden handle. I know now that it came from a case of beautifully crafted tools and devices for the application of pain and pleasure, and that she was an expert in their use.

Jimmy took another photograph of the two women as Mrs de Haan looked at it and exhaled audibly in the silence that followed.

Georgina's voice was commanding. 'Firm strokes on the buttocks. That is what is needed. You will be naked and must submit with joy to the redemption the tawse offers you. As I am applying the punishment, I want you to think about your maid bathing and let your imagination run free. That will ensure the most effective remedy for your unnatural urges. And to ensure you are fully contrite, I will affix these to your nipples before we start.'

She held up her left hand and dangled two delicate brass clamps, each with a short chain attached, below which a shiny weight the size of a small marble hung.

She fixed the older woman with another devastating look, part dominance, part sympathy, then reached out again and stroked her neck. When she spoke again, her voice was much softer, almost caressing. 'You do trust me, don't you?'

Mrs de Haan seemed not to have heard. For some moments she stared at the tawse, and when she looked at Georgina again, her attractive face was wreathed in indecision. 'But fully naked in front of you? It is shaming.'

'What you did is shaming,' came the uncompromising reply. Georgina seemed to pause and think before continuing in a low voice. 'Very well. If the nudity is an embarrassment, then I will strip naked as well. Then we will be equals. In fact, I will lead the way.' With one of her trademark shocked grins, she turned her back and said, 'My buttons, if you please.'

As the Dutchwoman still hesitated, she looked over her shoulder and spoke again, her voice back to its dominating timbre. 'Elena, are you serious about redemption or not? Come on!'

I could see how she was smoothly switching between sympathy and judgement, and the poor woman, upset and confused as she was by her feelings about the maid, was kept constantly off balance. It was a lesson I was to learn well.

Mrs de Haan obediently unbuttoned the back of the sleek green dress and helped Georgina out of it. She looked utterly delicious in no doubt carefully chosen undergarments of red silk. She told me later they were from Paris, and indeed I had not seen anything like them in England, and certainly not in rural Devon. The top was a lacy camisole with narrow shoulder straps. As she moved, her nipples stood beautifully proud, two high points in the silky material. Below, her loose lace-trimmed drawers were short, finishing half-way up her thighs.

The Dutchwoman gasped and said, 'You look wonderful.'

'Given the circumstances, I'm not sure that's the right expression,' was the dry reply from Georgina as she moved behind her and quickly unbuttoned her dress. The undergarments revealed were of a more conventional design, and without further ado, and still working from behind, she lifted the camisole up and over Mrs de Haan's head.

They were facing the mirror at this point – no accident, I am sure – and as her heavy, dark-nippled breasts swung into view, Jimmy stood and clicked again with the camera. The drawers followed quickly, then her shoes and stockings, so that within a minute she stood naked and embarrassed in front of the mirror. She still had an excellent figure to match her fine face, and I felt my own interest stir as I looked at her smooth white skin and the dark thatch at her groin.

'I think Mr de Haan is rather foolish,' murmured Georgina. 'You are a woman who deserves considerable attention in the bedroom, not none at all.' I saw her slowly stroke her finger down her back. Mrs de Haan shivered and looked confused but stayed silent.

'And now …' She picked up the clamps. 'Your nipples need to be erect when I put these on,' she continued and lifted the right breast and sucked it into her mouth. I saw the older woman's shocked expression, but then her head bent back slightly, and her mouth widened as Georgina sucked and licked her. It seemed to me she took rather longer than needed before moving onto the other one. Then, moving quickly, she clamped each nipple and gently let the weights hang.

The older woman gasped in pain, instinctively moving her hands upwards, but Georgina grasped them both and looked her in the eyes.

'Remember, some pain is necessary for contrition and redemption,' she said firmly, pushing them back to her sides. She held up the tawse. Jimmy clicked.

Mrs de Haan eyed it. 'What do you want me to do? Shall I stand here?'

'Yes, in front of the mirror so you can watch yourself receiving due punishment for the pain you have caused Our Father with your perversions. Put your hands behind your head. And remember, you deserve this.'

Mrs de Haan did as instructed and I watched her breasts lift and part as she raised her arms, the weights moving gently. Georgina positioned herself to her left, holding the tawse in her right hand, and looked at the other woman, who was breathing audibly as she asked another question.

'What about you? You said you'd be naked too.'

'All in good time.'

She raised the tawse and brought it down with a sharp slap on the Dutchwoman's buttocks, smiling briefly as she heard the resulting cry of shock. 'I think it best if you thank me for each stroke. That way we ensure a penitent attitude is maintained. Please call me Mrs Beaufort whilst I am administering the punishment, and on no account move from this spot until I say you may.'

She swung again, and Mrs de Haan gasped as the tawse met her soft flesh before exclaiming, 'Thank you, Mrs Beaufort.'

'Good. Twenty strokes, I think.'

She swung again and then again, settling down into a steady rhythm as Jimmy stood and took a number of photographs. I noticed that Georgina would sometimes pause at the top of her backswing for two or three seconds, and this was often when I heard the quiet click of the shutter.

Mrs de Haan watched Georgina in the mirror. Her breasts moved gently as she reacted to each blow, and the weights swung from side to side. After a number of strokes, I noticed that the gasps of pain receded, and her tongue appeared between her lips. Her nipples were fully erect, cruelly squeezed by the clamps and darkly aroused against the pale red flush that was spreading across her neck and upper chest.

It seemed that repentance was not the only emotion being generated by the tawse.

After twenty strokes, Georgina stopped. 'How do you feel?' she said. 'Were you thinking about the maid as I asked?' The other woman nodded, seemingly unable to speak. 'Turn around. You may watch me remove my undergarments, but you must take no pleasure from it.'

As she turned, Jimmy and I were treated to a fine view of her buttocks. They were bright pink across both cheeks, with an occasional fine red line where the edge of the tawse had marked the flesh. I noticed her hand discreetly stroking them to try to assuage the stinging, which must have been profound.

In two swift movements, Georgina pulled her camisole over her head and wriggled out of her drawers. Both garments were thrown onto the floor. I heard Mrs De Haan's gasp of surprise and barely suppressed one myself as I saw her fully nude from the front.

Georgina had a beautifully proportioned body. Her shapely, pert breasts were crowned with delightful pink upturned nipples, and her belly, hips, and thighs seem to flow seamlessly from one to another. But there were two further and most striking things about her unclothed appearance. One was a large tattoo of a glorious red and green Chinese dragon, which occupied the left side of her ribs and belly. It was the size of a dinner plate and curved away out of sight around her side.

As if that was not enough, I realised with a shock that her cunny was hairless. Even from my hiding place some twelve feet away, I could clearly see the delightful plump lips and cleft of her most intimate parts. She posed briefly in front of Mrs de Haan before smiling and picking up the tawse again. Jimmy took another photograph.

'It's rude to stare. Even if you enjoy it.' She said this in a girlish flirty tone and grinned wickedly, then reached out, gently stroking the leather strap across the older woman's belly before flicking it upwards onto the weights, which swung under the impact. There was a gasp of pain as she continued speaking. 'On your hands and knees, bottom in the air. Quickly now, if you please.'

'Mrs Beaufort. Georgina, I …' But the Dutchwoman's attempt to speak was quickly cut off.

‘I saw you looking at me just then, Elena, and it is clear that more contrition is needed. I promised you repentance and a cure, and that is what I am going to give you. Now, get down onto all fours.’

With a muted whimper of surrender, Mrs de Haan obeyed, kneeling on the thick Turkey rug and then bending forward so her breasts hung down, the weights swinging from side to side as she got into position.

Georgina placed a cushion below her head. ‘Rest your face on that and part your knees.’

From our position behind the mirror, we were treated to a glorious view of the older woman’s rounded white-and-red buttocks raised into the air as she positioned herself according to Georgina’s instructions. Her cunny lips were visible in the dark hair between her legs, and I was conscious of a strong desire to pleasure myself as I watched the next stages of the treatment. I wondered if Jimmy was hard. It was difficult to imagine him not being so when presented with the extraordinary tableau on the other side of the mirror.

‘Another twenty strokes, I think, and remember to keep thinking about your naked maid,’ said Georgina, and without further ado she bent over and swung the tawse, which connected with a flat slap across both cheeks.

‘Thank you, Mrs Beaufort,’ she cooed, as the only sound from Mrs de Haan was a moan.

‘Thank you, Mrs Beaufort,’ came the echo, muted a little by the cushion her face was buried in.

The punishment continued until, on the eighteenth stroke, Georgina stopped. The poor woman’s bum was now bright crimson and streaked with lines, and I could see the cushion was wet from her tears.

'Elena, are you becoming aroused?'

Georgina put the tawse down and gently stroked a hand over her buttocks. It drifted to the top of the crack that led to her exposed pink bum hole and thick hair below. I watched, willing her on, as she slowly traced her finger downwards until it slid into the thatch. She moved it gently around, and Mrs de Haan shuddered and gasped.

'No, please, Mrs Beaufort. You mustn't do that. It's sinful,' she whispered in despair.

'But you are so wet, Elena. See how easily my finger slides into you. Do you feel no remorse at all? Why, anyone might think that you secretly enjoy being beaten by another naked woman. Are you not ashamed?'

'I am sorry, Mrs Beaufort.'

The muffled sob was barely audible as Georgina continued speaking in the same vein, her hand movements becoming more and more pronounced until she was steadily masturbating the older woman, who moaned and moved her hips, the combination of pain and pleasure produced by her stinging buttocks and stimulated clitty clearly driving her to distraction.

'Poor Elena. So confused. I think you need reminding of the simple realities of life,' said Georgina, picking up the tawse again. I thought she would resume the beating, but instead she grasped the leather strap and held up the handle. As she showed it to Elena, Jimmy took another photograph. 'A hard fucking is what you need, and fortunately for you, I have a fine implement here.'

Elena looked at the long, thick ebony shaft and moaned again, although whether with desire or despair was unclear. What was clear, however, was that Georgina had established complete control over the woman. Moving back to her rear, she knelt beside her and gently rubbed the end of the handle up and down her slit. 'Take your punishment, Elena. Take it like the penitent woman you are.'

Then she drove the tawse handle into her with one long deep thrust.

The older woman screamed and raised her head, but as a joyously grinning Georgina began to vigorously move her hand backwards and forwards, the cries turned to gasps and finally moans of submission. Her head fell back onto the cushion. I watched, deeply aroused and frankly rather envious of the treatment she was receiving.

She climaxed quickly, crying out in Dutch, but Georgina did not falter. In fact, if anything, she increased the rate and vigour of her movements. As Elena's second spend approached, she slid her thumb deep into her bum hole, which was enough to send her over the edge again. This time her deep passion produced not cries of pleasure but guttural animal grunts as she hungrily thrust backwards onto the glistening shaft, sucking it deeper and deeper as the muscles in the backs of her thighs flexed and worked.

Riveted to the scene before me, I realised that Georgina's skilful treatment had peeled away every layer of civility and decorum from the older woman, leaving only the base desire that nestles in the heart of all of us.

At last she withdrew the handle and Elena collapsed into a heap on the rug, her hair awry, eyes vacant, and expression wild, as though she was barely present in the room. Georgina gently removed the nipple clamps and then lay over her and kissed her long and hard. I could see her mouth was open as she worked her tongue around the Dutchwoman's mouth. She murmured some things in her ear that I did not catch, but clearly it was a further instruction of some kind.

Elena, completely subservient now, lay flat on her back. Georgina straddled her face, her knees level with the woman's shoulders.

'My turn, my darling,' she whispered, settling lower. 'Pleasure me with your mouth.'

Jimmy took two photographs in quick succession as the older woman obeyed without demur. Cupping Georgina's lovely bum, she raised her mouth and her tongue went to work. Georgina gasped and her head went forward as she looked down, and her hips started to move and quiver.

'That's it, my darling. Pleasure your mistress. I am going to spend on your face. You know that's what you want, isn't it?'

Georgina was pulling on her nipples as she muttered this seemingly to herself, but as her spend built, she became yet more dominant. Reaching down with both hands, she grasped Elena's head and began to forcefully slide her cunny backwards and forwards over her mouth, riding her mercilessly.

Jimmy clicked the final two photographs as she did this. The very last, as I subsequently saw, showed Georgina, head back and spine arched in ecstasy as she ground herself into Elena's face and her spend engulfed her.

Chapter Five

Georgina and Jimmy continue my education.

Seven days after observing Georgina and Elena de Haan, I moved into Arundel Court with the public position of maid and companion to Mrs Georgina Beaufort. It transpired that the house was larger than it seemed, and I was given a comfortable set of rooms on the second floor comprising a bedroom that looked out of the front of the house, a snug sitting room, and a bathroom, all on the same corridor.

Georgina's bedroom was not the one that I had seen the week before, as this was kept for clients only. Her own room was further down the first-floor corridor with a fine view out of the rear of the house and across some gardens towards the River Thames.

Jimmy's room was on the ground floor at the rear, on the opposite side of the main corridor to the kitchen door. Next door was the room where he developed the photographs. Various storage rooms and a back yard completed the main parts of the house, although Jimmy told me there were extensive cellars and a floored attic above my rooms. He cooked our meals, which we ate together in the kitchen, and a local woman came in for a few hours each morning to clean and tidy and take the laundry away.

I asked Georgina about Jimmy's background and she replied, 'He came with the house.' When I persevered, she said, 'He works for Hector. I once asked him about his life before that, and he declined to reply. We left it at that. I would do the same if I were you, Mary. We live in the present and look forward to the future at Arundel Court …'

Thus our household was arranged.

I was excited and more than a little nervous about my new role. Mr Wyatt had been delighted at my acceptance and had explained that I would live as a member of the household and would be paid a monthly sum as a retainer. When he mentioned how much that was, I was surprised and delighted. With no living expenses and a good income, I would be in a position to add to my current savings safely deposited in Farthings Bank head office in Leadenhall Street.

'You will need some training, my dear,' said Georgina on the second morning as she looked at me over the breakfast table. 'One needs to be something of an actress in our line of work, as well as becoming proficient in many physical skills.' As she emphasised the second part of her sentence, that amused, slightly outraged smile spread across her face, and as usual, I found myself smiling back at her.

'I am keen to learn, Georgina, and if the evening with Mrs de Haan is anything to go by, I am in need of considerable tutoring. I place myself in your hands.'

'And perhaps we will place Jimmy in yours.' She said delightedly and turned to him as he washed the dishes behind us. 'What say you, Jimmy? Are you prepared to assist with the beautiful Mary's education?'

He glanced at her, then caught my eye for a much longer look before saying, 'What man wouldn't?'

'One might say Jimmy is uniquely equipped to further your knowledge, Mary.' She giggled in a stage whisper across the table. 'We must begin classes without delay. What an exciting prospect.' Then, raising her voice again, she continued. 'But before that, one or two other changes are needed, I think. Have you ever considered cutting your hair short?'

'No, I haven't. It's been this French plait for as long as I can remember,' I replied.

'I think perhaps we should cut it so that your lovely neck is showing and create a fringe across your brow to give those extraordinary green eyes even more power.' She leant over, undid the ribbon, and ruffled my hair so that it fell loose at the back, then combed it forward with her fingers onto my forehead. 'Yes, that will be most effective, I think.' She led me over to a small wall mirror and showed me what she had in mind.

I nodded in acquiescence. 'If you think so, Georgina. I have confidence in you.'

So it was that later that day I emerged from a ladies' hairdressers with a fine new and rather unconventional hairstyle. Looking back, and with the advantage of time, it is best described as a 1920s bob, short at the back and with a low fringe, but at a time when most ladies of fashion wore long hair ornately piled high on their heads and domestic staff had a plait or a ponytail, my short cut was eye-catching. And Georgina was right; it did show my eyes and neck off to fine effect. I was delighted with it, and my confidence in her guidance was strengthened accordingly.

'You cannot use your real name, my dear,' she told me as we walked back to Arundel Court. 'Mary is all right, but we must choose a new surname as your working name. Do you have any preferences?'

I said that I did not.

'I am sure that you will be successful, and I hope you will be lucky. So perhaps the Latin word that means those two things would be a good choice. From now on, you will be Mary Felix.'

Alongside a review of my wardrobe and a discussion about cosmetics, the other items we talked about at some length the following day were Georgina's little secrets, namely her tattoo and her bald private parts. Sitting together with a bottle of madeira, she explained that it was a good idea for the clients to be a little shocked.

'It builds up the mystique and eroticism of the moment when they see us naked for the first time. A body tattoo and one's cunny on full display, these are things of fantasy, Mary. They erase any last-minute hesitation on the part of the client.'

'But the shaving?' I queried. 'How is that achieved without assistance?'

She led me upstairs to her bathroom and picked up a small metal device. 'This safety razor was invented in America a few years ago. It is quite different from a traditional cutthroat and makes shaving much easier and safer. And the type of shaving we require possible. With a small hand mirror, of course.' She touched my arm. 'Mary, I do hope you're not shocked at all the things you have seen and heard over the past few days.'

I took the razor from her and inspected it. 'I am here to learn, Georgina, and all this is fascinating. Perhaps I should try?' I brandished it in her direction.

'It is best done during a bath, so perhaps later or tomorrow.' She said this with a casual air, but her eyes flashed as she drew close, lowered her voice, and put her mouth so close to my ear I could feel her breath on my newly exposed neck. 'Perhaps I should help you the first time. I am experienced, after all.' My head whirled and my heart thudded, but suddenly she had turned and was walking out into the corridor. 'Come along, much more to talk about.'

I followed, feeling distinctly off balance. I was beginning to understand why Georgina was such a successful seductress. She had a way of drawing near and backing off, each time getting a little closer and lingering longer until you were sure that one time she would not retreat. And when that happened, you would joyously surrender and be hers in every way.

I could barely wait.

Downstairs, the conversation turned to tattoos. 'Now is the time, Mary. They take at least three weeks to heal, so there should be no delay,' she informed me.

'Does it hurt?' I asked.

'In truth, yes, a little, but the rewards are worth it.'

'I must admit yours is very impressive, and I do like the idea of being in polite company with a scandalous secret.'

She roared with laughter. 'That is it, Mary, that is it exactly. Many is the time I've been at a boring reception talking to some dry old stick and wanting to whisper to him, "I've got a red dragon tattooed on my belly and a shaved cunny. Would you like to see them?" And once in a while, one of them does.' She raised her eyes at me in naughty delight as she said this.

I laughed as well. 'Very well, Georgina, a tattoo it is.'

As a consequence of this discussion, two days later the three of us set out in a cab, heading to Limehouse in the east end of London. I was glad that Jimmy had accompanied us, for when the cab drew to a halt in a crowded street, the atmosphere was a world away from Sussex Street.

Just fifty yards ahead of us, the road ended at the River Thames, and a tangle of masts and funnels from ships of every description filled the gap between the tall warehouses that lined the end of the street. A cacophony of noise assailed our senses as costermongers and street traders bawled out the desirability of their wares, and the smoky air was filled with a range of odours, from exotic spices to far more unpleasant elements. We were noticed immediately by a gang of raggedly dressed children, who ran up and began pestering us for alms.

'All right here, then?' the cabbie called down. Then he added in a lower voice, 'Keep your eyes open. With the ladies and all.' This was privately addressed to Jimmy as he paid him.

But having brushed the urchins aside, Georgina was already heading for a narrow alley between two dilapidated buildings. We followed, and within moments the noise of the street began to fade. She banged on a red door set low in the wall to our left, which opened quickly.

'We're here to see Mr Chan,' she said, addressing the old woman who appeared and we entered a long, low, and dimly lit hall in what was clearly a very old building. I could hear Chinese music coming from somewhere, and a sweet musty smell mingled with jasmine assailed our nostrils as we turned left into a small sitting room.

'Opium,' whispered Jimmy in answer to my raised-eyebrow query.

An elderly Chinese man was sitting at a desk smoking a battered yellow pipe, pen in hand. I could see a simple drawing in black ink in front of him. He looked at us, then fixed his eyes on Georgina and smiled as he stood up.

'Mrs Beaufort. We meet again.'

'Good morning, Mr Chan,' she said, walking forward to shake his hand. 'This is my friend Mary Felix. She would like a tattoo, and as you worked so satisfactorily for me, I have come back to see what might be arranged.'

He nodded slowly and looked at me without speaking.

'Is this your wife, Mr Chan?' I asked, gesturing vaguely at the old woman, primarily to break the silence and interrupt his stare, which was becoming rather oppressive.

'His mother, dear,' giggled Georgina. 'He's not as old as he looks, but opium, well, it ages people.'

Mr Chan smiled bleakly at this and pulled a blank piece of paper towards him. With a few swift strokes of the pen he drew the graceful outline of two unclothed female bodies, one a frontal view and one from the rear. Then he held out the pen to me.

'Draw it, please.'

Georgina and I had settled, largely under her direction, on a snake, which would twist across my torso and finish low on my belly. This I now drew as a line commencing under my left breast and curving under its partner and then under my arm. I picked up the line on the rear view and showed it curving down across the base of my shoulders to reappear on the front image. It then described a full circle of my belly button before dropping down to finish directly above the neat little ink stroke Mr Chan had drawn to illustrate my cunny.

He nodded. 'Snake?'

'Yes, a snake. Like this.' I drew two parallel lines and sketched in a diamond pattern between them. 'Yellow, black, red, yellow, black, red. And so on.'

He picked up the pen again and drew a snake's head with a long forked tongue twisting out of it and showed me. Then he added a thin snake body and coloured it in a yellow, black, and red diamond pattern. He looked up again, his eyes questioning.

'Yes, I think so. Georgina, what do you think?'

'Wonderful, my dear. You will be quite a sensation with your pet serpent.'

I will draw a veil over the rest of the day and two that followed, which were without a doubt the greatest ordeal I had endured in my life up to that point.

The pain as Mr Chan worked on me was such that by the first afternoon I was reduced to imbibing jasmine tea with a much-diluted measure of opium in it to numb my senses. As well as reducing the agony, this had a curious effect on my mind. Even though I felt dreamy and somehow lifted out of myself, I found I could recall the events at the house the previous evening with a clarity and intensity that was in effect a complete reliving of them.

As you will hear, this was a mixed blessing.

After supper, Georgina had suggested to me that it might be time for a bath. She did this with a raised eyebrow and a quizzical smile that clearly indicated to me that what she had in mind was a trial with the safety razor, and I willingly agreed.

We went upstairs to the bathroom on the first floor, which was reserved for her exclusive use. It was a pleasant room with a wooden chair, wash basin, and a small dresser upon which a range of oils and unguents were displayed. The walls were painted a pale terracotta, and the bath was tucked into an alcove space rather like a doorless wardrobe. The taps were positioned centrally on the wall side, and, after closing the door with a distinctive click, Georgina turned them on and added some sandalwood oil, which quickly filled the room with a rich and distinctly eastern aroma.

'I'll help you with your dress, my dear,' she said, unbuttoning the back. I slipped it off and she hung it on the back of the door. I turned and looked at her, half expecting that she too would start undressing, but I was to be disappointed, as she merely gestured at my underclothes and smiled. I slipped out of them and stood before her, naked and suddenly shy, my heart beating strongly. It was the first time she had seen me in such a state, and I saw hunger flash across her eyes as she smiled at me.

'Oh, Mary, you are delicious. Utterly delicious.'

I climbed in and she sat down on the chair, watching and talking as I leant back in the hot water. After a while she stood, picked up a large sponge from the dresser shelf, and showed it to me.

'From the Pacific Ocean. They grow under the sea and are collected and dried by the natives. Lean forward and let me wash you.' She knelt down and dipped it into the water, then worked some soap into it before slowly stroking it across my back. Then she washed me all over, taking her time and concentrating, almost as though it was a ritual cleansing of the kind I had read about in books. It was a delightful sensation, and as I stood and she gently worked the sponge over my buttocks and inner thighs, I shivered a little.

'And finally here,' she said, drawing the warm soapy sponge down my bum crack and onto my cunny. She gently rubbed it backwards and forwards as I gasped and spread my legs a little, willing her onwards.

'That's very nice, Georgina,' I whispered, hoping to encourage further intimacies, but she just smiled and put the sponge down.

'I'll get the towel,' she said, standing and reaching for it. One part of me could have screamed with frustration, but another part appreciated the game she was playing. I was beginning to understand that she was training me. Showing how layer upon layer of desire and anticipation could be developed until the climactic fusing of two souls became not just possible but inevitable.

This was seduction as a fine art, and I was a willing pupil.

'Sit down in the chair, Mary,' said Georgina. She was holding a pair of scissors. 'Open your legs, my darling. Let me trim you so we can apply the razor.' I obeyed, letting her kneel between my legs and watching as she gently and carefully cut my dark thatch until there was just a short fuzz across my groin. She held up a hand mirror to show me the results.

'See, Mary, already we are beginning to see your true beauty. And now the razor.'

Picking up the soap, she lathered it into the sponge again, which she spread across my cunny, rubbing it in gently. She handed me the razor and placed the mirror in my other hand.

'Hold it so you can see what you are doing and gently scrape the lather away.' I did just that, slowly shaving the remaining hair away and dipping the razor in the bath from time to time to clean it. The sensation was unusual and stimulating, and I found working with the mirror quite difficult, but at last the task was complete.

'Get back into the bath for a moment and wash the soap off,' Georgina instructed.

I complied and dried myself, then she led me naked to a long freestanding mirror in the corner, and I stood and looked at myself in my new hairless state. I was thrilled. My cunny showed clearly, two plump lips either side of a deep cleft, with my clitty peeping from its summit.

Georgina looked at me in the mirror for a long time, saying nothing, just holding my hand and smiling, almost sadly. Finally she handed me a soft silk dressing gown and said, 'Let's go into my boudoir, Mary.'

I walked barefoot down the corridor and turned into the lovely room in which I had seen Mrs de Haan reduced to quivering submission by Georgina's dominatrix skills. She followed me in. The room was warm but empty, a fire burning in the grate. I glanced to the left through the double doors that led into the bedroom. They were open, and with a beating heart I saw Jimmy sitting on the big bed, wearing a richly decorated dressing gown of his own. He was looking at me.

'Here we are, Mary. Just the three of us,' said Georgina and led me into the bedroom.

Jimmy stood up silently, his face serious. Georgina pulled off my robe, leaving me standing naked and newly shaved six feet from him.

'It's time for the next element of your education, Mary,' she said. Then she addressed the tall man in front of me. 'She is yours, Jimmy. Probably the most desirable woman in England. Enjoy her.'

With two quick paces he crossed the space between us and put his hand underneath my chin, lifting my face to his.

'Good evening, beautiful,' he said, then kissed me hard. I kissed him back, mouth open and heart racing, my passion rising as I felt his stiffening cock through the thin material of his robe. The prospect of congress with such a muscular and potent man was intoxicating, and I felt my head begin to swim in anticipation. Especially as Georgina showed every intention of staying to observe us.

His big hands roamed all over me, lifting and parting my buttocks before squeezing my breasts hard. As he stepped back to look at them, I slid the robe off his shoulders. It fell to the floor, revealing his magnificent torso. I ran my hands over his chest, which felt like it was made of sheet steel, but when I reached down to grasp him, he slapped my hand away.

'No,' he grunted, then bent forward and engulfed first one, then the other nipple, licking, then biting and squeezing, working his hands over them hungrily. It was arousing but also painful.

'Gently, Jimmy,' I murmured breathlessly.

His eyes met mine momentarily, but I saw no tenderness in them, and there was no slackening in his lustful assault on my breasts. If anything, the reverse. At length, he looked downwards and slid his hand onto my belly and then in between my legs, pushing my thighs apart so my new nakedness was exposed to his gaze. He grunted with satisfaction as his rough hands discovered my wetness and my erect clitty. Again I reached for his cock, eager to feel him, but again he slapped my hand aside.

'No,' he repeated, then slid two fingers inside me, his other hand grasping and squeezing my buttocks so I was held firmly as he drove his fingers in and out. The rough treatment continued for some time, alternating between my breasts and cunny, until he suddenly pushed me to a kneeling position. I gasped in surprise as my face came level with his swollen cock, and I barely had time to register its prodigious size before he grasped the shaft with his right hand and placed his left behind my head.

'Open your mouth,' he instructed.

I obeyed, opening my mouth as wide as possible and just managing to accommodate his cockhead as he slid it in. He grunted with pleasure and placed both hands on the back of my head. His hips started to thrust, and within moments I was not sucking him; rather, he was fucking my mouth. He continued using me for his own pleasure in this way, occasionally removing his cock and rubbing it over my face before sliding it back in. I felt both used and aroused beyond measure and managed to slip one hand between my legs so I could stroke my clitty as I serviced him.

Across to my left, I could see Georgina had removed her clothes and was leaning back in an easy chair, her left leg lifted onto the arm. Her fingers were slowly stroking her exposed cunny as she watched us. She looked me in the eye and smiled lasciviously but with no warmth.

'Fuck her now, Jimmy,' she said.

He bent down and picked me up effortlessly, then walked over to the bed and placed me on the coverlet. Kneeling between my legs, he pushed them wide apart, leaving me naked and defenceless against the coming assault. His cock was both magnificent and terrifying, a towering thick shaft skinned back and ready. He looked at my cunny for a long moment and smiled but made no eye contact with me.

'Sweet,' he said.

Suddenly, I was aware of Georgina next to the bed with something in her hand. Bending forward, she obscured him for a moment or two, but when she leant back again, I saw a narrow leather strap pulled tight and encircling the base of his cock.

'I want to watch her being used. Fuck her hard, Jimmy. Take your pleasure and don't hold back,' she instructed him.

He did not reply, just knelt forward and drove into me, deeper and thicker than anything before. I arched my back and screamed as he penetrated me, but he ignored my cries and settled into a steady, fast rhythm. I wriggled desperately, trying to accommodate him as best I could, but it was clear that my pleasure was of no concern to him at all. Lust had stripped him of all sensitivity, just as I had seen Mrs de Haan reduced to the same state some days earlier.

On and on he pounded until sweat was running freely off his chest. I licked it up, nuzzling and biting him on the neck, my fingers deeply embedded in his muscular back and my legs spread wide. I spent multiple times, and far away I could hear someone crying out and wailing loudly, but it was only as he paused and changed position that I realised it was me.

He raised himself into a kneeling position and drove forwards again. Now my heavy breasts were exposed to his gaze, and he watched them swaying rhythmically up and down, the brown nipples standing proud as he fucked me, before reaching out and squeezing them hard.

Georgina was still standing by the bed, masturbating openly as she watched his cock plunging into my shaved cunny lips. I met her eyes in surrender, hoping for some connection, but she just smiled and shook her head at me before urging him on with the most profane language I have ever heard, her voice hoarse with lust.

Finally, she gave him a further instruction. 'On her knees now, Jimmy.'

He disengaged, his cock springing out of me like a jack-in-a-box, before powerfully flipping me over onto my tummy and then lifting me at the hips so I was on all fours. He pushed my legs apart and my shoulders down onto the bed.

‘Wait. I want to see,’ said Georgina. Looking in the big mirror to my left, I saw her lean over and have a long look at my exposed cunny and bum, then felt her fingers probe me briefly. She reached up and gave Jimmy a long open-mouthed kiss before taking hold of his cock shaft. She swiftly undid the leather strap and threw it onto the floor, then guided him into me.

In this position, his penetration felt deeper than ever, and I climaxed powerfully again, crying and moaning into the pillow as he fucked me. On and on he went, his hands gripped tightly onto my buttocks as his thighs battered away until at last, with an animal howl, he came inside me, a prolonged shuddering orgasm. Then he collapsed onto my back, his thighs still jerking and his face buried in my hair as we rolled over to lie side by side on the bed.

I was shaking and spasming all over. My poor cunny felt as though it had been pounded with a tawse, and my arms and breasts were bruised where Jimmy’s rough treatment had left their mark. As for himself, his back was torn and bleeding from my fingernails, and he was panting for breath and wild eyed, as though he had fled the devil himself. He lay next to me and took my hand in his as Georgina slipped onto the bed on my other side.

As I lay there looking at the ceiling, tears started to flow, and I quietly sobbed. My lovemaking had always been passionate but also consensual and loving, each one pleasuring the other. But Jimmy’s dominant aggression had shocked me. I had been used by him with no thought of my own feelings and left sore and bruised both physically and emotionally.

Georgina let me cry for a while, then began to kiss my shoulders and neck gently, her hands soft and caressing. At last she spoke quietly to me. 'I am so sorry, dear Mary, but that was a necessary lesson. Your lovers to date have been your own choices, and with your looks, you have been able to control them, whether you realised it or not. Our work is different. Hector is prepared to pay for us to live in this high style because he understands that sometimes what we do is distasteful and occasionally worse.'

I turned my head on the pillow and looked tearfully at her without speaking as she continued, her voice soft.

'We are women with beauty and above-average desires, Mary. We wield these weapons for king and country just as soldiers use muskets and swords, and sometimes we are wounded in action. It is possible a client will treat you like that, and you must be able to cope with it.'

She picked up the corner of one of the robes and dabbed at my eyes. 'Now come and have a whisky and soda by the fire. You have seen how a powerful man can easily dominate a woman if he chooses. When we are rested, I will show how a woman can do the same to a man. Be assured, you will have your revenge on Jimmy tonight.'

Donning our robes, we moved through to the boudoir, rather shakily in my case, and sat around the fire. Slowly, I started to feel better. I was also coming to terms with the fact that although Jimmy had been brutal, I had spent intensely as he took me. And I had found the fact that Georgina was watching and pleasuring herself very arousing.

For his part, Jimmy said very little. It was noticeable that he didn't apologise for his treatment of me and I resolved to take full advantage of whatever opportunity for revenge Georgina had in mind. We became peckish, and Jimmy was dispatched down to the kitchen to bring us up some sandwiches. When he had left the room, Georgina crossed to a cupboard, and returned with a black leather case. She placed it on the table in front of the settee and opened the lid. I gasped in surprise at the contents.

It was lined with plush red velvet into which, in custom shaped recesses, a number of devices were embedded. I saw the tawse that had proved so effective on Mrs de Haan and its partner, which had a longer, narrower strap, plus the two nipple clamps sitting snugly side by side. But what was most remarkable were two ivory cocks, one about six inches long, the other around eight inches. They occupied the middle of the case, and neatly packed below was some kind of soft leather harness. I was to learn later that Georgina called these devices Lord Hardwick and Doctor Bone. The final elements running round the outside of the case were four black cords each about half an inch in diameter.

'My box of tricks,' said Georgina, rolling her eyes in delight. Reaching down, she picked up the cords and handed one to me. 'Made of silk. Feel it.' It was about two feet long and as soft as running water. I slipped it around my fingers and looked at her, a question in my eyes.

'Restraint by consent is a powerful stimulant for some people. Even if they don't know it before they visit me.' She laughed and looked horrified simultaneously, and as usual I found myself smiling back at her outrageousness. Then she snapped the case shut and put it back in the cupboard. 'We'll have a look in there another time,' she said. Then, as footsteps sounded on the stairs, she draped all four cords across the table, spacing them equidistantly, like four railway lines.

Half an hour later, Jimmy was naked and spread-eagled on the big bed, his hands and feet tied by the silken cords to each corner, a deep filled pillow under his bum so his hips were raised and splayed. I was kneeling on his left and Georgina was on the other side. In contrast to Jimmy, we were both still wearing our robes, although my breasts had a habit of falling out every time I leant forward. I had noticed Georgina eyeing them on several occasions.

Reaching down, Georgina began to stroke and then squeeze his balls. He responded with a muted sigh. 'I'm just wondering how unkindly we should treat him when we consider how rough he was with you,' she said. Then she removed her hands and gestured to me.

I reached out and gently stroked his ball sack with my right hand. I understood well enough what was required of me and intended to enjoy it. 'Well, that's a good question, Georgina. I mean, I could be gentle with him like this, but then, he wasn't gentle with me, was he? He was very rough indeed. So perhaps something similar would be appropriate.' With this, I squeezed hard and his balls appeared between my fingers and thumb. I tapped them with my other hand, and he moaned.

Georgina clapped delightedly. 'Look at the way they're pushed up like that, as though they're trying to escape. Perhaps they know what's coming, Mary.' She slipped her hand around his shaft and began to steadily pump her hand up and down it.

I am sorry to admit that I rather indulged myself for the next twenty minutes. Three times I removed my hands and watched as my beautiful and increasingly aroused companion pulled and sucked his cock until he was at the point of climax. Then she released him and I ruthlessly squeezed and spanked his balls. The pain from my ruinous hands prevented him from reaching fulfilment on each occasion, and his cries and moans filled the room as he strained against the silken bonds.

For much of this time Georgina kept up a running commentary, talking first to me and then to Jimmy. She clearly enjoyed such oration, and the ruder and more profane it got, the more and more stimulating she found it. The contrast with her civilised decorum in the drawing room could not have been greater, and my vocabulary was considerably expanded as she gave vent to her feelings.

At last she picked up the previously discarded leather strap and fixed it tightly around the base of his shaft.

'I must ride him, dear, for my own pleasure,' she said to me, throwing off her robe and straddling his cock. I watched her lips distend as it sank into her, and she began to slide backwards and forwards. 'He still can't come until we say so, Mary. That tight little strap will stop it getting out no matter how much he wants to,' she gasped.

She climaxed quickly, grunting and leaning forwards, her hands on his chest as her delicious bum bounced and thrust, wet slippery noises coming from her cunny. I found watching her enormously arousing and slipped a finger between my legs, but to my disappointment, I was still too sensitive and bruised to partake of that particular entertainment. I said so to Georgina as she slid off him. She made a little pout and addressed Jimmy.

'Poor Mary is still sore from your brutish attentions earlier on. Never mind; I am sure we can think of another way to entertain her. Why don't we fetch the little bottle of massage oil that is sitting on the shelves in my bathroom?'

Jimmy stirred. 'No, Georgina, please, not that. Enough now. You have both had your fun.'

'I'll be the judge of that. Be quiet.' She nodded to me and I left, returning quickly with a small blue phial of oil.

'Now kneel between his legs, dear,' she instructed.

Jimmy strained against the bonds. 'Georgina, please …' but she cut him off.

'She has to learn, and you must behave. You have had your pleasure; now be quiet.' Then, addressing me, she added, 'Oil his cock and balls, Mary.'

Once in position, I poured a little of the unguent into my hands and slowly worked it over him, paying special attention to his swollen cock head.

'Now slide your fingers down underneath his balls and rub the oil around his bum hole.'

Concentrating, I followed her instructions.

'Gently work your first two fingers into him. Put them in about two inches and press upwards. You will find a gland like a swollen soft walnut just there.'

Intrigued, I complied, ignoring his gasp as I penetrated him. My fingers went in easily and I found the lump as she described. As I moved my fingers gently over it,

Jimmy's reaction was electric. He moaned deeply and his cock strained and lifted from his stomach.

'That's it, Mary,' said Georgina, grinning at me as I slid my fingers out again. 'Jimmy's little secret. Although all men have such a thing. When directly and continuously stimulated, it produces a most powerful ejaculation. If the stimulation continues, the man will keep producing spunk until he is utterly drained. In every way.'

'But Jimmy cannot come while the strap is on him,' I pointed out, acting the earnest pupil as I stroked his balls.

'I know.' She giggled and clapped her hands with glee. 'I promised you revenge, and this is it. Put your fingers in again and gently massage the gland.'

I complied, steadily working my fingertips over the swelling for some time. After his treatment of me earlier, Jimmy's agonised cries were music to my ears, and I thoroughly enjoyed the power I had over him. Georgina slowly dragged her nail down the shaft of his cock. It strained in response, and I heard him mutter, 'Please, Georgina.' She laughed and looked at me.

'Do you see now, Mary? In our line of work, you must always be wary of the strength and power of a man, but we have our ways too. Poor Jimmy would agree to anything if only we weak and pitiful ladies would just release that cock strap and let him come. Anything at all.'

I took pity on him. 'Shall we see it now, Georgina?' I reached down and untied the tight leather band, then slid my fingers back in and started to massage his gland again whilst firmly pulling his balls back so the shaft rose to near vertical.

'That is it, Mary. Oh, look how delightfully his cock is jerking. I think he's going to come without us touching it.' Georgina's fingers were busy between her legs as she watched.

We both stared with wide-eyed anticipation as it throbbed and strained. Tied down, stretched out, and hips raised high as Jimmy was, it seemed as though every individual muscle and sinew in his body was vibrating like corded steel.

I felt his bum tighten on my fingers as the gland and then the tube below his balls started to pulse. I pressed my thumb onto it, feeling exquisitely powerful as I watched his tortured face.

'Oh God, yes, Mary, don't stop. Empty me out.' He pleaded and twisted in his bonds, and then, with a sudden aching cry of surrender, he let fly.

The first two spurts passed directly over his head and hit the wall behind him, then three more splattered onto his chest as he roared and strained against the ropes.

'Keep going, Mary,' instructed Georgina calmly as the initial spasms eased. Then she leant over him and encircled the end of his cock with her thumb and index finger. Slowly, she drew them back and forth, not touching the shaft at all and focusing solely on its slippery head.

Powerless in his bonds, Jimmy cried out and came some more, less powerfully this time. Georgina grinned lasciviously at me as it spread across his stomach.

'Plenty more where that came from, Mary. Keep working him.'

I pushed my fingers deeper, pressing more firmly and pulling on his balls encouragingly. Jimmy groaned at the further stimulation. 'That's enough,' he whispered.

'I think you can give us a little bit more. Squeeze his balls hard, Mary. Do they feel empty yet?'

'Not yet, Georgina. After all, it was only minutes ago that he was pleading to come,' I said in my strictest voice, feigning irritation as I worked away.

She giggled in agreement. 'One last effort, Jimmy. Come on, show Mary what you can do.' She wrapped both hands around the shaft of his cock and began to wank it mercilessly. The poor man pleaded and thrashed his head about, but sure enough, after three relentless minutes of our combined attentions, he began to spasm and spend again, begging with us to stop even as he did so. This time it was little more than a dribble, and when we finally released him, he was soft.

Georgina rubbed her hand across his chest and stomach, then reached upwards.

'Open wide, Jimmy,' she said firmly. 'Show Mary what you like.' As he obeyed, she wiped her spunky fingers over his lips and pushed them into his mouth. He sucked them clean. She turned to me and in a stage whisper said, 'That is naughty Jimmy's other secret. He likes cock almost as much as he likes cunny. A fact that has proved rather handy in the photography department on more than one occasion.'

Chapter Six

Edward de Haan receives bad news and Lord Bridport recruits a housekeeper.

Edward de Haan sipped his morning coffee and considered the note which had arrived at his office in the Dutch embassy some twenty minutes earlier. It had been hand delivered, and the messenger was waiting for a reply downstairs. It was a short message, handwritten in black ink on plain, good-quality paper.

Mr de Haan,

I beg you to attend on me at the Athenaeum Club at half past two this afternoon, where you will learn something to your personal advantage. The porter will have your name.

Yours sincerely,

William Munroe

He leant back, idly eyeing the portrait of Queen Wilhelmina on the wall opposite, and wondered if an unknown relative had died and left him a legacy or whether some other unexpected windfall might be in the offing. He certainly did not recognise the name of the sender.

Then he frowned slightly and pursed his lips. More alarmingly, it might be something to do with the clandestine network of informers he was steadily constructing across Whitehall. Men whose hunger for money outweighed their patriotism and who provided a steady flow of useful intelligence about the inner workings of the British Empire. On more than one occasion, his friends in the Boer community in South Africa had been appreciative of information he had passed their way.

He leant forward and picked up a pen. Either way, it was an invitation of sufficient interest for him to quickly draft a short and positive reply, walk down the stairs, and pass it to the waiting boy.

At half past two he presented himself to Albert Hobbs, the long-standing porter at the Athenaeum, who eyed him with well-concealed distaste. De Haan was a tall man who dressed soberly but exuded an arrogance and moral superiority that did little to endear him to new acquaintances. The porter was used to summing up men in a single glance and made his judgement accordingly.

Not like Mr Munroe with whom the man was to meet. There was a gentleman of quality and no mistake, thought Albert as he led the Dutchman across the hall and up a grand staircase to a small meeting room. He knocked and opened the door.

'Mr de Haan, sir,' he announced and stood back to let him enter before closing the door quietly.

A well-dressed, grey-haired, clean-shaven man with an intelligent face was waiting inside. He smiled briefly and offered his hand.

'I am Munroe, Mr de Haan. Good of you to come at such short notice. I'm sure your duties at the embassy keep you fully occupied.' He gestured at a pair of armchairs placed on either side of a coffee table. 'Do sit down. Can I offer you a whisky and soda?'

When the drinks were served and the men were sitting opposite each other, Munroe smiled urbanely at him and started to speak again.

'It was your work for the Dutch Government here in London that prompted this invitation. I work for the British Government. Indeed, you might say we toil in the same field.' He paused and raised his eyebrows a little as if inviting recognition of this fact.

The man opposite smiled. 'You are involved in export and import permits as well, Munroe? Well, it is not the most exciting of things, but it needs to be done. Now, perhaps you can explain why you wanted to meet at such short notice?'

'No, not trade regulation. Espionage. That is your stock in trade, is it not?' Munroe leaned forward and fixed his eyes on the Dutchman. When he spoke again, his voice was cold. 'I am well aware of your attempts to encourage British government employees to betray their country, and, although your efforts have not been as successful as you might believe, I have decided that it is time for them to stop.'

Although shocked, De Haan affected surprise and then smiled across the table. 'Munroe, I can tell you sincerely that you are mistaken. Such activities do not form part of my responsibilities here. Or indeed of anyone else's at the embassy, for that matter.'

'Then you occupy a curiously senior position and a fine office for what is essentially a clerical role,' the other man retorted. Then he held up his hand and continued. 'But no matter, your protestations of innocence are of no interest to me. It is time to go back to Amsterdam, Mr de Haan, and to retire from public life.'

The Dutchman frowned at this.

'I say again, you are mistaken, Munroe. And I can assure you I have no intention of going back to Amsterdam. Retire from public life? You must have taken leave of your senses. In any event, you have no jurisdiction over me. I have diplomatic protection.'

'As you wish.' Munroe shrugged slightly and reached down to pick up an attaché case that was sitting by his chair. He opened it and removed a large manila envelope before replacing the case on the ground. Opening the envelope, he removed some photographs and appeared to quickly check the order they were in before turning the top one over and placing it on the coffee table facing De Haan.

'What is this?' The Dutchman leaned forward.

The picture showed his wife sitting next to an extremely attractive blonde woman in a richly decorated sitting room. The women were holding hands and the blonde was leaning forward as though talking earnestly to Mrs de Haan. A second picture appeared. Both were now standing, and his wife was looking at a leather strop of some kind which the blonde was showing her. She looked upset.

'What is this, I said, Munroe?' he demanded. 'Where did you obtain these photographs? His voice tailed off as two more pictures appeared. His wife was now naked and seemingly being beaten by the blonde, who was wearing her underclothes.

De Haan swore in Dutch and looked in outrage at Munroe, but the images kept coming, each one more horrifying than the last. His wife on her knees being whipped and then, to his horror, manually stimulated from behind by the naked blonde. In the next one, she was being deeply penetrated with the handle of the tawse, her ecstatic face turned towards the camera, mouth wide open and all decorum gone.

The last one showed the blonde woman, head forward and smiling, straddling his wife's face as she cupped her buttocks and eagerly reached upwards with her tongue. De Haan saw to his horror that the woman was hairless down there, and his wife's features were clearly recognisable. The blonde had a large dragon tattoo across her stomach and ribs, he noticed.

'My God, Munroe, who is that woman? What is the meaning of this obscenity?' All the colour had drained from De Haan's face, and his voice was now quiet.

Throughout the gradual display of the photographs, Munroe had said nothing, just calmly laid each one down in succession so they formed a double row across the table. Now he looked up and spoke.

'There are eight photographs here, but in total we have twenty and the film. Quite enough to send to the ambassador, the foreign minister in Amsterdam, and your mother in Haarlem. The rest we will spread about amongst your friends and colleagues. Perhaps even send a couple to the pastor at that church you both attend so devotedly.' He smiled thinly at that.

De Haan somehow seemed smaller, and yet the rage burning inside him was clear. 'May Satan take you,' he muttered, then inhaled as though to speak further, but Munroe interrupted, his voice authoritative and clear in the silent room.

'The British Empire is the most powerful the world has ever seen, and it is not run by fools. You have two choices, De Haan. Either resign, go back to the Netherlands, and retire from public life, or be disgraced to the point that suicide for the pair of you is the only option.'

He stood, collected the photographs, and replaced them in his case. The Dutchman watched him silently from his seat. Finally he spoke.

'How did you manage it? Without her knowing.'

'Your wife is an unhappy woman. We exploited that and we exploited her, and for that I am sorry. Do not punish her, De Haan. Your lack of attention meant she was distracted from a true course, and the other woman is extremely skilled. But never forget it was your actions which precipitated this; we are merely defending ourselves.'

He walked to the door and opened it, then turned and stared back for a long moment.

'Go home, De Haan, and take your troubled wife with you. Goodbye.'

*

The Fortune Domestic Agency in Bridport High Street was reached by climbing a long straight flight of stairs from the outside door. On reaching the summit, Mrs Virginia Welling turned to the right and walked along the landing towards a door marked 'Please knock and enter'. These actions accomplished, she presented herself to the secretary behind the desk, who looked up with a pleasant smile.

'Good morning. I am Mrs Welling, here to be interviewed for the post of housekeeper at Bancroft Hall.'

'Yes indeed, Mrs Welling. I'll just let Mr Fortune know that you are here.' But it immediately became apparent that an announcement would be unnecessary, as a voice called out from the inner office.

'That's fine, Amanda, send her in.'

'Mr Fortune will see you now, Mrs Welling.' The girl indicated a door to her left. 'Let me take your coat and hat first.'

The office that she entered was a large and pleasant room with a bay window that looked out over the high street. Behind an old oak desk, a man was standing, smiling. He was younger than she was expecting, perhaps in his mid-twenties, with dark blond hair and a moustache. He leant across the desk and held out his hand.

'Good Morning. William Fortune.' He paused and added dryly, 'The younger.'

'Virginia Welling, Mr Fortune.' She sat down as he indicated in an upright wooden chair.

William leaned back in his own chair and took her in with a brief but surprisingly sophisticated glance for one so young. He saw a woman in early middle age, quite tall and strongly built, with calm grey eyes. Her fine-boned face was framed by dark brown hair neatly contained within a tight bun, and she had a good complexion, he noticed, with lips that were particularly full and well shaped. Her dark blue dress was of good cloth and complemented her excellent figure without being showy.

A very attractive woman in the full bloom of her life, he concluded. All this was registered as he continued talking. 'My father sends his apologies, Mrs Welling. He is not well and asked me to conduct this interview on his behalf, and of course on that of Lord Bridport as well.'

'I quite understand and hope that he is soon on the mend.' Mrs Welling's voice was pleasant, without accent and firm, William noticed, and when she met his eye, her look was direct and clear. *Good*, he thought. *A strong character.*

'Indeed. Thank you. So, Mrs Welling, tell me about your current circumstances and why you think you are suited for the post at Bancroft Hall.'

The discussion continued for half an hour, and William became increasingly convinced that in the candidate before him he might well have found the solution to the unique problems that Bancroft Hall presented. At length he paused and drummed his fingers gently on the desk.

'Mrs Welling, you have acquitted yourself entirely satisfactorily, and I thank you for your candour. There are some things at Bancroft Hall, some aspects to the post, as it were, that I feel I must make you aware of before we go any further.' He stood and walked over to the door and pushed it shut before returning to his seat.

'Have you heard of Lord Bridport before, may I ask?'

'To be honest, no, I haven't.' She moved her hands in a gently negative gesture.

He nodded. 'You may, however, be more familiar with his name before he acceded to the title, when he was known as the honourable Percival Lyons, or better known, perhaps, as Captain Percy Lyons. Cast your mind back.' He saw her pause and think, then recognition appeared on her face.

'Oh. I see.'

'Yes, Mrs Welling. The very same Captain Percy Lyons who, as the popular press had it, led his men to slaughter in a vainglorious attack on a Boer position on the high plains of Natal. The pursuit of personal glory at the expense of his men, they said. Although around here you won't find much sympathy with that point of view.'

Mrs Welling shifted slightly on her seat as she absorbed this and then nodded firmly. 'Well, if that is all, Mr Fortune, I do not see that as an issue from my side, I can assure you. It is clear the man is brave, if nothing else.'

William grimaced gently. 'I fear that is not all. Not completely. When he was finally carried back by one of the few men still able to walk, he had received a bullet wound to the head. It healed in a manner of speaking but left him physically scarred and, I fear, mentally scarred as well. Put simply, Mrs Welling, he has a reputation as a reclusive and difficult man. Rumours occasionally circulate about events at Bancroft Hall that are distasteful at best.'

'Rumours, Mr Fortune?'

'Just so, Mrs Welling.'

She paused and looked at him, inviting further disclosure, but his mouth remained firmly shut, although she noticed he was blushing furiously. She inhaled and opened her mouth to ask him directly, but he interrupted her, speaking quickly.

'Mrs Welling, the post requires a firm and experienced hand, and I am confident that you meet the requirements very well indeed. I will telephone to the hall straight away advising them of such. If you would be so kind as to return here after lunch, I will then have made arrangements for your onward trip to Bancroft with the intention of meeting Lord Bridport and commencing your post immediately, assuming you are satisfactory to him.'

He stood and shepherded her into the outer office before quickly retreating to his lair and shutting the door.

'Congratulations, Mrs Welling,' said Amanda brightly.

The older woman stood and looked at her and then said, 'It seems I am accepted for the post. Mr Fortune spoke of rumours …?' She tailed off.

'Amanda, can you come in, please?' The voice carried through from the other room. The girl stood and moved towards the inner office door as she replied.

'Oh, don't worry about those. Just salacious tittle-tattle. Quite the disciplinarian, our Lord Bridport, it seems. See yourself out, will you?' With another quick grin, she disappeared through the door.

At four o'clock that same afternoon, the cab in which Virginia Welling was travelling was admitted to the grounds of Bancroft Hall by the lodge keeper at the south gate. Since her interview she had had plenty of time to reflect on the conversation with young Mr Fortune and, despite some minor misgivings about the nature of the rumours to which both he and Amanda had alluded, was well satisfied with the way things seemed to be working out.

Finding herself a childless widow aged thirty-two and of limited means, she had had little choice but to seek a respectable post as a housekeeper. Over three separate positions in the Southampton area, she had advanced her status by the simple expedient of moving to larger establishments each time.

Starting with a well-to-do surgeon and his wife, she had moved on to the owner of a successful chain of draper's shops before spending three years in her most recent role as housekeeper managing a staff of five on a small estate just north of the city.

On each occasion she had allowed herself to be persuaded to grant the gentlemen whose households she managed certain favours on the understanding that these would be quietly rewarded in financial terms. As a woman alone, she saw no reason not to partake in such activities if they were both pleasurable and profitable.

Her natural appetites and good looks had undoubtedly helped, and as she was subtle and discreet, the arrangements had been acceptable to all concerned. Indeed, the wife of the shop owner had admitted to her that she was glad to have another to share the burden of her husband's rapacious appetites. They had on more than one occasion all shared a bed together, an experience which Mrs Welling had found most stimulating.

Sadly, her most recent tenure at the estate had become increasingly difficult as the health of her employer had started to fail, and his wife, concerned for the integrity of her inheritance, had firmly suggested it would be best if she sought another place. However, as the cab emerged from a tree-lined carriageway and swung over a slight incline, she looked out of the window to the right and any lingering regrets faded.

Below her, Bancroft Hall lay peacefully in the late afternoon sunshine surrounded by wooded hills and open estate land dotted with fine trees. She could see a herd of deer grazing on the slopes to the right of the long three-storey Georgian frontage. A high cupola rose above the pillared main entrance, which was reached by a wide flight of steps. Three large windows were arrayed on either side, and above, on the first floor, there were twelve smaller ones, regularly spaced across the building.

From her elevated position she could see the house was shaped like the letter n, with two parallel wings extending to the rear at each end of the long frontage. A formal garden occupied the space between these and stretched further in the same direction before melting into a tangle of wooded paths and pleasure grounds. To the left of the main house, a cluster of roofs and walls indicated the location of the stables, outhouses, and a large kitchen garden.

She was delighted. Here at last, she reflected, was a place that she could settle and achieve the status that she desired.

'Front or back?' The cabbie's call interrupted her thoughts.

'Back, if you please,' she replied.

Two minutes later, she was standing at a tatty brown door ringing the electric bell. After a considerable delay, the door swung open, and she found herself looking at a tall and ruggedly handsome footman. Although she immediately noticed that he had not shaved that day and his uniform was neither clean nor pressed.

'Mrs Welling to see Lord Bridport regarding the position of housekeeper.'

He nodded. 'Yes, we heard you were coming. Follow me, if you please. You can leave your bag there for the moment.' He pointed to an alcove by the door. She did so and followed him through a number of twists and turns until they climbed a flight of back stairs and entered the main hall. They saw no one else, and the hall was silent.

Straight ahead she could see the front door, and to her left a graceful flight of stairs rose to a half landing before splitting to run up both sides of the hall to the first-floor. Above her, the great glass cupola allowed light to flood down, even as the sun was setting.

'Lord Bridport is in his study, I believe.' It was the only remark the man had made since they had met at the back door.

'Is that where he spends a lot of his time?' enquired Mrs Welling, attempting some small talk. But the servant just nodded and led the way down a thickly carpeted corridor to an oak-panelled door at the end. He knocked and entered without waiting for a reply. As he did so, the woman reached out and drew her finger across the top of a fine walnut side table. It was thick with dust.

She heard a brief muffled exchange and then the servant reappeared.

'You can go in now.' Then he edged past her and walked off. Drawing a deep breath and bracing her shoulders, she fixed a smile on her face and stepped through the door, closing it behind her. She had a brief impression of a large masculine room, but all her attention was focused on the figure sitting in profile behind a desk in the window. He was backlit by the fading light, and as she watched, he reached out and flicked the switch on a desk lamp.

'Good afternoon, Mrs Welling. Please come in and take a seat before me.'

Lit by the warm glow of the lamp, she could see that he was a fine-looking man with a strong profile, clean shaven and with short brown hair that was gathered into tight curls. She guessed he was aged around forty, like herself. He was wearing a Lovat green tweed suit, a cream-coloured shirt and a dark red knitted tie.

'I am Lord Bridport. Please ready yourself, madam.' After a slight pause, he turned to face her.

She inhaled and raised her head a little but managed to retain her warm smile as the extent of his injuries became apparent. The bullet had clearly impacted above his left eye and ricocheted backwards, removing half of his left ear and damaging the skin on his scalp to a degree that meant no hair grew around the scarring. It was a gravely disfiguring injury, and Mrs Welling felt immediate sympathy both for the young man so terribly damaged and the reclusive man he had become.

'It is a pleasure to meet you, my lord,' she replied.

He smiled sourly. 'Is that so? Then you must be a woman of rare character and fortitude, madam. Or blind.'

'I am not blind, my lord, and I would like to believe that the former is true. I am here because I hope to have the opportunity to demonstrate those qualities to you.'

He was silent at this for a moment, then continued. 'Very well, Mrs Welling. Young Fortune telephoned and spoke highly of you, so I will lay before you the size of the task here at Bancroft. When my father died six years ago, I inherited not just the house and estates but also a butler who lacked both the character and inclination to perform to the standard that this great place requires. Put simply, he was lazy and incompetent. For old times' sake, I put up with him for three years but in the end had to suggest honourable retirement was the only option. In his place, I recruited a younger and seemingly enthusiastic man whom I thought could take command below stairs. He too has failed, and in fact it was discovered by my accountants that he had been merrily fiddling the books to his personal profit.'

He sighed and placed his hands on the table as though thinking what to say next. The woman sat silently. She could sense a curious conflict in the man before her, as though dominance and submission competed constantly for the upper hand. As he continued speaking, she realised that this was indeed what he was suggesting.

'I will be frank with you. My injuries have affected my appearance, of course, but also my moods. I acknowledge that sometimes I am a difficult man to please. On occasions I manifest great passion and purpose and a desire to be in control most fully, and yet at other times my confidence melts away and I am strongly driven to assume a passive role. I am aware that I lack …' he paused and stared across the room for a moment before completing his sentence, 'consistency.'

She made to reply, but he spoke over her.

'The staff have become slack and lazy. Certainly the indoor staff, anyway. Outside, Ellerman the head gardener keeps his people in order and working hard. He is a good man, but inside I fear I have lost the initiative, and the house suffers as a consequence. As do I. The staff need direction and discipline. Firm discipline. I have tried, of course, but because of my inconsistency, my efforts have too often petered out. I have not seen it through – been unable, in fact, to see it through. Do you see?'

His anguished expression was painful, and she felt a burst of pity for him as he shuddered and shook his head violently before continuing.

'I feel sometimes as though I have a traitor living inside my head alongside my old self, working constantly to exploit my weaknesses and suborn my authority. I speak openly to you, Mrs Welling, because if we are to work together to recover matters, I believe you must have the full picture.'

She looked at him with her wide calm eyes and spoke in a low but clear voice. 'My lord, your honesty sets you apart from other men. What happened to you, it is unimaginable …' She tailed off, gesturing with her hands in her lap.

'I was humiliated by the press and harangued by my peers and the public for an act that was forced upon me by another. It wounded me as much as these physical scars, but I will be revenged yet, Mrs Welling. I have my strategy, rest assured.'

'And in the meantime, you wish me to assume the post of housekeeper and wield the stick in order to bring the house back to its former glory. Are we agreed on that, my lord?'

He stood and held out his hand over the desk. She took it and they shook hands. To her surprise, the skin-on-skin contact sent a little shock through her.

'We are, Mrs Welling. We are. I like the look of you, and you are quite right to mention the stick. I am great believer in physical discipline.' As he said this, his eyes drifted over her shoulder. Turning to follow his gaze, she saw an umbrella stand in the corner. A polished wooden handle protruded from it.

'Bring that over here, Mrs Welling,' he said. She walked across the room, letting him see the swing of her hips, and picked it out. Below the handle a stiff leather strap some fifteen inches long and two inches wide was attached. She placed it on the desk between them.

'A tawse, my lord,' she said.

Bridport looked at it, a smile appearing on his lips. 'When the cheating butler was discovered, I ordered him stripped and then whipped him with this in the stable yard whilst the staff looked on. Then he was made to walk naked from the house to the lodge, where his possessions were dumped in the road. I found the experience to be most satisfactory. But since then…' he shrugged and looked at her.

'Nevertheless, a salutary lesson,' said the woman approvingly. She pursued the conversation, curious to see where it would lead. 'And you wish me to use this to enforce my authority below stairs?'

'I do. I am resolved. No more weakness on my part. Henceforth everyone in this house is subject to the discipline of the tawse, Mrs Welling.'

There was a silence in the room before the woman looked directly at him and spoke. 'My lord, it strikes me that if you wish me to beat the staff when they transgress, I should perhaps have some experience of the way it is done.'

His eyes narrowed. 'Are you proposing that you beat me, Mrs Welling?'

The attractive woman smiled at this. His voice should have expressed outrage, but it was, in fact, calm and level. Again, she held his eyes for a long moment before answering, so he understood that such a course of events would not be unacceptable to her.

'No, sir. I am suggesting that you beat me.'

'You would permit that?' His eyes gleamed at her.

'My lord, I will be a firm disciplinarian with the staff, you may be assured of that. But as far as you are concerned, if it pleases you to chastise me at any time, then you will find me receptive and compliant.'

'Now?'

She smiled again and stood up, then walked over to the study door and locked it. In the silence, the click seemed abnormally loud. She walked back to the desk, picked up the tawse, and handed it to him.

'Now, sir,' she whispered.

A surge of excitement appeared on his face, and his voice assumed an unmistakable tone of command as he instructed her. 'On your naked buttocks, then, Mrs Welling. Please remove your undergarments and lean over the desk.'

'Certainly, my lord.' She reached under her dress, pulled down her drawers, and stepped out of them, then placed them on the wooden chair. With a long look at the scarred aristocrat, she leaned forward and rested her torso on the desktop.

'Perhaps it would be easier if you were to raise my dress, sir.'

He didn't answer her directly but placed the tawse next to her head. A second later, she felt her clothing being lifted, and a draft of cool air crept up her calves and then her thighs. She moved away from the edge of the table slightly and helped to facilitate the final stages by raising the front of her dress, whilst Bridport gathered the rest into the small of her back.

He exhaled slowly as her white buttocks were fully exposed to his gaze. They were flawless, he saw. Unblemished and full, in perfect proportion to the woman's strongly built body. He felt his cock stir at the sight and reached for the tawse, barely able to remove his eyes from her vulnerable pose.

Mrs Welling spoke. 'When you are ready, my lord, please proceed. I will be firm with your staff, so pray be the same with me. I suggest a good number of strokes so I may appreciate the experience fully.'

With no further ado, he swung the tawse firmly onto both cheeks. A flat smack echoed around the library and then another as the stroke was repeated. A third followed quickly. Mrs Welling gasped in pain as her buttocks started to sting. From his position behind her, Bridport could see a crimson flush developing. His cock was now at full stand, and he paused briefly to adjust his clothing before continuing. At the tenth stroke, Mrs Welling raised her hand.

'A moment, please.' She turned and faced him, leaning back a little onto the desk and still holding her dress high at her waist, seemingly oblivious to the view she was presenting him with.

He stared openly at the dark thatch at her groin. She saw he was flushed and guessed he was hard. 'Thank you. A brief respite was needed. You have a strong arm, my lord.' Turning, she resumed her position, but this time she placed her hands on the edge of the desk and her legs much further apart, then dipped her head and bent her back low so that her pink bum hole was clearly in view, with a glimpse of her dark cunny lips below.

'Punish me, sir,' she said.

The aristocrat swung the tawse again and again against her crimson buttocks. She stopped counting as he passed twenty and continued, but at last, with her cheeks aflame and tears of pain running down her face, she held her hand up and turned, only letting the dress fall after a short delay. She was very sore but also had to acknowledge to herself that the act of submission had left her deeply aroused.

'Thank you, my lord. That was most instructive.'

He stood wild eyed and flushed, the tawse hanging limply in his hand. Stepping forward, she gently picked it out of his hand and placed it on the desk, then stood close and looked up at his face.

'I cannot imagine the rejection and loneliness that you have had to bear from my female compatriots, my lord, but I am sorry for it. Let me take some of your anger and pain away, I beg you.'

She reached up and stroked the scarring on his face briefly, then slowly sank to her knees. Her gentle hands undid his fly buttons and eased his clothing down. He sighed but said nothing as she released his hard cock and stroked it, slowly at first and then more quickly, her hands practised and skilful as she worked him.

‘Let it all come out,’ she whispered. Her right hand moving quickly, she slipped the left behind his balls, cupping them whilst pressing upwards onto the tube that resides behind. He moaned and spread his legs wider, unconsciously giving her access, and she pressed harder.

His hips started to move as he panted rhythmically in response to her firm strokes. She worked relentlessly for some time, her fingers slick with his juices, until he gave a loud gasp as his climax approached.

‘Nearly there?’ she whispered, her voice intimate in the quiet room. She felt him start to jerk and pulse. ‘Ah, yes; here it comes now. That’s it; let it all go, my lord.’

At the last moment she sank her warm mouth over his swollen cockhead and swallowed it all, sucking passionately and sliding her left hand beneath her dress to finger herself to the climax she so urgently needed. When he finally quieted, she released him, then stood and put her underclothes on as he buttoned himself up.

Bridport looked at her in some embarrassment. Now that his lust was slaked, he did not know what to say or do. However, Mrs Welling was a match for the situation and gave him a warm smile.

‘Thank you, my lord. That was most enjoyable. I will go downstairs and assume my duties directly, if you would find that acceptable?’

Still bemused, he nodded silently. She crossed to the door, unlocked it, slipped through, and closed it quietly behind her. Bridport sat down in his desk chair and turned to stare reflectively out of the window. As he did so, a faint smile appeared on his face.

Chapter Seven

The tempting of the Earl of Culligan.

The Earl of Culligan was enjoying the spring sunshine in St James's Park in central London. Even though he had only arrived from Dublin a few days earlier, he had established a very pleasant afternoon routine encompassing a circuit of the lake and a stop for refreshment at a tea house on the edge of Birdcage Walk, the main road that led back towards Parliament Square. From his seat outside, he could see Big Ben rising above the trees. A steady stream of hansom cabs and the occasional motor car passed him, and in the park, finely dressed gentlemen and ladies mingled with clerks and office girls. He watched them, his mind drifting idly as he smoked a cigarette.

A couple detached themselves from the throng and headed towards the tables outside the tearoom. He noticed the girl straight away. Even though plainly dressed in maid's clothing and hatless, she was remarkably attractive, with unusually short dark hair that left her neck exposed. As she walked past his table, he was transfixed by her luminous green eyes and full lips. She gave him a glance and a quick smile, moving easily and gracefully, her splendid figure all too obvious under her tightly buttoned coat.

A beauty, no less. A full-blown English beauty, he thought to himself. They sat down at a table about ten feet from him, and he moved his chair a little and continued to study her discreetly. She did not look happy, he noted; in fact, her face was distressed, and as he strained to listen to their conversation, he had a good look at the man who was with her.

He did not like the look of him at all. A coarse-looking, strongly built fellow with a rough beard and thick dark hair, dressed in workman's clothes. As he watched, the man reached over the table and grasped the woman's upper arm.

She twisted away and he heard her say, 'No, I won't. And please let me go.'

He glanced around. The only other couple sitting outside had just left and were walking towards the pavement on Birdcage Walk.

A chair pushed back noisily, and he saw the woman was now standing rubbing her arm. She looked over at him, an unspoken appeal in her eyes. It was enough to spur him into action. Blood pumping, he rose and strode purposefully across to the table.

'Is this man bothering you, Miss?' he asked, before turning his glare on the man, who was now also rising from his seat.

'I don't really know who he is,' she said. Her voice had a thick West Country burr, he realised, as her words tumbled over each other. 'My mistress told me to meet her here at four o'clock, and when I was walking across the park, well, he just started talking to me and then followed me here. I told him I was busy, but he ignored that.' She lowered her eyes, clearly embarrassed. 'Then he made an improper suggestion. Wants me to go with him. I told him I am not that sort of girl. Then he grabbed my arm.'

Culligan turned to the man in fury. 'You absolute bounder. Get out of it, or I will raise my cane to you, sir. Go on. Away with you!'

But the man stared belligerently back and stood his ground. 'Oo are you, anyway? You ain't her dad, that's for sure.'

The Irishman drew himself up and hissed, 'I am the Earl of Culligan, and by God, sir, if you are not gone from this place in ten seconds then I will not be responsible for my actions.'

'Olright, I'm going. You probably just fancy a bit yourself, anyway. I know you toffs. Pretty girl, ain't she?' He leered across the table. Then, as Culligan raised his cane, he turned and shuffled off. They watched him go in silence.

'Dreadful man. Come to my table, my dear. What a terrible experience for you. What is your name?' Culligan gently took her elbow and steered her back to where his coffee pot waited.

'My name is Mary Felix, sir.'

'Well, as you heard, I am the Earl of Culligan, but my friends call me Alfred.'

'Oh no, sir, I couldn't do that. I'm just a lady's maid, and what with you being royalty and all.' She looked shocked at the thought.

He laughed, delighted by her naivety. 'I can assure you I am not of royal blood, Mary, just a common or garden Irish earl. And Alfred will do.'

‘Mary, is that you?’ a voice called out from behind him.

‘My mistress is here,’ said the girl, glancing over his shoulder.

He turned and just managed to stifle an exclamation. Another startlingly attractive woman was bustling over from the path. Her blonde hair was styled in tight ringlets and piled high, and she was dressed in a pale blue dress with a small matching hat and carried a rolled-up parasol. As she neared their table, he realised she was older than Mary – perhaps about thirty, he guessed.

He stood up to greet her and, as she met his eyes, for the second time in less than ten minutes he found himself bewitched. They were a bottomless shade of brown that seemed to ebb and flow in front of him as amusement, arrogance, passion, promise, and delight flitted across them in a beguiling kaleidoscope. He stared, momentarily transfixed.

In the background he heard Mary speaking and caught ‘the Earl of Culligan’.

She held out her hand and he shook it, rapidly recovering from his shock. She had a melodious and surprisingly deep voice that seemed to embrace him with warmth.

‘Mrs Georgina Beaufort, my lord. It appears we are in your debt.’

‘It was very little, I can assure you, Mrs Beaufort. I merely did what any gentleman would do.’

‘Yes, well, Mary has a history of getting into scrapes, I am afraid.’ She lowered her voice and whispered, ‘She got the looks, my lord, but she didn't get the brains to go with them.'

This confidence was accompanied by an arch look of such amused horror that the Irishman found himself grinning like a schoolboy in response, utterly charmed by the charisma of the woman in front of him.

As the story was told, to Culligan's surprise, Mrs Beaufort seemed sceptical about Mary's role in the matter and questioned her closely. With the maid wide eyed and pleading innocence, the earl felt he had to step in.

'Having seen the matter unfolding before me, I think I can reassure you that Mary was the offended party. On this occasion, at least.'

'Hmm, we'll see,' she replied, looking across the table at the girl. 'Mary has a chequered past and has not been with me very long. I have taken her on as an act of kindness after she was rescued from …' she paused here and met his eye, 'a place of low reputation.'

'Ah. I see.'

'Quite. Well, anyway, enough of this. My lord, you must come to tea tomorrow and give me an opportunity to thank you properly for your noble act this afternoon.' Completely captured by the adoring looks Mary was giving him and the extraordinary charm of Mrs Beaufort, Culligan found he had little difficulty in accepting.

At half past four the following day, a cab dropped him at the entrance to Arundel Court and, following the instructions provided by Mrs Beaufort, he walked down the alley to the square and knocked on the shiny blue door. Mary herself opened it and welcomed him effusively. After taking his coat, she led him into a pleasant salon with a large bay window at one end and a bright fire at the other. A large and very attractively framed mirror was attached to the wall, he noticed.

Mrs Beaufort was waiting for him and smiled. 'My lord. Welcome to our humble home. How very nice to see you again.'

He was again captivated by her eyes but managed a little bow and took a seat opposite her. 'Do please call me Alfred, Mrs Beaufort. We are all friends here, I'm sure.' He beamed at her and managed to encompass Mary in the look as well.

'Then you must call me Georgina. Will you join me in a whisky and soda?'

'I would enjoy that, Georgina, thank you.'

She nodded to Mary, who moved over to a table where Culligan could see a collection of bottles and glasses. Out of the corner of his eye he saw her carefully pour the whisky and then struggle with the soda siphon, clearly unfamiliar with its operation. However, at last the drinks were served, and after Mary had left, he and Georgina had a very pleasant conversation for half an hour. She was a good listener and asked him interesting questions. He told her about his Irish estates and the importance of his role in the Irish Government before suddenly realising that he had barely given her a chance to speak at all.

'That's enough about me, Georgina. Do tell me about yourself and how you come to be living here in this delightful house.'

'Before I do, one more question for you, Alfred. Would you care for another whisky?'

He hesitated. The first one had been very strong, and he was feeling it, but before he could refuse, Georgina added, 'Do have one. I think that I will.' Without waiting for an answer, she walked to a bell button and pushed it, and thirty seconds later, Mary appeared. 'Two more whiskies,' she said.

Again Culligan noticed that her tone was distinctly short with the girl, but he supposed that, as Georgina was another woman, she was perhaps immune to her extraordinary beauty. He also noted that her maid's dress was of good quality cloth and surprising well fitted, pulled in tight around her waist and flaring gracefully out over the swell of her buttocks. The top was cut lower than he would have expected, and the deep valley of her breasts was enticingly evident as she bent over the drinks table.

After the death of his first wife, he had partaken freely of the obliging Irish maids in service at his country seat on the outskirts of Cork. Some of them had been pretty, but nothing like Mary. Warmed and relaxed by the whisky, he watched as she walked carefully towards him, carrying his drink on a tray and smiling. He could see her nipples underneath the fabric of her dress and felt a stir of lust.

He reached out for the glass just as the girl stumbled in front of him. The tray tipped over, depositing the whisky in his lap, instantly soaking his trousers.

For a moment, pandemonium reigned as he stood up, frantically brushing with his hand whilst Mary wailed an apology, her hands at her face. Georgina leapt to her feet, her face suffused with fury.

'You foolish clumsy girl,' she cried. 'That is the second time in less than a week. What is wrong with you, child?'

'Oh, my lord, I am so sorry. Please forgive me.' The maid's plea was infused with rising panic as she stared at their visitor.

Culligan continued mopping with a handkerchief and replied, 'An accident, my dear. These things happen. It will dry in due course, I am sure.'

But Georgina was not to be mollified. Grasping Mary firmly by the arm, she steered her towards the settee opposite Culligan and sat down. 'I warned you that any more foolish behaviour would result in punishment, and I mean to keep my word.'

'Oh no, please, Mrs Beaufort, not in front of the earl,' pleaded Mary. But the blonde woman would not take no for an answer and pulled her forward. An astounded Culligan watched open-mouthed as Mary ended up braced face down over Georgina's knees.

'Apologies, my lord, but the time has come to teach this tiresome girl a lesson.'

So saying, she began to pull at the maid's dress, revealing shapely calves, then thighs, and finally a pair of wonderfully rounded and wriggling buttocks. She wore no underclothes, the earl noted, and again he was reminded of the smiling Irish maids who would lift their skirts for a shilling. He watched, fascinated and increasingly aroused, as Georgina, now in complete control, pulled the dress up onto her back, leaving Mary naked from the waist down but for a pair of laced black boots.

'Now then, Mary, perhaps after this you will be a little more careful, you clumsy girl.'

Raising her right hand, she began to firmly spank her buttocks, each flat crack echoing around the salon. Culligan stared, conscious of his rapidly swelling cock as Mary cried out and struggled most delightfully under the chastisement.

On and on it went until, faintly tanned though her skin was, the earl could see a strong red flush appearing across both cheeks. The maid was crying now, her face turned towards him as Georgina worked away, scolding and smacking with an enthusiasm that Culligan found arousing in itself.

Finally she stopped, breathless from her exertions. 'Stand up, child.'

Mary stood, and Culligan gasped as she turned to him. In her wriggling, the dress's front buttons had come undone and one of her magnificent breasts had fallen completely out. He stared at the dark brown nipple and unconsciously licked his lips. As if that was not enough, the garment somehow remained rucked up at the front, so that as she stood, there was a long pause before it fell back into place.

In that moment he had a glorious view of her cunny shaved bare and plump, and, even more extraordinary, what looked like a serpent's head tattoo appearing from under the dress, its long tongue flickering downwards towards the thick fold of skin at the top of her cleft.

'For heaven's sake, adjust your dress, Mary.' Georgina's voice broke into his spellbound open-mouthed reverie. His poor cock was achingly hard, and he fervently prayed that he would not have to stand up for the next few minutes.

But it was not to be.

'Alfred, please take off your jacket and let this tiresome girl sponge it dry.'

'I … er …' He tailed off.

'It is the least we can do. Mary, help him with it.'

Reluctantly, he stood and turned to face the fireplace, hoping that the awkward bulge in his trousers was not too obvious. However, he was amazed when, as Mary came behind him and reached around to take the jacket, she breathed quite deliberately on his neck and her hand gently squeezed his cock, sending shockwaves through him. It was so quickly and skilfully done that he was certain Georgina noticed nothing.

The blonde waved her away and out of the room before smiling at Culligan and resuming her conversation.

'My apologies again, Alfred. I am sorry you had to witness that unfortunate scene, but I do believe that firm treatment is needed for one's staff, and it is best done immediately.'

'Spare the rod and spoil the child, Georgina,' agreed Culligan, and the conversation moved on to other things.

It was only much later that night, as he was getting undressed to go to bed, that he realised there was a piece of paper in his jacket pocket. Unfolding it, he read a short note, written in an untutored childish hand.

Cum tomorrow at 2pm. She will be out. Bak door. M

He stared at it for a long time, a smile slowly breaking out on his face as his groin stirred in anticipation.

Chapter Eight

Earl Culligan succumbs and suffers the consequences.

The following day, with his heart beating noticeably harder than normal, the earl rapped firmly on the back door of Arundel Court with his cane. As it swung open Culligan could not help grinning with delight. The girl had changed into a low-cut red dress that suited her colouring, and with her short hair brushed and eyes glowing under her fringe, she looked utterly beguiling. A relieved smile suffused her face as she saw him.

'I thought you weren't coming, sir. Thought maybe you weren't interested in me.'

'No, no, Mary, quite the contrary,' he hurried to reassure her. The girl's naivety really was quite delightful, he thought. 'I was delighted to receive your charming note, and here I am.'

She stepped aside and said, 'Shall we go into the room where we were yesterday, sir?'

'If you like, and it is Alfred, please, Mary. You must call me Alfred.'

'Very well … Alfred.' She gave a delicious giggle as she tried it out. 'Fancy me being on first names with a member of the royalty. If only my mum could hear me.'

This time Culligan did not bother to correct her, partly because he was eyeing her delicious buttocks moving beneath her tightly fitting dress. He suspected that, as with the previous afternoon, she was wearing nothing beneath it, and his head swam at the thought.

Within moments he was sitting on the same settee as before, with the girl next to him.

'So your mistress is out, Mary?'

'Yes, Alfred, for all afternoon,' she said. 'Leaving me here all alone and bored.' She pouted a little, and Culligan realised belatedly that her red lips matched her dress. *Really, every part of her was perfect.*

'Then we'll have to entertain you somehow, won't we?' he remarked, his mind racing with possibilities. 'Tell me, Mary, why did you send me that lovely little note?'

The girl looked out of the window for a moment, apparently lost in thought. Then she seemed to reach a decision. She turned back to Culligan and took a deep breath before speaking, her words coming out in a rush, the Devonian burr strongly pronounced.

'When the mistress chastised me yesterday, I liked it that you were watching. Being a handsome milord and all. I imagined it was you doing it. That you were my lord and master and I had been a bad girl, and you were holding me down and spanking my bottom before having your way with me. It made me wet, Alfred. That is why I touched you, and why I sent you that note. I know it's naughty of me, but I'm a girl with strong desires ...'

She tailed off as Culligan, heart beating wildly, placed his hand on her knee and leant forward. 'My dear Mary, your honesty does you great credit, and I can assure you that I would like nothing better than what you propose.'

'Mrs Beaufort told you I'd come from, a place of low reputation. It's true. Gentlemen paid for my favours.' She hesitated and wrung her hands in her lap, 'And I was paid to provide them.' She looked at him, suddenly embarrassed.

A knowing smile appeared on Culligan's face. 'I imagine even in London a maid's wages are modest, Mary, but I am a wealthy man, and I am sure we can come to some arrangement. A generous arrangement.'

He looked at the relief flooding across her face and his heart leapt with affection at her simplicity and lack of guile.

'I would be very grateful, sir. Very grateful indeed.' She licked her lips. 'Would you spank my bottom now? Please, Alfred? I'd like it, but I'd best be naked if you do.'

Speechless, Culligan could only nod. With a look that spoke volumes about the pleasures to come, she stood up and walked over to the mirror. She looked at him in the reflection. 'I like mirrors,' she said, starting to slowly unbutton the front of her dress. 'I like what you see in them. I like watching myself. You can sit there and watch too, my lord.' She completed the buttons and gently pulled the top of the dress apart, then shrugged it down off her shoulders, stopping it at her waist.

'Saints alive, Mary, you are perfect.' Culligan stared open-mouthed at her nakedness in the mirror. Her breasts were quite extraordinary, and the tattoo added a level of exoticism to her beauty that made his head swim. His cock was straining, and he shifted on the settee but managed to remain seated.

Holding the dress with one hand, she cupped her heavy left breast and lifted it, staring open-mouthed at herself whilst she did so. Bending her head downwards, she stretched out her tongue and licked the fat brown nipple before sucking it into her mouth. It was fully erect when she released it, a good half of an inch long.

'That felt nice, Alfred,' she whispered.

'What about the tattoo?' he said faintly, his throat dry.

'They made me have it. At the place before. Do you want to see where it ends?

'Oh yes, I do, Mary. Most fervently.'

She giggled. 'Naughty, naughty, Alfred. Perhaps I should be the one spanking you.' Turning to him, she released the dress and stepped out of it to stand fully naked apart from her laced-up boots. 'They made me shave myself down there as well. The woman in charge said the gentlemen would like it, and they did. I have kept doing it out of habit. Do you like it, Alfred?'

He nodded, rendered speechless by the vision in front of him.

Smiling, she walked over to him, her breasts swinging gently. As if in a dream, Culligan stood and they kissed, long, passionate, and open-mouthed, their tongues entwined and pulses racing. His hands stroked her back and reached down to lift and squeeze her buttocks.

At length she broke off and said breathlessly, 'Take off your jacket and shirt, Alfred.'

He pulled them off with frantic haste.

'Now sit down on the settee just like Mrs Beaufort did yesterday.' He obeyed unhesitatingly. She leant forward, her breasts hanging down as she gracefully stretched out over his knee. Somehow in the process she managed to give his cock a firm squeeze through his trousers. He moaned in anticipation. 'Now then, Alfred. Chastise me firmly. Do not hold back.'

He raised his right hand and brought it down with a brisk slap onto her right buttock. The firm flesh rippled and flexed as he repeated the blow. He heard her sigh and relax, her legs spreading wider.

'Oh yes, sir. That's what I need,' she whispered.

He started to spank her, alternating between buttocks and delighting in her whispered encouragement. 'Oh yes, sir, that's right, punish me. I've been a naughty girl and need to be taught a lesson.'

For a further five minutes his hand steadily rose and fell as she wriggled and moaned and a deep red blush appeared across both buttocks. Finally, he stopped and gently pulled her cheeks apart leaving her exposed and vulnerable. He slid his fingers down and pressed, and her lips parted easily. His head swam as he felt how wet she was.

'Ye gods,' he whispered to himself in wonder, completely lost in the moment as he felt her respond.

'I think you need to fuck me now. Please, my lord. If you will.' Her voice was urgent.

'Stand up,' he said quietly, and as she rose, he stood beside her and tore the rest of his clothes off before they embraced and kissed. She reached down and grasped his shaft, slowly pulling it as her tongue explored the inside of his mouth. Then, gently disengaging from him, she lay back on the settee and opened her legs.

Culligan stared, spellbound. She was fully aroused and glistening, her large clitty standing proud. An erotic sneer appeared on her face as her hand crept downwards. 'Here you are, my lord. Here's your mark.'

All reason left the earl, and with a roar of passion he knelt between her knees, pushing them wide apart, his cock engorged and skinned back. She stared, eyes narrow with lust, then she reached out, grasped it, and pulled him forward.

They settled into a hard, fast, rhythm, her arms and legs wrapped around him as he pumped away. It could not last long, and, as he felt her spend, he came inside her, spasming repeatedly and crying out in ecstasy.

'Mary, Mary, my darling,' he panted as his mouth and lips caressed her neck. It seemed to him that he was coming alive for the first time in his life, and, as his cock remained rigid with excitement, he started to thrust into her again.

'Yes, my lord, more,' she urged as he possessed her.

At last they quietened and lay in each other's arms, staring at the fire and talking quietly. Engulfed in a post-coital glow, Culligan was utterly besotted. He felt his life had gone from black-and-white to colour in the space of two days, and Mary's intoxicating beauty and free-willed lovemaking had opened a new door in his life.

'When can I see you again, my darling?' he asked.

'Well, today's Monday, and Mrs Beaufort always goes out on Thursday evenings, Alfred. Will you come to see me again then?'

He kissed her deeply, marvelling at how agile and alive her mouth and tongue were. 'I will be here.'

'And you will be generous with me, Alfred? You did promise.'

'What you have given me is priceless, Mary, but rest assured I will provide for you.'

She sighed with satisfaction and snuggled into him. 'Thank you, Alfred.'

The next three weeks were the most extraordinary and delightful that Culligan had ever experienced. Mary's beauty and enthusiastic coupling left him walking on air, and he found she completely dominated his thoughts from early in the morning until late at night.

They had taken to using a bedroom on the first floor at Arundel Court which Mary said was not in use. The furniture was covered with dust sheets, but the bed was big and comfortable. As with the salon below, he noticed there was a large mirror on the wall, and a colourful deep-pile rug occupied the space between it and the bed.

On their third meeting, she had shyly shown him a black *attaché* case which she had stolen from her previous place of work. The contents had astonished him at first, but with her enthusiastic guidance they had experimented at length with the various devices.

Indeed, thinking about some of the daring new experiences she had introduced him to as they cavorted on the bed in front of the mirror made him shiver with delight and blush with shame in the same moment. For one so young, the girl was phenomenally skilled in the arts of love and, he had to acknowledge, he was receiving an utterly delicious education that left him in thrall to each new and outrageous suggestion she made.

The only cloud on the horizon was the fact that his stay in London was coming to an end and he spent considerable time planning ways to delay his departure.

One afternoon he was just leaving a meeting with some colleagues in the Irish Department in Whitehall when a clerk approached him.

'Excuse me, sir, there is a gentleman to see you. He's waiting in the Sandford Room.'

'Oh, really? What's his name?'

'A Mr William Munroe, I believe, sir.'

'Very well. I'll see him now.'

As he entered he saw a grey-haired gentleman in formal dress sitting in one of two chairs by a coffee table. A decanter of whiskey, a small jug of water, two glasses, and an ashtray were positioned upon it. The man stood up and smiled at him.

'Good afternoon, Lord Culligan. My name is William Munroe. I don't believe that we have met before, although I have heard fine things about you from our colleagues in Dublin.'

The earl smiled and took the seat indicated. 'That's kind of you, Munroe. You are in government yourself, then, I take it?'

'In a manner of speaking.' He nodded, poured himself a drink, and raised the decanter in an unspoken question. The man opposite shook his head.

'Cigar?'

'No, I won't, thank you. So, to what do I owe the pleasure, Munroe?'

The older man leant back in his seat and took a sip from his glass. There was a pause as he held it up to the window, admiring its colour. When he spoke, his eyes remained on the amber liquid.

'She's delightful, isn't she? Quite extraordinary.'

Culligan hesitated. 'Sorry, who is?'

'The lady with whom you have been spending such an agreeable time, my lord.' He met Culligan's eyes and smiled. 'Mary. Mary the beautiful and willing maid.'

The earl started in his chair and a look of consternation appeared on his face. He opened his mouth to speak, but Munroe held up his hand and carried on. 'No need to deny it, Culligan; we're both men of the world. Frankly, I envy you. I mean, what man wouldn't?'

The Irishman thought quickly. There was steely quality to Munroe that he had not noticed at first, and he sensed that bluster or denial was not the answer. But what to say? He spread his hands in a gesture of conciliation.

'I see you have me at a disadvantage, Munroe. I fear I must own up. But what gentleman has not considered a dalliance when away from home on an extended trip? No harm has been done. However, what I am not sure about is why my private life is any of your business.' His tone rose as he completed his sentence, shock giving way to anger at the cheek of the fellow sitting opposite. But instead of answering his question, Munroe asked him another.

'Tell me, when did you become sympathetic to the Irish republican cause, my lord?'

For the second time in a minute Culligan stared across the table, however, he managed to keep his voice even as he replied.

'I'm sorry, Munroe, but you either have the wrong man or you have taken leave of your senses.'

'I think not. A simple trap was set. You were provided with false information about planned military deployments in the southwest of Ireland.' He paused and extracted a cigar from his jacket pocket, struck a match, and lit it. Culligan remained silent as he did so, trying to look calm whilst at the same time thinking furiously. When the cigar was fully alight, Munroe continued.

'We know this information is now in the hands of certain senior members of the republican movement. I also know your new wife strongly sympathises with the aims of these people. Put simply, Culligan, I am satisfied that you passed the information to your spouse, who in turn passed it to the Home Rule fanatics. I am also sure that having done it once, you will do it again. We can't have that, I'm afraid.'

Culligan glared at him, his body tense with fury and alarm. 'That is a preposterous assertion, Munroe. Who are you, exactly? You should know that I am extremely well connected here in London, both within the government and at court. If you continue to make such suggestions I shall have no hesitation in bringing my influence to bear on your life and your career. I can ruin you, sir, in a matter of weeks.'

Munroe smiled bleakly and ignored his outburst. 'You have a chance to retire quietly and with honour. We might even organise a medal of some kind, but understand this, my lord: your days in His Majesty's Government are drawing to a close.'

His face suffused with anger the earl pointed a finger at the man sitting opposite and hissed a reply as voices passed by in the corridor outside. 'I have no idea who you are or what your position is, and yet you presume to threaten me in this way? Rest assured I will find out who you are and put a stop to you.'

The man with the grey hair and the distinguished face remained seated and looked at him, seemingly unperturbed by the Irishman's furious response. 'I take it that is a no to voluntary retirement, my lord?'

'Damn your eyes, it is.'

'As you wish.'

He picked up an *attaché case* that was sitting to one side of his chair, drew out an envelope and withdrew a handful of photographs. He started to place them on the table in a line.

Culligan glanced at the first photo and then, as each one was revealed, a rising sense horror overcame him. The first picture showed him and Mary sitting at the outside table of the café in St James's Park. The second showed them sitting in the salon at Arundel Court.

Mary was wearing the dress she had worn when he had visited her clandestinely for the first time. In the third picture she was not wearing anything at all apart from her boots and was lying across his knees. His hand was raised, and he was smiling as he spanked her.

'What the devil, Munroe? What is this? How did you get those photographs?' he managed to stutter.

But the man opposite did not reply, just placed five more photographs on the table. showing him and Mary in a variety of poses, mostly taken in the upstairs room with the dust sheets over the furniture.

'The mirror, Culligan. Doesn't Mary love the mirror?'

'My God, she's one of yours.'

The earl slumped back in his chair, appalled at the images in front of him but, if anything, more horrified by the terrible realisation that his darling Mary, his sweet, wonderful obsession, was nothing more than a courtesan.

They sat in silence for a long moment. When Munroe spoke again, his tone was sympathetic. A candid acknowledgment of the truth from one man to another.

'You have been seduced by an expert and utterly irresistible heart-breaker, Culligan. There is no shame in that, and there is no reason why these photographs cannot remain private. They will be kept securely and will not be released to what one might call interested parties. Your wife, for example. But you must resign immediately, my lord. That is the price.'

The Irishman stared at Munroe, a deep and powerful rage building within him. Partly it was anger about what the man in front of him was demanding, but even more it was the fact that he had been manipulated. In one short moment, his hopes and dreams of some sort of a life with Mary had cruelly collapsed, and he now saw he had been played like a fool from beginning to end.

Five hundred years of ruling-class entitlement and arrogance drove his fury.

'I won't pay your price, Munroe. Send your damn photographs to my wife. I'll warrant she likes being married to a wealthy earl much more than she cares about an indiscretion with a whore such as this.' He smiled grimly. 'As for the rest of them, show those to any man and he will clap me on the back and tell me I'm a hell of a fellow. I'm calling your bluff.'

He sat back and folded his arms.

Munroe smiled at him. The man had a bit of backbone after all. Shame that he was a traitor to his country. With a shrug, he slowly placed the remaining photographs on the table.

'Oh God, no,' Culligan whispered. Unable to stop himself, he reached out and picked one up. He was stark naked, on his hands and knees on the big bed. Mary was kneeling up behind him, also naked and looking quite magnificent. She was smiling to herself as she swung the tawse against his buttocks. The camera had clearly caught his joyful grimace.

Munroe handed him two other pictures. He took them, barely able to focus as his cheeks burned with shame. In the first, he was still in the same position, but Mary now had an ivory cock in her hand and was looking directly at the camera. Her eyebrows were raised in amused horror, as though inviting the viewer to encourage her.

The second image showed him slewed round, his buttocks at an angle to the photographer. Mary had buried the cock deep in his bum hole and was holding it in with the flat of her palm. With the other, she had reached between his legs and was wanking his stiff cock. She was laughing.

'Being married to a man who has made a stupid but understandable mistake is one thing, Culligan. But being married to a gross pervert who indulges in such practices is a rather different matter. Especially if these images reach your society friends. Imagine the gossip at your club.'

'You fucking bastard.' The words rang clear in the silence of the Sandford Room.

Munroe sipped his drink and gestured at the earl. 'Do try this; it's excellent. Irish, I believe.' He permitted himself a small smile before continuing.

'Resign from the government immediately, Culligan, and retire to your estates in in Ireland. If you refuse, then these photographs will be released to all the people you hold most dear. Frankly, suicide will be your only option.'

He stood up, placed a card on the table and looked down on the earl. 'Telephone me by seven o'clock this evening with your immediate resignation. If you do not, you will be overtaken by events that cannot be reversed. Good afternoon.'

He paced to the door, opened it, and passed through, closing it with a soft click. The Irishman remained sitting in his chair, staring blankly ahead but seeing nothing.

Chapter Nine

The pursuit of Dietrich Brunner.

The remainder of that first year in Arundel Court passed quickly. I was commissioned by Hector on three occasions: twice with a man, once with a woman. The results proved satisfactory, and both Georgina and Hector commended me for the way I had adapted to my new role.

Georgina and I finally became lovers. I think we both knew it was inevitable, and perhaps because of that, neither of us had rushed matters as the year unfolded. However, late on a hot September evening in 1901, I came out of my bathroom having enjoyed a cooling bathe to find her sitting on my bed, a curiously vulnerable expression on her face.

She had been away in France for three weeks on a secret commission of Hector's, and on returning that afternoon, I had noticed how strained and tired she looked.

'Here I am,' she said quietly, meeting my eyes and smiling almost sadly. I understood immediately and went to sit down next to her on the bed, picking up her hand as I gently leant against her.

'How was Paris?' I asked. 'Really, how was it?'

She stared across the room and stayed silent for a long moment, then said, 'A good man died. A brave man. And I only just escaped myself.'

'Oh, Georgina, my darling, what happened?' I squeezed her hand and she returned the pressure but only shook her head, and when at last she turned to me, I could see tears in her eyes, her deep distress all too obvious. I gently pushed her down onto the bed and lay alongside her, holding her close and comforting her with my body in that age-old way as she cried it out. Whatever happened in Paris – and she never told me – had deeply affected her, and for a long time afterwards she just lay in silence, her arm across me, as I stroked her hair and told her quietly how wonderful she was.

'I love you, Georgina,' I finally whispered.

She stirred and raised her face to mine. 'And I love you, Mary.'

We kissed, slowly and tenderly at first, both aware, I think, that those moments were the start of something uniquely important for both of us. As our kisses became more passionate and our gowns were slipped off, I felt more as though a great engine hitherto undiscovered within me had finally roared into life. And, fully released, my mind and body opened up as one, and I felt her respond accordingly.

When we finally climaxed together in a huge release of energy and love, it seemed as though the world had melted away and the only things in the universe were my electrified body and my darling Georgina, whose mouth and hands had driven me to raptures that I had never experienced before with a man or a woman.

Much later, we lay entwined and uncovered, telling each other small quiet secret things and occasionally laughing together as we listened to the muffled sounds of the London night drifting in through the window.

My darling Georgina and I were together for another forty years. We both had many other lovers and, of course, our work for Hector, but after that still, hot, London night, we both understood that we were two people but one life, and our love transcended any other events that might befall us.

*

'Excuse me, sir, may I share your table with you? It is very busy in here today, what with Christmas being around the corner and all.'

Dietrich Brunner, *vice consul* at the German embassy in London, glanced up at the girl standing at his table and then around the tea shop off Regent Street where he habitually lunched. A slight shadow crossed his face. He preferred to eat alone, but the room was crowded, so he had little choice but to raise himself in his seat slightly, nod his head and agree.

'Of course, Miss. My pleasure.'

'Thank you, sir.' She placed her tray with a cup of tea and a bun on the table and sat down opposite him. 'I am Mary Felix.' She smiled winningly across the table.

Brunner realised she was a startlingly pretty girl. She had an unusually short haircut with a low fringe and striking green eyes, and when she unbuttoned her dark brown coat, he could not help but notice that the plain blue dress she was wearing revealed the beginnings of a deep valley between her breasts.

'Brunner. Dietrich Brunner,' he replied. In spite of himself, he held her eyes a little longer than necessary. She really was quite exquisite, he thought. Out of the corner of his eye he saw both of the men sitting at the next table staring quite openly at her.

'Well, it's nice to meet you, Mr Brunner. I've just arrived in London and am trying to make new friends whenever I can.'

The German smiled wryly. 'And succeeding, I should imagine, Miss Felix.'

'Well, everyone seems very friendly, I must say, although my mother said you can't always trust people just because they seem nice.'

'That is sound advice, I would say,' Brunner replied, still slightly bemused her exceptional beauty.

To his surprise, he found the girl drew him into a conversation which he quite enjoyed. Speaking in a soft and curiously intimate voice, she told him she had grown up in an inn in the southwest of the country and was now working as a lady's maid and companion to a wealthy widow. She seemed very interested in his role at the embassy and congratulated him when he told her he had married a year earlier.

'To a German girl, Mr Brunner?'

'Of course. My wife's maiden name was Irene von Schmitt, and she is the daughter of the Baron von Schmitt, the German ambassador here in London. We met when I came over here two years ago.'

'My word, a fine marriage, Mr Brunner. You must have exciting prospects.'

'I hope so, Miss Felix. Time will tell.' He did not add that his new wife was a plain, petulant, and self-regarding bore or that he was tired of the sight of her already. The truth was that, desperately short of suitors and far from Berlin, her parents had been relieved to see her married off to the son of a respectable and well-to-do, if not noble, family.

Brunner's own parents had been equally delighted as, at thirty-six years old, balding and slightly stooped, they were not sure their only son would marry either. Certainly he had shown little interest in the various girls in his circle in Hamburg as a younger man.

As for himself, Brunner had reached the conclusion that marriage was necessary for progression in the diplomatic world and on arriving in England had rapidly realised that Irene von Schmitt was in many ways an ideal candidate, especially as the support of the baron would be of untold value to an ambitious man.

The gentle West Country voice interrupted his thoughts. 'You must know London society very well, Mr Brunner, with lots of glamorous friends and diplomatic parties.'

He smiled and shrugged. 'A little, perhaps, Miss Felix, but the life of a vice consul is not all cocktail parties and receptions.' He puffed out his chest a little. 'Much of the work is dealing with the German court and government in Berlin, and some of it is highly important and confidential. There is much I cannot discuss, I'm sure you understand.'

This produced a most pleasing look of respect from the beauty facing him as she widened her eyes in admiration. 'Oh my word, I'm sure that must be true. You must be very clever to be given such responsibility. And here I am, just a lady's maid from Devon talking to you.' She giggled and leaned forward. Brunner noticed the men next to him stir as the light caught the curve of her breasts.

They continued to talk and eat as she daintily cut up her bun. She asked what Germany was like, and he told her a little about growing up in Hamburg. 'It is a most handsome city with lots of canals, Miss Felix. Perhaps you will have a chance to visit at some point.'

'I do hope so, Mr Brunner, but for now I am just looking for someone to show me round London's sights. I find sometimes men bother me when I am out on my own, and it would be such a help to have a fine strong fellow at my side …' Her voice tailed off as she met his eyes.

'I see. Is there no one else in the house? No other servants?'

She seemed disappointed at his response and pouted a little. 'Only Jimmy, my mistress's man. He's nice enough but a stranger to London as well.'

Brunner noticed the clock on the wall above the counter. He was surprised at how much time had passed. 'Alas, Miss Felix, I wish I could help you, but my time is fully occupied with affairs of state. And they are calling to me now, I'm afraid.' He pushed back his chair and stood up.

'Oh, of course, Mr Brunner. A man of your importance.' She held his eyes as they shook hands. 'Perhaps I'll see you again.'

He nodded and clicked his heels. 'Perhaps. Good afternoon.'

The girl watched the tall balding figure pass between the rows of tables before buttoning up her coat and following him two minutes later. Every male eye in the room watched her progress from the table to the door.

The following week, Brunner was again lunching in the tearooms and noticed the girl enter. His eyes creased in silent amusement at the covert and overt glances she attracted from the other diners. She looked over to him and waved, and he nodded back. Even though there were spare tables, she came and sat with him, and, to his surprise, he found he was pleased at the envious looks this produced from the other men in the room.

'We meet again, Miss Felix.'

'I thought you might be here. Hoped so, in fact, Mr Brunner.' Again that winning smile and soft voice, and again the unbuttoning of her coat to reveal a décolletage that strained the bounds of respectability. But she seemed quite unaware of this as she chatted away to him.

'I looked up Hamburg in my mistress's encyclopaedia and it sounds quite delightful. I hoped you'd be pleased with my researches.' They talked some more about the city, and it was clear she had been busy looking up places of interest so she could discuss them with him. Brunner was rather charmed. There was undoubtedly a naive eagerness to please about the girl which was most endearing.

Finally, he asked, 'And how are you getting on with your search for a gallant escort to help you explore the sights of London?'

She frowned gently. 'Not very well, I'm afraid. Jimmy is not interested in me at all, and I only have one afternoon off each week. I know that my mistress is generous, but it is hard to meet new friends in a city where you don't know anyone.'

'I hope you consider me a friend, Miss Felix.' Brunner was surprised with himself for saying so, but the words were out before he could think about them. Within a moment she had reached across the table and slipped her hand into his, her face lighting up.

'Oh, but I do. I definitely do. It is such a shame you cannot spare some time to spend with me. Why, you could even come and look at the house I live in. It is very grand and interesting and in a quite private place. You could come when my mistress and Jimmy are out, so we could have good look round. Downstairs and upstairs.'

Her green eyes gently raked him over as she concluded this sentence before finally adding quietly, 'I seem to have been on my own for rather a long time, Mr Brunner. It makes a girl restless.'

The German swallowed and looked down at the table, where their hands were still entwined. *Any other man*, he thought. *Any other man in this room would be pulling her out onto the street.* 'It is a great shame, Miss Felix, but I have no time. My duties …' He shrugged.

'Yes, that is a shame. A disappointment even, Dietrich.' She used his name for the first time. 'But never mind, we must restrict our delightful conversations to the Colonial Tearooms.' They chatted for another ten minutes before he left.

Over the next ten days, he met Miss Felix a further two times, on each occasion politely declining an invitation to 'come and see the house' during their conversations.

Her disappointment was palpable, and he sensed a slight confusion behind it. Mary would not be accustomed to being turned down when she made such an offer, especially as her invitations continued to carry the prospect of intimacy. He was both flattered and amused by this and once again reflected that most men would be throwing their hats into the air with joy and calling for a hansom cab in short order.

However, a week later everything changed when he left the German embassy late one afternoon. Whilst standing at the kerb waiting to hail a cab, he heard a familiar voice call out, 'Why, Mr Brunner, good afternoon.' He turned to see Mary and a companion walking towards him.

'Miss Felix! What a pleasant surprise. What brings you to Belgrave Square?'

'Well, I finally persuaded Jimmy here to accompany me on an exploration of some parts of London I have not yet seen. We took a cab over here and intend to walk back to Arundel Court. Jimmy, say hello to my friend Mr Brunner from the German embassy.' She rolled her eyes delightedly and continued in a stage whisper, 'He is a very important man, Jimmy, so we must be nice to him.'

'A pleasure to meet you, sir.' Jimmy smiled and extended a hand, the West Indian lilt in his gravelly voice audible even to the German.

Brunner was transfixed. The man was a god in human clothing. A good six feet three inches tall and well dressed, his skin was dark but not black. And the face, oh, the face was like chiselled mahogany, with high cheekbones, proud lips, and a strong jawline in perfect proportion. A passer-by might have remarked what a profoundly striking couple he and Mary made, but as he stared, the German forgot Mary even existed.

'A pleasure to meet you too. A great pleasure indeed.' It was all Brunner could manage in the moment.

Their eyes met and they held a look for a long moment before parting hands. Brunner's heart was beating like a drum as Mary chattered to him, but in truth he could hardly concentrate on what she was saying. Finally, he dragged his attention back to her.

'I'm sorry, Miss Felix, what were you saying?'

'Oh, just that it is so fortunate we have met you, as Jimmy has received a letter from Germany about his brother, who lives in Stuttgart, but it is in German and none of us in the house can read it. He is worried it might be urgent news. Would you read it for him and put his mind at rest?'

'A letter, you say? Translate a letter? Of course, I'd be happy to, Jimmy.'

'Thank you kindly, sir. I would greatly appreciate that.' The big man smiled at him.

Before he knew it Brunner had been firmly guided into a hansom and they were trotting briskly towards Trafalgar Square. During the next fifteen minutes she kept up a cheerful conversation with both men about such mundane matters that they had little to do but agree with her from time to time.

Brunner tried not to stare at Jimmy but did meet his eyes a couple of times and smiled warmly. He was delighted to receive a similar response from the other man, who seemed amused by Mary's chattering. Indeed, sitting in the darkening cab, the German felt that he was already establishing a connection with her companion.

'Surrey Street.' A voice from above indicated they were close to the house.

'Just halfway down, please, cabbie,' called Mary, and the hansom pulled to a halt thirty yards from the entrance to Arundel Court. They stepped down and walked along the alley and into the square.

'Here we are, then, Mr Brunner. As you are with us, we'll go in the front.' With that, she led the way up the steps and opened the door with a key. They walked to the right of a wide staircase and down a handsome corridor floored with black and white tiles, passing a door on the right-hand side. At the next door, Mary paused and turned to their guest.

'My mistress is not expected back until later, but we'll just use the kitchen rather than the sitting room, if that is all right.'

He nodded. 'Of course, Miss Felix. I quite understand.' A slight scent of sandalwood reached his nostrils and he felt quite heady and off balance, intensely aware of the presence of the powerfully built man standing close behind him. They entered a pleasant and well-equipped kitchen with a large oak table in the centre. Around the walls there were various cupboards, draining boards, and well-stocked shelves, and a wide wooden worktop stretched the length of the room on the left-hand side.

Brunner sat down at the table as invited, and Jimmy opened a cupboard and brandished a bottle and glasses. 'A brandy, Mr Brunner?'

'Perhaps a small one, thank you.'

'And you, Mary?' he asked.

But the girl had opened a drawer and seemed momentarily distracted. 'Jimmy, I put the letter in here this afternoon, but it isn't here anymore. Did you take it back?'

'No, but here's a note from Mrs Beaufort.' He had picked up a piece of paper which was sitting in the middle of the table. Unfolding it, he read it out loud.

Dear Jimmy,

I recall that one of the ladies whom I am meeting early this evening has a German mother, so I am sure she will speak the language herself. Accordingly, I have taken the liberty of taking the letter about your brother with me, as I know you are anxious about its contents.

Hopefully I will return later with a translation and reassuring news.

Regards,

Georgina Beaufort

Mary turned to look at the German, clearly very embarrassed. 'Oh dear, Mr Brunner, we seem to have kidnapped you in vain,' she said. 'I do apologise.'

He shrugged. 'Your actions were well intentioned, and I would have been very happy to have assisted Jimmy. But hopefully all will be well later this evening.'

Jimmy sat down next to him with two glasses of brandy. 'Well, please have a glass or two with us before heading home, sir. A toast. To interesting new friends.' He met Brunner's eye as he said this, and the German felt his pulse race again.

The three of them sat around the table and chatted most pleasantly for a while, then suddenly Mary stopped mid-sentence and slapped her hand on the table. 'Oh no.

I forgot that Mrs Beaufort asked me to collect a dress that she intends to wear tomorrow morning.' She looked at them both and, standing up, added, 'It won't take me long. Have another glass and I'll be back in a quarter of an hour.' With that, she left the room.

Jimmy stood up as well and took a step to the worktop where the brandy bottle was standing. He picked it up and raised his eyebrows at Brunner in an unspoken question.

'Yes, thank you,' the German replied. Jimmy reached over and filled his glass with a generous measure, then replaced the bottle and leant back against the worktop. Their eyes met. Suddenly the atmosphere in the kitchen was electric.

'Fifteen minutes,' said Jimmy thoughtfully. His eyes glinted as a wicked smile appeared on his face. 'Well now, let's see here.' With that, he slowly undid his belt and loosed his breeches before reaching inside. Brunner gasped in shock as he pulled out his cock and balls and then leant back, both hands braced on the wooden top behind him.

'My God, what are you doing?' he spluttered, transfixed by the sight.

Jimmy smiled knowingly. The German's shocked face was a picture, but there was excitement there as well. The shaft was rapidly thickening and lengthening, and as Brunner watched open-mouthed, it climbed steadily until it was horizontal to the floor.

'What if Mary comes back?' Brunner whispered, briefly eyeing the door before returning his gaze to Jimmy's groin.

'Then you better hurry up and hold it. Forbidden fruit, Mr Brunner. We both know you want to.'

'I don't know, I really don't. I mean …'

'Come here.' The voice was a command. Brunner stood as though in a daze and walked forward to stand to one side of him. He slowly reached down and wrapped his fingers around the shaft. 'That's it. Now wank it, Mr Brunner. Make it nice and hard.'

With a whimpering noise, the German complied, rapidly becoming completely absorbed in his task. Within a minute, Jimmy was fully erect and uttering little groans of encouragement. 'Oh yes, that's right. You've done this before, haven't you, Mr Brunner? What a bad man you are.' He reached down and let his hands run across the front of Brunner's trousers and smiled. Brunner looked up at him, his face flushed and eyes wide.

Jimmy continued speaking as his hand steadily worked away. 'You're getting as hard as me, aren't you? Make me come and then I'll suck you off before Mary comes back.' His fingers quickly unbuttoned his white shirt and pulled it open. Wrapping his arm around the German's head, he gently pulled him onto his chest. 'Lick my nipples.'

Brunner willingly complied as his hand sped up. The big man leant back further, pushing his hips forward, groaning as his climax started to build. Suddenly the sound of the front door slamming echoed down the corridor and a cheery call came through the half-open kitchen door.

'I'm back. Only me.' By the time Mary entered the room, both men were sitting at the table with a glass of brandy in front of them. Brunner was amazed that the foolish girl noticed nothing, as he could see that Jimmy was sweating and his shirt was incorrectly buttoned up at the front. He was sure he must also look dishevelled, but fortunately the girl did not stay with them.

'Closed.' She pouted. 'The shop was closed, and now I'll have to persuade Mrs Beaufort that another dress would be more suitable for an art gallery viewing. I'd better go and look one out.' She looked at Brunner directly. 'I am sorry again that we have inconvenienced you, but at least you've had a chance to meet Jimmy, and I do hope we shall see you again.'

With that, she smiled prettily, shook his hand, and left the kitchen. Moments later, they heard the sound of her footsteps running up the stairs.

Chapter Ten

Dietrich Brunner receives an offer from William Munroe.

At eleven o'clock the following evening, Brunner lay in bed, his hands behind his head, and reflected on the past twenty-four hours. His plump and tiresome wife snored lightly next to him, and he found his distaste at having to share a bed with her was growing ever stronger, especially after the extraordinary events of the afternoon.

The previous day, he had left Arundel Court shortly after Mary had gone upstairs but only after Jimmy had kissed him passionately, squeezed his cock through his trousers, and told him to return at three o'clock the following day.

'They'll all be out then. Mrs Beaufort is going to play cards with her friends, and Mary is going with her. So we'll have time,' he had said, leaving the implications hanging in the air.

So, with a beating heart, Brunner had knocked on the door to Arundel Court at three exactly and Jimmy had welcomed him, then led the way straight upstairs and into a bedroom that seemed to be unused. The furniture was covered with dust sheets and the bed itself was also draped in a large white sheet that covered the mattress. A large mirror was attached to the wall behind the door, Brunner noticed.

The next hour had been the most intense, exhilarating, and pleasurable he had ever experienced. He smiled in the darkness as he remembered the sheer debauchery Jimmy had encouraged as their passions burned. He had seemed to be particularly stimulated by the mirror and insisted that Brunner watched in its reflection as he sucked his cock and then placed him on all fours and fucked him in the ass on the floor rug right in front of it. The man was alarmingly well-endowed, but so keen was Brunner to oblige that he had withstood the pain and let the powerfully built man possess him ruthlessly.

Even though he was still very sore from Jimmy's attentions, Brunner shivered with pleasure at the memory of the afternoon and smiled in the darkness at Jimmy's parting words to him.

'Come back next week, Dietrich. Same time. They'll be out again.'

The following days passed achingly slowly. Brunner simply could not get Jimmy out of his mind, possessed as he was by powerful memories of their lust-filled afternoon and eager for more. He lunched every day at the Colonial tea rooms in the hope that Jimmy might accompany Mary there, but in the event, neither of them appeared.

On separate occasions both the ambassador and his wife commented on his distracted demeanour, and he was forced to concentrate and behave as normally as possible, even though he felt as though his whole world had been turned upside down. The rushed and guilt-ridden fumbling of his younger days felt far removed from the full-blown passion he had experienced with Jimmy, and he spent a great deal of time thinking about how things could be arranged so that they might spend as much time together as possible.

At last, with beating heart, he rang the bell at Arundel Court. His beaming smile of welcome disappeared as the door was opened by a grey-haired man in late middle age. Clean shaven and formally dressed, he smiled at Brunner's confusion.

'Herr Brunner, welcome. My name is William Munroe. Please come in.' Then, as the German hesitated, he added, 'Yes, I know you were expecting Jimmy. He has been called away, I am afraid. But never mind. I think a conversation between ourselves would be useful'.

Moving aside, he gestured for Brunner to enter and led the way to the first door on the right. They entered a large and pleasant salon with a bay window and a settee placed in front of a brightly burning fire. A decanter of brandy with two glasses and an ashtray sat on a low table. Munroe indicated that Brunner should sit down, and then, without asking, poured two generous measures.

Taking his seat opposite, he looked at Brunner, smiled, and extracted a case of cigars from his inside pocket. He offered one to the German with raised eyebrows and, when he shook his head, shrugged, and lit one himself. Brunner went to speak, but Munroe held his finger up as he puffed the cigar alight before leaning back and speaking, his eyes remaining on the glowing tip.

'You upset Mary, you know. She was quite put out that you were so able to resist her overtures. It was,' he paused and finally met Brunner's eyes, 'unprecedented.'

Brunner moved uneasily in his seat. 'What is this ...?' But the man opposite continued unabashed.

'After the fourth meeting, she realised what the issue might be and felt it might be useful for you to be introduced to Jimmy. And so it turned out.'

'Who are you? How do you know these things?' asked Brunner.

Rather than answering, the man opposite picked up an *attaché* case that was lying under the table. Removing a buff-coloured envelope, he extracted a set of large photographs and placed six of them one by one in a line on the coffee table facing towards the German.

Brunner stared in horror as each one was revealed. They were graphic images of himself and Jimmy pleasuring each other. Each one seemed worse than the last, their passion recorded unmercifully by the camera.

'No, no, no. What is the meaning of this? How did you obtain these? Mein Gott, Munroe, have you no shame?'

'Not really, Brunner, no. But then neither do you, it appears.' The older man smiled bleakly and gestured at the table.

'Does Jimmy know?' spluttered the German. But even as he asked the question, he knew the answer. Suddenly he understood it all, from the first meeting with Mary in the tearoom to the delirious excitement of the scene in the kitchen and the debauchery in front of the mirror the following day.

'Jimmy knows,' said the grey-haired man quietly.

‘So it was all a deception.’ Brunner raised his hands to his face and rubbed his eyes as images of a delightful future with Jimmy disappeared before his eyes. ‘For what purpose? Blackmail? Is that your sordid game, Munroe?’

The Englishman tilted his head upwards and exhaled a plume of smoke, which rose high into the room. ‘In a manner of speaking, yes, but not perhaps quite as you are expecting. Certainly not money.’

‘What, then?’

‘Put simply, Herr Brunner, I am offering you a choice between two options. The first is that I arrange for a selection of the photographs we have of your illegal gymnastics to reach the Baron von Schmitt, your wife Irene, the German foreign minister in Berlin, your parents, and your friends. I think you can guess what their reaction would be.’

Brunner stared at him as Munroe continued. ‘The alternative is that from time to time you and I will meet and have a pleasant talk about life in the German embassy, your news from Berlin, the instructions you have received, and the plans and priorities of your government.’

The German’s eyes narrowed. ‘You expect me to betray my country?’

Munroe shrugged. ‘That is a very harsh way to put it. I would prefer to see it as a change of masters. And one which could be to your benefit, I believe. Are you an ambitious man, Brunner?’

‘What has that to do with it?’

‘If you choose the second option then, with a moment’s thought, you will realise that it would be in both our interests for you to progress as far as possible in your career. The higher you rise, the better. You take my point, I'm sure.'

Anger showed on the German's face for the first time. 'No, I don't. And who the hell are you, Munroe?'

'I work for His Majesty's Government. Let us leave it at that, shall we?'

'Have you no honour, Munroe? No dignity? What do you say here in England? It is not cricket?'

He was rewarded with another bleak smile. 'I'm a Scotsman and don't play cricket. Think about it, Brunner. When we meet, you will provide me with inside knowledge of the workings of German foreign policy and, from time to time, I may ask you to find out specific things or answer particular questions.'

The German stared at him in grim-faced silence as Munroe paused and continued.

'But here's the thing, Brunner. I will reciprocate by giving you useful information about our own activities that will be new to your government. This intelligence might not have the same value, but nevertheless it will seem to Berlin as though you are performing an effective role here in London and that you are a man with excellent and discreet contacts within Whitehall. In short, we will make you look good.'

He paused again and knocked the ash off the end of his cigar, then puffed luxuriously and leaned across the table, his voice clear and direct.

'We would expect you to be the German ambassador here in London within six months. That is the big prize for you, Brunner. The demise of the Baron von Schmitt and your tiresomely bovine wife can be arranged in a way that makes it look like a tragic accident. By then, you will be the obvious choice to replace him.'

Brunner's eyes bulged as he struggled to take in what Munroe was saying. His shock at the apparently casual removal of his wife and his superior quickly dissipated as the possibilities became apparent to him.

Munroe saw all this and nodded in approval.

'I see you are starting to appreciate what I am offering you. It would be a good life here, Brunner, with all the benefits of an ambassadorship. A grieving widower putting his feelings to one side and bravely assuming the responsibilities of a great post. You will be lauded by London society and, of course, as a newly single man, you would be free to pursue a wide range of interests in your spare time.' Munroe met his eye and smiled.

'Could I still see Jimmy?'

'No. Jimmy is in the past for you. However …' Munroe reached into his jacket and withdrew a pocket book. Writing a few words on a blank page, he tore it out and passed it over.

The German glanced at it. 'Thirty Cavendish Square. Wentworth. What is this?'

'At that address you will find a private club where men with your interests meet and enjoy each other's company. It is run by a very sympathetic and understanding management. Wentworth is the word you quote at the door to gain entry.'

Brunner rubbed his face with his hands again and leant back, exhaling deeply. Expecting another session of unbridled lust with the delicious and muscular Jimmy, he instead found himself being offered a choice between appalling disgrace and a fundamental betrayal of his country. And yet, he mused, the possibilities of the latter option were rapidly becoming clear to him. Munroe was right. He could envisage a very fine life as the German ambassador in London. He stared out of the window, thinking hard, before looking across the table and meeting the other man's eyes.

'It seems you leave me little choice.'

'Oh no, Brunner. I am giving you a choice, make no mistake about that. You are in this situation because of your own weakness, and you must choose whichever option best serves you at this moment. Utter disgrace, or great success as the German ambassador to the Court of St James. You must embrace one or the other. That is what is on the table.' He smiled and glanced down at the photographs. 'Quite literally, as it happens.'

'Very well. I accept your terms, Munroe.'

'Wholeheartedly, Brunner?'

'Yes. Despite what you say, we both know I have no choice. But the offer you have made me is not without its attractions. You may consider me "on board", as you British say.'

'Excellent.' The Englishman stood and stretched out his hand. Brunner did the same and they shook. 'And now a toast.' He filled up the brandy glasses and handed one to the German. 'To the new German ambassador and his invaluable service to the British empire. And, of course, happy New Year. May 1902 be a successful one for both of us, Brunner.'

Interlude

An excerpt from the London Times, March 17th, 1902.

A Tragedy in Regent's Park

It is with great regret that we report the occurrence of a terrible motor car accident yesterday afternoon on the Outer Circle of Regent's Park, near London Zoo. The German ambassador, the Baron von Schmitt, his wife and daughter were enjoying an outing in their Daimler Benz vehicle when it exploded with no warning. The subsequent conflagration engulfed the unfortunate occupants, and police report that three bodies have been recovered and taken to Baker Street morgue.

The baron was a well-known motor car enthusiast and the vehicle had been recently imported from Germany. Your correspondent has spoken to a number of motor car engineers, and the prevailing view amongst these esteemed gentlemen is that the fuel line cracked, allowing petrol vapour to spontaneously ignite.

The German embassy has issued a statement declaring their shock and grief at the tragedy, and we offer them our most sincere condolences. It is understood that Herr Dietrich Brunner has been appointed Chargé d'Affaires at the embassy and will temporarily assume the duties of ambassador whilst new arrangements are put in place.

Chapter Eleven

A storm breaks in London.

Virginia Welling sipped her tea, eased back into the comfortable armchair in her parlour at Bancroft Hall, and permitted herself a small smile of satisfaction. There was little doubt that since arriving the previous spring she had used her time at the hall to excellent effect, making wholesale changes to the staff, laying down new rules for the running of the household, and developing a relationship with Lord Bridport that might be described as one of mutual convenience and support.

She genuinely liked the wounded aristocrat and had considerable sympathy for the way he had been treated by the press, his peers, and the public. The physical and mental injuries he had received made him unpredictable and quick to anger, yet at other times he withdrew into his shell so deeply that she almost needed to lead him by the hand through these bad patches.

In this, she knew, the fundamental kindness at the heart of her own character served her well, and she had felt increasingly protective towards her master as the year had progressed. At the age of forty she had the sense to realise that, as the housekeeper of one of Dorsetshire's great houses, she had reached her peak and made every effort to secure her position by making herself indispensable to his being.

After the events of her first meeting, this had inevitably included a powerful, if sporadic, sexual relationship. They tried to be discreet, although the spontaneous nature of their passion made this difficult at times. She suspected their liaisons were common knowledge amongst the servants and, in consequence, also in the little village of Bradstock where the hall was located. But as her affection for Lord Bridport grew, she cared not.

In short, as the summer of 1902 slipped by, she considered that Lord Bridport had found himself a capable, kind, and obliging housekeeper whose loyalty grew with each day and who was well satisfied with her lot. And if she occasionally allowed herself a vigorous dalliance with Thomas, the craggily handsome footman, who was the only surviving member of staff from her arrival, then so be it.

She sipped her tea and eyed the tawse hanging from a hook on the back of the door. A shiver ran through her as she remembered a private punishment handed out to one of the maids in this very parlour some two weeks ago. The reasons had been contrived but the consequences delightful, as the squealing half-naked maid had proved deliciously co-operative and imaginative in her efforts to commute her punishment and retain her place at Bancroft.

She knew that she should not be indulging herself but, as she was in sole command below stairs, the urge was sometimes irresistible. Memories of the bed she had shared with the shop owner and his wife had prompted her curiosity about sapphic love, and she had gladly explored it. A handsome strong footman or a co-operative pretty maid? Both offered a pleasing distraction from the cares of running a great house. She smiled as an image of the three of them together in her big bed appeared in her mind. One for the future, perhaps, after the girl had been further corrupted.

She raised her dress and eased her legs apart, then slipped her hand down her drawers, slowly pleasuring herself as she reflected that soon it would be time to approach the lord and admit that she had once again been weak and deserved to be placed under the discipline of the tawse. Her hand busy, she came gently and quietly and uttered a long sigh of satisfaction. Life at Bancroft Hall was fine indeed.

Meanwhile, in his study upstairs, the aristocrat in question had come to a decision. The insufferable Bertie had finally acceded to the crown of the British Empire over a year ago, and he had waited long enough – twenty years, in fact. It was time to act.

Crossing to the door, he locked it, then walked across to a shelf on the far side of the room and lifted out a set of false books, revealing a safe built into the wall. He unlocked the door and swung it open. Inside were various papers, bank drafts, and a large sum of cash. These he ignored and instead reached underneath to extract a thick manila portfolio, which he carried back to his desk. He opened it and placed a set of photographs onto the polished walnut surface. He shuffled through them, smiling all the while, before selecting four. The remainder he returned to the safe, then replaced the false books and put the safe key back in its normal place.

He sat down at his desk and pulled a piece of writing paper from a holder. Picking up his pen, he turned and stared out of the window for a minute, as though seeking inspiration, before leaning forward and starting to write.

Half an hour later, the footman collected some large buff-coloured envelopes from his master's hand in the study.

'Please post these immediately, Thomas. Take them into the village.'

'Very good, my lord.' As he left the house by the back door, he glanced down at the address of the top one. It read:

His Excellency Herr Dietrich Brunner

The German Ambassador

23 Belgrave Square

London SW

and was marked 'Strictly private and confidential, for His Excellency's eyes only'.

*

The following morning Brunner, looked up as his assistant knocked and entered his impressive office.

'A confidential letter for you, Ambassador, marked for your eyes only.'

'I see.' Brunner held out his hand and took the letter as the aide came to a halt opposite his desk. 'Thank you. That will be all,' he added, doing his best not to eye the young man's backside as he turned and walked back to the door.

In the time since he had been promoted to ambassador, Brunner had got used to receiving confidential mail from his masters in Germany, but this, it seemed, was not one of those. He turned the envelope over in his hand. It was larger than a normal personal letter, made from good paper, and addressed in pale blue ink in a fine hand.

Intrigued, he reached for his paper-knife and slit it open. A sheet of unfolded, unheaded, writing paper and a single photograph slid out. As he reached for the letter, he glanced at the photograph, did a shocked double take, then, utterly stunned, picked it up and stared at it for a long time.

'Mein Gott,' he muttered, astounded. 'Mein Gott.'

He picked up the letter and read it through quickly before re-reading it very slowly and carefully. Finally he put it down on his desk, leaned back, and exhaled loudly as he stared through the window of his first-floor office. Outside, the leaves on the trees in Belgrave Square were starting to fade and show the first hints of autumn, but he saw nothing of this, transfixed as he was by the contents of the envelope.

At length he started to smile, and before long his amusement had given way to open laughter. He looked at the photograph again and then stood and walked to the window, staring down at the people on the pavement below, his mind working busily. Dear Lord, life contained some surprises, and the one that had just fallen into his lap was a bombshell of the most extraordinary kind. He needed to think very carefully how to handle it.

*

Two weeks later, Hector Wyatt was surprised to receive a note from Dietrich Brunner. It was the first time it had happened. The note was short and to the point, and not without interest. It must be something significant to warrant such an approach he mused.

M.

I have news that will interest you. Please meet me at the usual place at 7.00 p.m. tomorrow evening.

Yours, B.

At the appointed time, Brunner arrived at the Athenaeum and was escorted into the small room where they normally conducted their business. Munroe was waiting for him, a glass of brandy in his hand.

'Evening, Brunner,' he said affably as they shook hands. 'A drink?' He poured a measure and handed it over at the German's assent. They sat, and there was a pause as both men sipped their drinks and placed them on the table.

Munroe leant back and crossed his legs. Over the months their relationship had developed reasonably well. Since the fatal motor car fire that had led to his appointment as ambassador, Brunner seemed to have completely come to terms with his ambivalent role, and it was fair to say that the men, though not close friends, were at least relaxed in each other's company.

This evening, however, he sensed a change in the atmosphere. The man opposite seemed ebullient and was smiling in a way that was faintly ominous. He mentally prepared himself for difficult news.

'You wanted to see me, Brunner? Something important, I imagine?'

'I have to confess, Munroe, that I feel I will enjoy this meeting with you somewhat more than those in the past,' the German replied, his smile becoming more obvious. 'Two weeks ago, I received an astonishing communication. The delay in discussing it with you has been because of my need to make Berlin aware of its nature and to receive instructions. All that has now taken place, and matters are in hand. Rest assured, my friend, were I merely the German ambassador, the British

Government would remain completely unaware of the events that are about to unfold. However, I find myself unable to resist bringing you in on the secret, as it were.'

Munroe's unease had been growing as Brunner delivered this little speech. The man was clearly very pleased with himself.

'Well, this is all very intriguing, Brunner. And what exactly is the nature of this great confidence?'

'It is particularly pleasing, given the nature of your original entrapment of me, to pass this to you for your perusal.' He took an envelope from his case and pushed it across the table.

Munroe picked it up, slid his hand inside, and extracted a single photograph. He looked at it and uttered a startled exclamation, then, appalled by what he saw, stared harder, hoping that he had made an error. Finally he looked up. His face was slack with shock as the grotesque implications of what he was looking at started to career through his mind.

'A fine likeness, and taken some years ago, I imagine. When he was clearly in his prime.' The German chucked delightedly. 'The tables are turned, Munroe. Tell me, how does it feel to know that another holds a photograph that will destroy everything that you hold dear?'

'How much?' said Munroe flatly. 'How much do you want for it?'

Brunner reached across the table and gently removed the photograph from his hands. 'Alas, it is not mine to sell. And in any event, even if I did extract an extortionate price from you, I am told this is merely one of a number of similar pictures.'

A shudder ran through the man opposite. 'So what do you want? Why have you shown it to me?'

'For my own simple pleasure, Munroe. Revenge is a dish best served cold, they say, and looking at your face now, I suspect they are right. A letter accompanied the photograph when it arrived at my office.'

'Who sent it?'

'Apparently a member of your aristocracy. A senior member, they claim, but unnamed. This individual advised me that a portfolio of similar photographs is in his possession and that he intends to conduct an auction amongst interested parties. The highest bidder will secure ownership, and they will be free to do whatever they wish with them.'

'So you are not the only person in receipt of such an envelope?'

'That is the implication of the letter, yes. My government will be bidding, of course. The feeling in Berlin is that such inflammatory material could be very useful during periods of diplomatic tension.'

Munroe stared at the German. 'The auction. Do you know where and when?'

'Regrettably, I am not in a position to disclose that information.'

The grey-faced man nodded grimly, unsurprised, and then met his eye. 'But you do know, I assume?'

Brunner said nothing for a moment, then spoke. 'Actually, no. Having informed my masters in Berlin, I find myself – what do you say in English? Ah, yes – "out of the loop".'

The man opposite him frowned. 'What do you mean by that?'

'Berlin are sending someone. I believe they have an individual in mind, because that person is familiar with the British aristocracy and may even know the seller. The intention is for this person to try and negotiate a sale before the main auction – in effect, to take the goods off the market by securing them before the other bidders arrive.'

'I see. And they are coming to London?'

'Correct.'

'Is that where the negotiation will take place?'

'As I say, I do not know.'

'How will arrangements be made?'

'Again, Munroe, I cannot say until my colleague from Berlin arrives. I assume there will have been some further direct communication, as the sender of the letter included instructions regarding a reply.'

'Who are they sending?'

Brunner laughed. 'My dear Munroe, too many questions, I'm afraid, and I cannot answer any of them, so it's no use trying to turn the screw.' He reached forward, picked up his brandy glass, and stood up. 'To intrigue and revenge. Enjoy your evening, my dear fellow.'

He drained his glass, picked up his case, and left the room, chuckling to himself.

Munroe poured himself another large measure and leaned back in his chair, eyes narrow in his haunted face as he thought furiously.

*

The following day I had just returned from a pleasing stroll around St James's Park in the late summer sunshine when Jimmy entered the sitting room.

'Mr Wyatt telephoned twice whilst you were out, Mary. He says to ring him back most urgently.'

My daydreams of amusing flirtations with the eager beaux in the park faded abruptly. 'Did he say what he wanted?'

'No. He asked for Georgina as well, but as you know, she is in Harrogate until Friday. He was told but had forgotten, it seems.'

'Indeed.' Georgina was very discreet about her family antecedents, but Jimmy and I had worked out that she probably only had one close living relative and that they lived in that handsome town. More to the point was Jimmy's remark about Hector forgetting. He never forgot anything as far as I knew.

I crossed to the telephone and, with a mild frisson of excitement, gave the operator the number. A male answered it immediately, if rather rudely, I felt.

'Yes?'

'This is Mary Felix. Mr Wyatt asked me to telephone him.'

'Ah yes, Miss Felix. You are to come here as soon as you can. At once was the instruction, in fact.'

That is the trouble with telephones. One cannot see one's interlocutor. I was not used to men being short with me, and I felt slightly piqued at his brusqueness.

'Is that so? And where exactly is "here"?' I replied in a rather chilly tone.

He briskly gave me some directions, just the once, and then rang off without saying goodbye. Fortunately I managed to find my way to the blue-painted door in a small cul-de-sac off Whitehall. I think the main building was the Home Office but am not sure, even to this day.

As instructed, I opened the door and climbed the stairs that led directly to the first floor. As I arrived at the top, I saw that the space opened out into an entrance lobby where a man in a dark suit was sitting at a desk bending over some papers. My main impressions were of a mousy complexion and wire-framed glasses. He looked up and met my eye.

'Miss Felix, I presume?'

'Then you presume correctly.' I raised my chin at him and did not smile. I recognised his voice as the man from the telephone – indeed, the cursed instrument was sitting on his desk – so we could dispense with unnecessary courtesies, I felt.

He stood up. 'If you'll just wait there for a moment, I'll inform Sir Hector that you're here.' As he looked at me, he did break into a warm smile, but I remained aloof. *Too little, too late, my friend*, I thought. *Learn your lesson.*

But more to the point, 'Sir Hector'? Neither he nor Georgina had ever mentioned that he was a Knight of the Realm. As I waited I passed the time idly imagining him peering out from the battlements of some misty Scottish castle whilst hairy tartan-clad retainers tossed cabers and danced reels for his delectation. The image was so pleasing to me that I was still faintly smiling as the receptionist, now becoming more friendly by the second, showed me down a thickly carpeted corridor and into Hector's office.

One look at the man banished whatever traces of amusement remained on my countenance. He looked ten years older, grey and drawn. Also he was in his shirt sleeves, which took me rather by surprise, as at Arundel Court he was invariably formally dressed. He stood.

'Mary, welcome. Thank-you for coming. Please take a seat.' I crossed to the low table he indicated, and he joined me, sitting opposite. 'Tea?'

'Thank you, Hector.' He nodded to my escort, who disappeared with alacrity, pulling the door closed behind him. 'You don't look well. Whatever is the matter?' I asked.

He paused and met my eye, then looked away for a moment as though searching for inspiration in the large and lovely seascape that hung on the wall to my left. It showed an East Indiaman in calm sunlit waters off a palm-lined coast. Perhaps he would rather be there, in that peaceful place, I thought. In the silence, I glanced around the rest of the room. It was large and well decorated, with two windows letting the early afternoon sunlight form oblongs on the green carpet, but before I could complete my observations, he started speaking.

'All of our conversations are confidential, Mary, but what I am about to tell you is secret. Very secret.' He paused and stared at the picture again. I realised that it was a habit, a place to go when thinking hard. 'We are facing a crisis. Perhaps the most notable single issue that I have ever had to deal with. You know me as the man who commissions your amorous tasks, and make no mistake, your work for me is important and helpful, but it represents just one small aspect of my responsibilities. As I explained to you when we first met, Britain has its generals and admirals to deal with the armed forces of foreign nations. I deal with matters which present a more subtle problem. I am the stiletto rather than the field gun.'

'I recall the conversation, Hector,' I affirmed before he continued.

'At present, we find ourselves confronting a hidden situation that threatens the very heart of the way the empire is perceived and therefore governed. It is a clear and distinct moment of danger in the history of our great nation.'

My heart went cold. From his expression and manner I could see that this was not idle hyperbole. He was deadly serious. As I went to speak, there was a brief knock and my new admirer entered with a tray, leading to a delay in further conversation. As you can imagine, I used this time to speculate on the nature of the threat. Was war about to be declared?

As the door shut and I poured out the tea, he resumed speaking.

'Last evening I became aware of a certain portfolio of material the content of which, if it became public knowledge, would be a disaster for the empire. It is going to be the subject of a bizarre but all too real auction, where the highest bidder will be free to do what they like with it. We cannot allow that to happen, and therefore we must obtain it before others do. I believe that you may well have a role in that mission.'

I was startled at this but managed to ask the obvious question. 'Can you not simply outbid the others? Surely with the financial resources of the empire …' I tailed off as he smiled sadly and shook his head.

'Alas, Mary, we have not been invited to bid. It seems the current owner, whoever they are, wishes us ill, and this is the method they have chosen. We are excluded. Which is where you might come in.'

I felt a surge of excitement. Like Georgina, it seemed I was to be given a wider brief.

'Our one advantage is that the seller does not know we are aware that the auction is planned, but any action we might take is hampered by the fact that we do not know where or when it will take place. We do know one of the participants, which is the German Government, so I imagine the other bidders will also be representatives of nations who, on occasions, are not our best friends.'

I took a wild guess. 'The French, do you think?'

'Yes, possibly, Mary. They would have their reasons.'

'Not least the Fashoda incident a couple of years ago, when they were publicly forced to back down by the British,' I suggested.

He looked at me with a new respect. 'I see you keep abreast of current affairs. And yes, that might be a factor. Certainly, had the French been in possession of the portfolio at that time …' He shrugged.

'It is that powerful a lever?'

'Yes, I believe it is. I suspect there may be Spanish interest too. We remained technically neutral during the recent Spanish–American war, but diplomatically we backed the United States, and they haven't forgotten that in Madrid.'

'What do you want me to do?'

'Hold yourself in readiness to travel at a moment's notice. I have other people to call on, but something tells me that at some point, your unique talents might be needed.' He smiled at me and added, 'For king and country, Mary.'

‘What about Georgina?’

‘She is travelling back tomorrow, so will be at Arundel Court by the evening.’

I hesitated and looked at the man opposite. ‘It’s just that she’s more experienced at this sort of thing, Hector. I worry that I might let you down.’

But he was staring at the East Indiaman again, lost in thought. Then he turned to me. ‘The Germans intend to try and do a deal with the seller before the main auction takes place. We must identify the individual they are sending to conduct the negotiation. To that end, I sent a confidential cable to our ambassador in Berlin last night asking if any senior members of the court or government had left Berlin in a hurry over the past week. I am awaiting a reply. Once we have that, then we can start to make plans.’

I decided to ask an impertinent question. ‘How do you know all this, Hector?’

He smiled grimly. ‘An old friend of yours, Mary, and more particularly of Jimmy’s. Enough said. Remember not to speak of this outside this room. I mean it, Mary. Not even to Georgina. I will talk to her as soon as I can.’

Shortly afterwards I took my leave and, with a head full of very worrying thoughts, walked slowly back to Arundel Court.

Chapter Twelve

Further events in London.

Cablegram from the British embassy, Berlin.

20 Sep 1902/Wyatt Home Office/Confidential.

Von Bulow left Berlin for Kiel Dockyards 18 Sep/Von Thielman left for Bavaria 19 Sep/Countess von Straum left today destination unknown/others believed in Berlin or at home/ends Blenkinsop

Hector Wyatt stood in his office staring at the cable, thinking hard. It was nine o'clock in the morning the day after his meeting with Mary and the second day after the bombshell news from Brunner. He walked over to his desk and sat for a minute writing on a cable form before pressing a bell push on the corner of the desk. Moments later the door opened and a tall saturnine man in his mid-thirties entered.

'Morning, Brown. Collect all the information we have on the Countess von Straum, if you would. Quick as you can – within the hour. Not just our files; have a word with the Foreign Office. They might have something too.'

'Certainly, Sir Hector.'

'And send this to Blenkinsop in Berlin, would you? Straight away.' The man took the piece of paper from him and nodded before departing. As he walked up to the cable office, he glanced down at it.

20 Sep 1902/Blenkinsop Embassy Berlin/Confidential
Please advise all available information about Von Straum/Immediate/Wyatt

*

Henri Allermen had been a railway porter at the Gare du Nord railway station in Paris for forty years. Very little moved or excited him anymore, but the little procession approaching from the taxi rank caused him to turn to his fellow worker and give him a nudge.

'Now there is a sight for sore eyes, Bastien. If we were a few years younger, eh?'

His colleague looked up and after a moment's delay whistled quietly in approval. 'You know who that is, don't you? The Countess von Straum. Supposed to be the most beautiful woman in Europe, they say. High up in the German court, friend of the Kaiser and all that.'

'How do you know?'

'My wife. She follows the society columns. She's shown me a photograph of her.' Further discussion was curtailed by the approach of the man leading the party of three.

'You there – we need porters for our luggage. It is by the taxi rank. We are for the train to Dieppe and then London.' Henri grimaced at his harsh French accent but nodded and started to move, as did Bastien. Where wealthy aristocrats were concerned, the tip was the thing.

The man was not tall but very wide and strongly built. His brown woollen suit was well cut and tailored in a south German style, and both it and the green waistcoat strained to encompass his frame. Henri thought there was something odd about his face and realised that he was completely devoid of hair – no eyebrows or any locks creeping down below his green alpine hat.

Behind him the countess stood, imperious and gloriously beautiful, her pale, flawless face framed by deep auburn hair styled in loose ringlets. Unusually for a redhead, her eyes were a piercing Prussian blue and shone with a fierce intelligence that Henri found distinctly intimidating. Not a woman to cross, he thought, but certainly one to worship. She was wearing a dark blue travelling coat and matching wide-brimmed hat that Henri reckoned probably cost a year's salary for him and Bastien together.

'Very good, sir. If the maid will just show us where it is, we will collect it. The boat train is on platform seven, sir. We will meet you by the first-class carriages.'

The man nodded his assent, as did the countess, who had clearly understood the exchange. They turned and walked off, leaving the two men to follow the maid towards the baggage. There was a lot of it, and both men were fully loaded as they struggled up the platform. Looking up, Henri saw the man give them a wave. He was standing by an open train door and the countess was just disappearing inside.

'We will take this one and this one for the journey. The remainder you may place in the luggage compartment. Get in, Agnes, and see your mistress is settled.'

'Yes, Herr Lindemann.' The woman slipped past him and mounted the steps.

Henri glanced up at the window of the carriage. The countess was looking down at him and their eyes met. He touched his cap in a small salute. Nothing more, he thought. They are Germans, after all. The woman nodded and smiled back, and the elderly man suddenly felt as though a ray of sunlight had pierced the roof of the station. Her face was exquisite, he thought.

'That will be all, then,' said the man as he handed over a tip. 'Thank you, porter.'

'She is a beauty, though, Henri, isn't she?' said Bastien as they strolled back down the platform.

'I'm in love again, mon ami,' laughed his friend, raising his voice as, with a loud hiss of steam and powerful puffs, the long train started to pull out of the Paris station, heading for Dieppe and the cross-channel ferry the following morning.

*

21 Sep 1902/Wyatt Home Office/Confidential

Countess Annetta von Straum/age 39 famous beauty/widow of Count Manfred von Straum/inherited large estates in Bavaria/not remarried/noted bloodstock breeder/court favourite in Berlin/believe trusted confidante of Kaiser/maybe more/query confidential role as Gov emissary/believe capable and effective/rumours of passionate but discreet nature/more follows/ends/Blenkinsop

Wyatt was sitting at his desk staring at the cablegram when Brown knocked and put his head around the door.

'I have some news on Von Straum if it is convenient, sir?'

The Scotsman gestured for him to come in and sit in front of the desk. He pushed the cablegram towards him. 'What can you add to that?' The man read it carefully and then pulled a notebook out of his pocket, flicked to the right page, and began to speak.

'There is very little beyond a name in our files, but the Foreign Office have come across her a few times in diplomatic negotiations. No formal role as such, but quite often just present in the background, if you see what I mean.'

'An advisor, then?'

The man screwed his face up. 'Not exactly, sir. The impression the FO had was that she is employed when a more unconventional approach to, ah, difficulties in the affairs of state is needed.'

'Meaning what exactly, Brown?'

'In Geneva last year, the Germans were on the wrong end of a deal being thrashed out to agree new tariffs. There were rumours the Swiss knew something embarrassing about the German delegation and were cracking the whip. The countess arrived late, and within a week the Germans had what they wanted, and the lead Swiss negotiator had, shall we say, fallen from grace, sir.'

Wyatt smiled. 'Not above a bit of dirty dealing, then.'

'A practical woman was the implication, sir. Not afraid to use her God-given talents. There are faint rumours of other similar events and at least one suspicious death. All unsubstantiated, though.'

Sir Hector walked to the window and looked out. He stood silently for some time, then turned and said, 'It's her, Brown. I think the Kaiser's sent the countess. Find a picture of her and bring it to me. And prepare to travel. I think we will have you down at Dover meeting the ferry from Dieppe. Incognito, please. You'll need to follow her.'

Over the following two hours, things moved with brisk efficiency within the office. Brown reappeared with a picture of the countess, which Sir Hector looked at and whistled quietly. If ever she and Mary were in the same room together, any gentlemen present would be in seventh heaven, he thought – always assuming their wives were not there, of course.

Brown, now attired in the manner of a comfortably off merchant and wearing a neat false moustache and horn-rimmed glasses, headed off to the station to catch the first available train to Dover.

Wyatt's instructions were simple. 'I'm assuming she'll come to London, but we don't know for sure. I want to know where she is staying tonight as a priority. And let me know who is travelling with her. I imagine she'll have a maid, but who else is in the party?'

When the man had left, he sat quietly for a while, jotting his thoughts down on a notepad. From these emerged a series of questions, which he then refined down to two simple tasks.

Establish where and when the auction is to take place.

Identify the seller and those who will be bidding.

Definitive action could not be taken until he was in possession of the answer to at least one of these questions. He tapped his pencil on the pad, deep in thought as he ran through the resources available to him and the various scenarios that might elicit the information he needed. In the end, there was one obvious solution which would almost certainly give him what he required. He simply had to place someone into the scene, and, as the other bidders were unknown, the route in was via the Countess von Straum and her party.

He was more or less certain that she would be travelling with a maid, as he had mentioned to Brown. On that basis, he reasoned that he could start planning without further delay. He rang the bell on his desk and seconds later the clerk appeared.

'Would you telephone Miss Felix and ask her to meet me here at seven this evening?'

'I will, Sir Hector.'

'And ask Captain Ransome to come in, would you?'

'Certainly, sir.'

The Earl of Culligan could be forgiven for not knowing the man who entered the Scotsman's office some five minutes later, as he was unrecognisable from the roughly dressed and course-voiced rogue who had pestered Mary in St James's Park the previous year. Of medium height with short brown hair combed straight back off his face and clean shaven, he was neatly dressed in a dark suit, white shirt, and a Coldstream Guards tie. He emitted an air of quiet competence which resonated silently around the room.

'Sit down, Ransome. I think I have a job for you, and it's going to need a fair amount of skill and a bit of luck to pull it off.' He spent the next ten minutes outlining what he had in mind and the end result he was looking for. When he had finished, he asked the man opposite what he thought.

Ransome stroked his chin reflectively. 'Seems to me it's all about the timing and being ready to respond to how the other party behaves, sir. If we need to do sufficient damage to take her out of the picture without killing her, then an accident is a risky thing to quantify. We might do too much, or then again, not enough.'

'So what do you propose?'

'Perhaps something along the lines of a Mickey Finn might be a better option. If the person in question becomes violently ill, then she will be unable to fulfil her duties, and a replacement will have to be sought. I would have thought we could manage that reasonably well in whatever hotel the countess's party ends up staying in this evening. Under the circumstances, it is almost inevitable that they will seek assistance from the hotel management. We can then pick things up from there.'

*

At seven o'clock I once again reported for duty at Sir Hector's offices. He looked better; much more energised and perky. I had prepared and dressed with some care, so was slightly put out when his eyes twinkled and he spoke.

'Mary, I have some bad news for you. Your crown as the most beautiful woman in London may have been usurped, albeit temporarily.'

With this, he handed me a photograph. I looked at it and raised my eyebrows. 'My word, Hector, she is indeed a beauty.' And she was. I felt a little tingle somewhere delicious just looking at her.

'The picture does not do her justice, I'm told, as she is a redhead with blue eyes. One of my men followed her clandestinely from Dover and admitted to me that he is already quite besotted.' He smiled. 'I hope he is joking, but I am not sure.'

'And why are you showing me?' I asked as I handed the photograph back to him.

'This is the Countess Annetta von Straum, friend of the Kaiser, and occasional emissary for the German Government. She is now in London and staying with her maid and her general factotum Max Lindemann at the Savoy on The Strand. You will recall our conversation about the portfolio yesterday. It is my belief that she is here in town as the German representative to bid in the auction. Although, as I mentioned, we understand that she will attempt to finesse the situation by acquiring the portfolio before the other bidders are present.'

'So you have identified the German bidder? Well done, Hector. That was quick work.'

'Our embassy in Berlin was helpful, and I cannot say I am certain, but we must act quickly, so I am making the assumption that that is the purpose of her arrival here in London. Of course, we still do not know the vital details of where and when the discussions will take place.'

'Here in town, though, you think?' I replied.

'Yes, almost certainly would be my guess.' He was looking at me and smiling now. 'But we need to know for sure, and to that end I am proposing a course of action that will enable us to place you right alongside the countess. As such, you will be in an ideal position to eavesdrop on events and keep me informed as she pursues the next stage of her plans.'

My heart pulsed and a little surging thrill of both fear and excitement ran through me. 'What do you mean?' I asked. His smile became something of a wolfish grin.

'You will become lady's maid to the Countess von Straum.'

There was a pause as I took this in and then started to babble as a rising sense of panic engulfed me. 'But how could that be achieved, Hector? Surely she has a maid accompanying her already. And anyway, I call myself maid and companion to Georgina, but as you yourself know, that is a fiction. We live as close friends, not mistress and servant.'

His eyes crinkled. 'Yes. So I am given to understand,' he remarked evenly.

I looked at him for a moment, then continued my protestations. 'Even if you could contrive such a thing, I'm really not sure that I could pull it off. She will be used to grand houses and professional staff of the highest order. Whereas I – well, I am a courtesan, Hector. Albeit rather a good one.'

'But you can play a part, Mary, and very well, I've heard. When we have finished this conversation, you will spend some time with a lady who runs a domestic service employment agency. She will show you the ropes in terms of what an aristocratic lady in this country would expect of a lady's maid.'

That sounded helpful; nevertheless, I remained alarmed. But as I opened my mouth to voice other concerns, he spoke over me.

'As to how the thing will be arranged, it is best if you do not know. That way if you are ever questioned about it, you can genuinely plead ignorance. Suffice to say that you will be on the books of the lady whom you will meet shortly and will be put forward to fill the vacancy on a temporary basis when the need arises.'

*

An hour later, just as Mary was being introduced to the proprietor of the Canning Domestic Agency in an office just off Whitehall, Alaric Ransome walked up to the reception desk in the Savoy hotel. Glancing around, he took in Brown still in his merchant's outfit sitting reading a copy of the *Times* while keeping an eye on the comings and goings in the beautifully appointed hall. They did not acknowledge one another.

'Captain Ransome to see Mr De Vallery,' he replied in answer to the clerk's enquiry.

'Of course, sir. I will inform the hotel manager that you are here.' He disappeared around a corner and returned two minutes later followed by a smiling moustachioed man in his fifties. He was impeccably dressed in a high wing collar, dark jacket, and pin-striped trousers and looked experienced and sophisticated.

They exchanged introductions and De Vallery led the way to his office.

'How can I be of service, Captain Ransome? On the telephone, you mentioned your position at the Home Office and that you wished to discuss a matter of state. Are we to be honoured with a notable guest?'

'Not as such, but I am interested in one of your guests, De Vallery. The Countess von Straum and party, who arrived this afternoon, I believe.'

'Ah yes, a most beautiful and charming lady. We are delighted that she chose the Savoy.'

'Is she staying long?'

'Alas, just one night.'

'And do you know where she is going next?'

The urbane man opposite him looked uncomfortable. 'Captain Ransome, it is most irregular to divulge information of that nature, but in any event, I do not think we are aware of her future travel plans. Might I ask, what is the nature of your interest?'

Instead of answering, Ransome removed an envelope from his jacket pocket and handed it to the manager. 'Before we go any further, would you mind reading that?'

The hotel manager removed a single sheet of paper and did so, his eyebrows raising as he got to the end of the short body of text and saw the well-known name typed underneath the signature. He handed it back, his face having lost some of its professional bonhomie.

'I see you have friends in high places, Ransome.'

'And low ones too, sadly. I can assure you that the co-operation we are requesting is very necessary. And I am also going to have to ask for your utmost discretion. Now then, what we need from you is this.'

The captain leaned forward and began to speak.

Whilst this conversation was taking place on the ground floor, upstairs in the Thames Suite the countess was making her wishes known to her maid with regard to the evening's arrangements.

'I will dine with Herr Lindemann in the main dining room at half past seven. After I have gone down, make arrangements to eat in your own room, Agnes. You may order something from the menu. Attend on me here at ten o'clock, when I will be retiring.'

'Yes, my lady. Thank you.'

'In the morning, I shall rise at eight o'clock, so attend on me then. We leave for the German embassy at ten o'clock in the morning, and I will be with the ambassador until lunchtime. The train from Waterloo departs at quarter past two in the afternoon. Please ensure everything is packed and transported to the station on time.'

'I will, my lady.'

Later that evening, the kitchen supplied a room service order for one of the modest rooms designed for the servants of the occupants of the suites. Tomato soup followed by fillet of lamb in red wine sauce and trifle to finish. As the uniformed boy charged with delivering this feast approached the service lift, to his amazement he was quietly accosted by the hotel manager.

'That'll do. You give that tray to this gentleman. He will see it delivered. You can go back to the kitchen.'

Slightly in awe at finding himself in the presence of the great man himself, the boy silently handed over the food to a smiling, calm-looking man in Savoy livery whom he did not recognise. The man nodded wordlessly, turned, and strode towards the lift.

'Go on, boy.' De Vallery gestured gently towards the service doors and then walked off towards the reception hall. Everything happened quietly and without fuss.

In the lift, Ransome quickly placed the tray of food on the floor and removed a small phial from his inner jacket pocket. He poured half of it into the soup and stirred it in with his finger. The remainder went over the lamb, where it rapidly became blended with the red wine sauce.

Three minutes later he knocked on the door of Agnes's room, and when she answered, he smiled most charmingly and handed over the tray.

'Bon appetite, madame.'

*

The following morning did not go according to plan in the suite occupied by the Countess Annetta von Straum. The previous evening she had enjoyed a fine dinner and perhaps a little too much wine with Max, but still had enough willpower to smilingly but firmly rebuff his suggestion that he join her in her suite once Agnes had gone to her own room.

'No, no, Max. We are here to work and must not become distracted by other considerations.' In truth, she did enjoy an occasional energetic encounter with her muscular, masculine, and devoted bloodstock manager, but she was careful that it did not become a regular occurrence. Judging by the adoring looks Agnes had been giving him lately, she was also sure that he had been spreading his favours in that direction anyway. It was typical of her that she had concluded their evening with a final remark.

'Remember I do not approve of liaisons between my staff, so leave Agnes alone from now on.' Then, stepping forwards, she had placed her mouth close to his ear and whispered, 'And leave yourself alone too, Max. Let the pressure build up a little. I like it most when you are nearly bursting and take me hard.'

The man had shuddered as she had smiled and stroked his cheek, then shut the bedroom door in his face.

At eight-fifteen she stirred and glanced at the travelling clock then stiffened as she realised the time. Muttering an unladylike curse, she sat up in bed and reached for her dressing gown. Crossing to the door, she unlocked it and looked down the corridor. At the far end and seemingly a long way away, a bell boy was sitting at his desk, ready to address any needs the guests on his floor might have.

'Come here.' The imperious voice carried easily to him and, looking up, he leapt to his feet with alacrity and hurried down the corridor. As he approached, he could not help noticing that her nipples were erect underneath the robe.

Blimey, she was a beauty, he thought, even though her mouth was pulled into a tight angry line.

'Yes, my lady?'

'My foolish maid has overslept. Go and find her and tell her that if she wishes to retain her position, she will be here in five minutes.' With that, she slammed the door shut.

The bell boy had no idea which room the maid was occupying, so he dashed downstairs and explained the situation. Accompanied by the reception manager, they made their way to the maid's room and the senior man rapped firmly on the door. There was no answer. A further knock produced the same result.

'This is no good. I'm going to open it,' he said and produced a master key, unlocked the door, and eased it open. 'Madam, are you decent?'

But madam was not decent. Not decent at all. She was lying on her stomach on the single bed with her head leaning over the side, apparently unconscious. One arm was touching the floor, her fingers dragging in a large pool of vomit below her head. A tray with empty plates had been placed on the dressing table, indicating that she had eaten in her room the previous evening.

Muttering a quiet cry of alarm, the manager stepped forward, closely followed by the boy, who was trying to take in every detail of the scene for the benefit of his fellow workers in the staff kitchen later. He knelt down and placed his arm on her shoulder.

'Madam, can you hear me? Madam?' There was no response. He stood up and looked at the boy. 'Raymond, walk quickly to the reception. Do not run. Report quietly what is happening. Tell the staff I said to call for the doctor, and then come back here. I will try and revive her in the meantime.'

Raymond nodded and blurted out, 'Is she dead, sir?'

'No, you fool, she is breathing, but clearly she is very ill. Go now.' He gestured at him and the youngster turned and fled the room.

Twenty minutes later a furious and hastily dressed countess was sipping coffee in her suite while De Vallery explained the situation to her. Max Lindemann was standing by the fireplace.

'… and so the hotel doctor is in attendance now, my lady, but I fear the poor woman will not be fit for work for some time. Days, I expect,' he concluded regretfully, his face a picture of sympathy and concern.

The countess stared out of the window, considering his remarks as an early autumn shower beat noisily against the glass. *Time was of the essence*, she reflected. It was essential that she had the longest possible period to negotiate privately with the seller of the portfolio before the auction. She turned and summoned a piercing, blue-eyed, glare.

'Is it food poisoning?'

A pained shadow crossed the manager's face. 'At the Savoy? Certainly not, madam. Many people ate the same food as your maid last night, and we have had no other incidents. It is some other virulent illness, I expect. When one is travelling …' He gave a slight shrug and opened his hands wide. 'We are, of course, extremely sorry. If there is anything the Savoy can do to assist, the resources of the hotel are at your disposal.'

'Then you had better find me a new maid. We leave London this afternoon and cannot delay our travel plans, so I look to you to arrange something with a domestic agency.'

She saw the man hesitate only slightly before nodding. 'Of course, madam. And where is your destination?' he asked.

'Remind me, Max,' she said, turning to her companion.

When he had replied, she said, 'Ah yes, of course,' then drew herself up to her full height. 'This is a serious inconvenience to me, Mr De Vallery, and I hold your hotel responsible. Please ensure that a maid is in place at my destination in time for my arrival this evening. I do not intend to dress for dinner on my own. Furthermore, I do not expect some clumsy local girl with fat fingers and mud on her boots. Do I make myself clear?'

'You do, my lady. I will attend to it immediately.' With that, he bowed himself out and hastened back to his office. Captain Ransome was waiting for him, smoking a cigarette.

'Well?'

'She has a meeting at the German embassy this morning and leaves London this afternoon. We are to provide a new maid at the destination, to be there in time to help her to dress for dinner.'

Ransome smiled. 'Once a countess, always a countess, eh, De Vallery? And where are they going?'

'It is in Dorsetshire. A place called Bancroft Hall.'

Chapter Thirteen

Bancroft Hall.

'Bridport. Now arriving at Bridport.' The guard's cry echoed plaintively through the train as it slowed and approached the station in the mid-afternoon sunshine. An increasing profusion of dwellings lined the track as the undulating Dorsetshire countryside gave way to cottages and then buildings made of warm brown stone. I must confess my heart was beating more fully than usual as I dismounted and walked through the ticket office, carrying my single suitcase. A modest number of passengers were with me, and they quickly dispersed as we reached the main entrance of the station.

On the train, I had had a chance to get my thoughts in order and take stock after the frantic rush that had resulted from Captain Ransome's telephone call from the Savoy informing Hector of the countess's plans.

When I answered his early morning summons to 'come straight to the office and bring a bag', Hector and his assistant Brown were leaning over his desk looking at a large-scale map of the area around Bridport. Without preamble or greeting, Hector had looked up and addressed me.

'It's not London, Mary. The countess is travelling to Bridport later this afternoon. From there, we believe they will make the short hop to Bancroft Hall, family seat of

Lord Bridport, formerly known as the honourable Percy Lyons. I now think that is to be the location of the auction.'

There was a pause whilst they both eyed me as though expecting some reaction to this intelligence. Slowly it rose to the surface. The name Percy Lyons rang a vague bell that got steadily stronger as I stood there.

'Captain Percy Lyons of Boer War fame? The man who led his men to certain death on the Transvaal?' I asked.

Hector nodded. 'Yes. Well done, Mary. The very same, and now succeeded to the title after the death of his father.'

'And you think he is the man behind this?' I said doubtfully. The man had been portrayed as a fool but not a traitor, as I recalled.

Hector hesitated for a moment. 'You may remember the venom with which he was treated by the press and the general public and, in the end, his own set as well. Ostracised from society, by and large.'

I nodded. Even though I had been young at the time, I recalled seeing my father spluttering with rage and ranting about the 'damned glory-seeking fool' as he read the newspaper reports of events.

'The thing is, Mary – and I bid you to remember our conversation about confidentiality – Captain Lyons, now Lord Bridport, had cause to be deeply angry at the time, and still does. The order for the attack effectively came from an individual of very high status who was not in the army but was on a private visit to see the British Forces. Over a drunken dinner in the officers' mess, the valley was discussed as a possible assault route onto the

Boer hilltop positions. Witnesses speak of Captain Lyons being dismissive, saying the route was obvious and suicidal, but as the discussion became more heated, he was more or less accused of cowardice by this individual in front of fellow officers. Placed in an impossible position and goaded beyond endurance, he led his men up the valley at first light the following day. The story goes that his commanding officer gave an order forbidding any assault, but by then it was too late. Lyons and his men had gone.'

I listened in surprise to this, but Hector had not finished.

'The attack was ambushed, and of the one hundred and fifty men who entered the narrow valley, only fifteen straggled back once darkness fell. The men who returned talked of him leading from the front with great distinction and pressing home the assault even when it was obvious it would fail.'

He sighed and nodded at Brown, who took up the tale.

'Lyons was grievously wounded in the head, and although he recovered, there was scarring – quite awful scarring, apparently – that left him disfigured. The attack was successfully hushed up at the time, and Captain Lyons was pensioned off because of his injuries and retired to Dorsetshire. To be frank, he was broken both in mind and body, and there it would have ended. But a journalist from the *London Times* heard rumours about the assault and the high-status individual involved, which persisted through the early 1880s. Some of Lyons's fellow officers were deeply angry, as you can imagine, and things leaked out. The reporter kept digging around, and the slaughter was eventually heavily publicised in London some years after the event.'

Hector interjected again. 'Seeing that the issue was not going to go away, and realising the implications for the individual concerned, the powers that be panicked. They laid the blame on Captain Lyons, leading the press to believe that he had acted out of a lust for glory and personal aggrandisement. The result of this deceit was that eight years after it happened, in the space of a just few weeks, the poor man went from being a respected ex-army officer who had suffered grievously for king and country to a glory-seeking fool.'

I stared at him. 'So a brave man was sacrificed so another could avoid censure.'

He shrugged. 'They ensured the trail led to the current Lord Bridport and no further. The individual who was really responsible for events that day was never mentioned in any reports.'

'And who was that high-status individual, Hector?' I asked, a vague suspicion forming in my mind.

'That I cannot disclose, Mary.'

I persevered, though. 'But is it reasonable to assume that this current threat to … I think you called it "the perception and government of the empire" is linked to this mysterious individual who was present all those years ago in a mess tent on the Transvaal?'

Sir Hector Wyatt had not been in the civil service for years without learning a thing or two about obfuscation, as his answer illustrated. 'What you assume with your rather astute brain, Mary, is your own business,' he remarked, dredging up a pale smile from somewhere. 'But it's not difficult to see that Lord Bridport has no reason to admire the higher echelons of London society and the government. It wouldn't be hard to imagine a man such as he seeking some kind of retribution.'

I nodded and said, 'But the attack became public knowledge in 1888. Surely that would be the obvious moment for revenge. Yet only now, in 1902, does he seek retribution. Why wait so long after the event? What would be the reason for that?'

He stared at his seascape for a long moment. 'Who knows, Mary? Who knows?'

Well, Hector, I thought, *I am pretty certain you do.*

At this point there was a knock on the door and a man entered. A well-built, competent-looking man with a hard-set face, aged in his forties. He moved like an animal. *A predator*, I thought.

'Ah, Mary, may I present Captain Alaric Ransome, late of the Coldstream Guards but on permanent secondment to our office. He undertakes various practical tasks for me and will assist you with yours.'

'Miss Felix.' He nodded his head at me, did a double take, and smiled slightly. A familiar reaction. As we were all still standing, he ignored the available chairs and positioned himself next to the desk.

'And what is my task to be?' I raised my head and asked this a little coolly, as Hector was clearly holding information back, and, for a woman, not being in full possession of the facts is a heinous place to be. It is not our fault; it is evolution. I know that because I read it in a book.

Needless to say, Hector didn't notice my irritation as he replied. 'The countess's maid is now incapacitated and unlikely to recover in the short term. She has been taken to a place of safety, where she will remain. The Savoy hotel has been charged with finding and supplying a replacement maid to await the countess at her destination this evening. In turn, the hotel manager had been happy to delegate this task to ourselves. So, through the good offices of the Canning Domestic Service Agency, you will depart for Bancroft Hall this morning in good time to assume your role as lady's maid later today.'

'And what exactly is it that you require of me, Hector?'

'To be our eyes and ears in the enemy camp, Mary. Your immediate priority will be to gain the trust of the countess so that she feels able to speak freely in your presence. After that, you must try and find out when the auction is to take place, who is bidding, and, of course, make every attempt to locate the portfolio in question, which must be secreted somewhere in the building.'

Although this did not take long to say, it felt like rather a long list to me.

'Hector, I am not experienced in this work. Perhaps Georgina …' I started to say, aiming to return to the theme that had been bothering me ever since our discussion two days earlier. But he held up his hand.

'No, Mary. Georgina cannot play the role of a lady's maid. You are the right person to do this. We all started in this business somewhere. We all have our abilities and innate talents.' He paused and gave me a slight smile. 'And you have yours, Mary, and they are considerable. Play to your strengths. That is the best piece of advice that I can give you.'

During our discussion I had already noticed Brown sneaking a couple of speculative glances at me, and to my irritation I noticed the faintest of smiles appear on his face as Hector said this. Perhaps it was my nerves or maybe the suspicion that he knew what I did and was judging me for it. Either way, I am afraid I raised my chin and glared at him.

'Is something amusing you, Mr Brown?'

'No, no, Miss Felix. Not at all.'

'Well, I distinctly saw you smirk, so something tickled your fancy, I think.'

'No, you are mistaken.'

But his expression had turned a little too sardonic for my taste.

I fixed my eyes on his and walked forwards slowly, unbuttoning the front of my close-fitting dress as I did so. I wore nothing under it, and as I came to a halt in front of the desk, I eased it apart and then off my shoulders, showing him my naked breasts sitting high and full. He spluttered and pulled back a little, but I kept my eyes fixed on him as I stroked my long brown nipples, which stiffened obligingly.

Gasping gently, I licked my lips and gave a little wet sob before whispering, 'Ah, that feels nice. I think they need to be sucked now, Mr Brown. Would you suck them for me? Please, my darling? Then, when you've got me nice and wet, I'll bend over so you can fuck me from behind if you like. I'm shaved bare down there, so you can watch it going in.'

The atmosphere in the room was suddenly electric as the three men all stared open-mouthed. I closed my dress, buttoned it up again, and gave him a gentle smile.

'That was just the mildest indication of my particular talents, Mr Brown. In your wildest dreams you cannot imagine the places I could take you if I so chose. Especially as I am quite naked beneath this dress. Sadly for you, you can be absolutely certain that you will never have that experience. Never ever.' To my satisfaction, his eyes boggled and he blushed scarlet, seemingly unable to respond.

'Bravo, Miss Felix, quite magnificent.' Captain Ransome broke the silence, laughing delightedly. 'You are indeed a spectacular talent, and I salute you.' His trousers seemed a little distended, I noticed.

I nodded my head to him in appreciation and then met Hector's eyes. They were crinkled with amusement as he spoke. 'Yes, well, Mary, as I say, play to your God-given strengths. I can't help feeling that you'll make something happen. I hope Dorsetshire is ready for you.'

*

'Miss Felix, is it?'

The voice interrupted my thoughts as I stood alone on the threshold of the station. Looking in the direction from which it had come, I noticed a large, closed car standing some twenty feet away and an accompanying uniformed chauffeur setting off towards me, a broad smile of welcome on his face.

Well, most men wear a broad smile of welcome when they see me for the first time, so I set little store by it; nevertheless, I smiled back. In fact, this was not difficult, as I realised that our friend was distinctly easy on the eye. He was about thirty years old and a good six inches taller than me (I am five feet two inches in my bare feet; did I mention that?), with short curly blond hair and a strong masculine face. A trim dark green uniform and shiny brown knee-length boots completed the ensemble, and, all told, he appeared to be a most acceptable escort. Distinctly so.

'I am William Stone, chauffeur at Bancroft, Miss Felix. I'm here to take you to the hall.' He leaned forward and took my case from my hand. 'May I?'

'You may, Mr Stone.' I released it and we walked over to the motor car. I had travelled in London a few times in such a vehicle, but they were still quite rare, so I must confess my interest was piqued. 'This is a fine machine,' I remarked, and indeed it was.

'It's a brand new Mercedes Simplex, Miss Felix, just arrived from Germany. Lord Bridport is interested in motor cars.'

'Oh, really? I thought he didn't leave the estate?'

'Now who told you that, Miss?' He stood and looked at me curiously.

I silently cursed myself for a fool. The chauffeur would naturally assume that as a new staff member, I had no knowledge of affairs on the estate. 'They mentioned it at the agency when they spoke to me this morning,' I said airily. 'Anyway, Mr Stone, do show me how it works. Where do I sit? In the back?' It was a foolish thing to say, I knew that even as I finished, but I was already flustered by my earlier mistake, darn it.

He met my eye and I saw a keen intelligence flash momentarily across his face. 'No, Miss. You sit up front next to me. The back is for His Lordship.' Then he laughed and to my alarm added, 'Have you been a maid for long?'

'Where are you from, Mr Stone? Do I detect a Devonian accent like mine?' I asked as I climbed up to the seat, ignoring his enquiry.

'That's right. Barnstaple,' he replied, but we both knew I had dodged his previous question, and I strongly suspected that he would not forget it.

Once we had managed the intricacies of the narrow streets of Bridport and were bowling along the high road for Dorchester at a thrilling pace, I asked him how long he had been at Bancroft Hall.

'Not long at all, Miss Felix. I arrived last week with the motor car, as it were, driving it here from Dover and assuming the position of chauffeur on arrival. I have a room over the stables, along with the grooms.'

'And what are your impressions of Bancroft Hall? Tell me about Lord Bridport and the staff.'

'Curious about your new position, eh? Well, that's fair enough.' He went on to tell me a little of what I knew already about events in South Africa and the injuries and then the press and publicity. Then he added, 'You are wrong about him not going out, though. I've driven him around a few times. We avoid towns, but he enjoys an outing in his motor car for sure.'

'Does he talk to you when you're out?'

Again that sideways look and a questioning smile. 'He's a lord and I'm a servant. He tells me where to go and I take him. That's it.' His answer was brutally short.

I stared ahead and sighed inwardly. If I had set out to give the impression that I wasn't used to being a maid, I could hardly have done a better job, I thought bitterly. There was silence for a while. In spite of my anxiety, I really was enjoying the ride and could not help noticing that Mr Stone handled the vehicle with an unhurried skill. Competence in a man is a singularly attractive characteristic I reflected as I glanced over at his profile.

We passed though the small village of Bradstock, which he explained was the nearest settlement to the hall, being about two miles away by road, but he added that a more direct footpath ran from the grounds to the village, taking about twenty minutes to walk. I noticed a solitary inn called the Highwayman. In London I had been reassured to hear that Captain Ransome would be 'billeted incognito in the village' to render assistance if required. I assumed he would stay there.

'And what of the other staff, Mr Stone?' I asked. 'The household is managed by a housekeeper, I believe. A Mrs Welling?'

'That's right. She has been there about a year and a half, I think – seems all right. Mind you, there are one or two rum …' He grinned and tailed off. 'Well, you'll meet her soon enough. This is the south lodge now. There is a west lodge further round, which is better if you're heading Dorchester way.'

The gate was open, so we turned in, and a man appeared out of the single-storey building and gave us a wave as we passed. Ahead, the carriageway led straight and true through a long avenue of chestnut trees, and in the far distance I could just see it turned right and dropped down out of sight.

The chauffeur grinned at me. 'Here we go, then. I always give the girl her head on this stretch. It's a good surface.'

Sure enough, the Mercedes begin to surge forwards and I was pressed back into my seat a little. As our speed built up, the air rushed past us, and I was obliged to grasp my hat, even though it was secured with a very robust hatpin.

'Fifty miles an hour, Miss Felix,' he cried out, pointing at a dial in front of him.

'Very impressive,' I called back, smiling, and indeed it was deliciously exciting to be rushing through the trees at such a pace. I felt a sudden exhilaration at the confidence Hector had in me and the importance of my mission. It would be all right somehow, I knew it would.

Well, I hoped it would.

*

Three hours later I was sitting at the supper table in the servants' dining room. The people present were trying to discreetly observe me in exactly the same way that I was trying to observe them, so there was a fair amount of eye rolling and soup slurping going on. By that time I had met the main *dramatis personae*, so to speak, so allow me to run through them.

I should say that I had not met Lord Bridport at that point but had been given a brief tour of the house by Mrs Welling, the housekeeper, who had received a telephone call advising her of the situation and warning of my arrival. It was she who had sent the car to collect me, I realised, and I thanked her for this.

When we had first stood face to face, she had narrowly avoided saying, 'You are very beautiful for a maid,' but I could see her thinking it. In all fairness, she was a singularly attractive woman herself, tall and quite strongly built but with striking grey eyes in a soft feminine face which benefited from an excellent complexion. She did not smile much, but perhaps the weight of her responsibilities fell heavily on her.

Her manner was formal but polite, and I realised that as the lady's maid to an honoured guest, I occupied a strange position in the household. Definitely a servant but not technically under her command.

Alongside myself, Mrs Welling, and the chauffeur, there were ten other people arranged around the table. The cook's name was Julia Wolstenholme, and I liked her straight away, a short, jolly, and plump lady in her late thirties who, judging by the soup we were eating, was very competent. Next to her was Thomas Edwards, one of the two footmen. He was a good-looking fellow in a roguish way, tall and dark, and I noticed he treated Mrs Welling with a casual ease. I was surprised that she permitted this and wondered at the cause, although I had my suspicions. The other footman lived in the village and left before dinner each evening, so was not present; in fact, I had not yet met him.

Jane Rancroft, the kitchen maid, served us before taking her seat at the table. She was young, perhaps eighteen, slim and dark eyed. I noticed her casting the odd glance at Thomas in between her sneaky attempts to look at me. For some reason I instinctively did not like her.

We also had four outside staff in attendance, the first being John Ellerman, the head gardener. He was in his mid-fifties, I think, and was clearly a solid experienced man, albeit a quiet one. I later learned that he had served with Lord Bridport in the Dorsets and knew the truth about the Boer War events. In fact, he was the fellow who had carried him out of that hellish defile, so he was very loyal to his master. The undergardener was also present, and I was surprised to learn that there were a total of six other gardeners who lived in and around Bradstock and walked in every morning.

When I expressed surprise at their number, Mrs Welling answered, 'The gardens are extensive and are Lord Bridport's pride and joy, Miss Felix. Mr Ellerman and his men do a fine job of maintaining them in peak condition.'

But alongside the two grooms sitting at the end of the table, I have saved the best until last – the delicious Miss Elizabeth Baker, who was sitting opposite me and training to be the new maid of all work. Lizzy, as she was known, chattered away quite unselfconsciously and had recently joined the household after the previous maid had left – under something of a cloud, I guessed, if my feminine senses were working properly.

She was seventeen or eighteen years old and medium height, with cornflower-blue eyes and blonde hair that fell into unruly tight natural corkscrews. She was a country girl and looked it, with freckles over her nose and a deep golden tan that was the mark of long hours spent in the fields. She was lovely looking, completely natural and unspoilt, and I imagined she would smell of hay and honey up close. Given the chance, I might even try and find out, I reflected as we smiled at each other.

Day-to-day life in Bancroft took place within the long frontage of the building which was arranged on either side of the domed entrance hall. The first floor housed Lord Bridport's bedroom and seven other empty ones. Only Mrs Welling slept below stairs, having a parlour and bedroom situated close to the kitchen. The remaining servants' bedrooms were in the attic, and mine was the fourth door on a long uncarpeted corridor. At least there was a bathroom up there with hot and cold running water and some radiators. I knew that when many great houses had been modernised, the new facilities had not reached the servants' quarters. Everyone had a room of their own, which was a nice consideration, as the likes of Lizzy and Jane had probably grown up in crowded dwellings sharing with brothers and sisters.

'That is not to be opened,' Mrs Welling had remarked firmly as we stood outside my room. She pointed down the corridor to a stout wooden door that blocked the way. 'The men sleep in rooms on the other side of it and use a different staircase.'

'Quite right, Mrs Welling.' I nodded approvingly whilst thinking, *I wonder who has the key?*

But above all, the talk around the table was of the impending arrival of the Countess von Straum. William was to meet the train at seven o'clock, so she was expected outside the main entrance of the hall just before half past seven, according to the housekeeper.

'Lord Bridport will be there to welcome Her Ladyship and so will I. Mary, you had better be in attendance as well so you can meet her and commence your duties immediately. We have prepared the second-best bedroom for her, although we are not used to guests here and must be on our toes.' She looked around the table and the others nodded agreement, and I had a sense this had been discussed a number of times – understandably, perhaps.

'Does Lord Bridport entertain often?' I asked innocently.

Thomas answered with a brief snort of amusement. 'First time in ten years to my knowledge. People call occasionally, the doctor and lawyers and suchlike, but to stay over? Never.'

'And to think there's more coming next week,' interjected Lizzy. 'Two more houseguests, so we'll have three altogether. It's exciting.' She beamed unaffectedly as I absorbed this interesting piece of intelligence.

'When next week?' I asked as casually as I could.

'Friday, I understand,' Mrs Welling answered.

'Who's coming?' I asked. 'To make up the house party?'

'That is hardly our concern, Miss Felix.' The housekeeper stared at me. 'No doubt we will be told in due course, and in the meantime our job is to ensure the house puts on the best possible show, not to indulge in idle speculation. I hope you appreciate that.'

'Of course.' Another slip-up. I dipped my head to my food and let the conversation drift on around me. At least I now knew that the auction would not take place until at least Saturday week, and as today was Wednesday, that gave me ten or eleven days to complete my mission. Always assuming the countess was not successful in hers and spirited away the portfolio before the others even arrived.

*

At fifteen minutes past seven, I was waiting in the main entrance hall as instructed. I had changed out of my traveling outfit and into what I called my number two maid's dress, the one that was not designed for seduction, and had spent some time in my room washing and drying my hair. My experiences of the aristocracy, both when growing up in the inn and through my more recent work, had convinced me that many of them were lucky rather than worthy, but when meeting a German countess and friend of the Kaiser for the first time, one likes to look one's best.

I sensed rather than heard someone on the stairs and, at the same moment that I turned to look, Mrs Welling appeared from the service stairs down the short corridor to their left. Both she and Lord Bridport therefore arrived in front of me at the same time. For there was no mistaking it was he.

I have described his disfigurement earlier, so will not repeat it; suffice to say the contrast between the even and attractive features that formed three-quarters of his face and the great hairless scar that completed the picture was truly shocking. The poor man would have terrified a child.

'Hello, Lord Bridport. I am Mary Felix, the countess's new maid,' I said brightly, completely forgetting myself. Maids do not introduce themselves to lords. For heaven's sake, no; of course they do not.

That this was indeed the case was confirmed by a sharp gasp of outrage from the housekeeper. Appalled with myself, I clenched my fists and stared at the floor, feeling very small and stupid in the huge high-ceilinged entrance hall as she spluttered and struggled for words. Thankfully, His Lordship gently stretched out a hand to quiet her.

'When meeting me for the first time, I find it useful to allow people a certain latitude, Mrs Welling. Especially in one so comely.' He smiled at me. 'I am indeed Lord Bridport. Welcome to Bancroft, Miss Felix. I trust you will enjoy your work in this house.'

Well, I had charmed him, and I wasn't even trying. Honestly. It was obvious from the wide smile and the way he reached out to shake my hand. His grip was warm and firm. I met his eyes and did my best to convince him I was a wonderful person in mind as well as body.

But lords do not shake maid's hands either, and as I glanced to my left and saw the look of thunder on Mrs Welling's face, something fell into place in my mind. I realised that I might have acquired an admirer, but I had also made an enemy. In thirty short seconds.

Further developments were curtailed by the sound of tyres on gravel as the Mercedes swung into sight through the glass panes of the porch.

'Door, Miss Felix,' the housekeeper rasped, letting me know quite clearly that we would be discussing this scene again at a later date.

I leapt forward and opened it, then stepped back to allow Lord Bridport to stride through. Mrs Welling followed and gave me a look that would have curdled milk.

Chapter Fourteen

I meet the Countess von Straum and make an enemy.

Our little procession emerged onto the steps of the portico as the motor car came to halt. William Stone leapt down and opened the rear door for the countess whilst the man I assumed to be Max Lindemann climbed out on the other side. I glanced at him briefly, but as the countess emerged, all three of us stared at her.

In the soft rays of the setting sun she looked utterly captivating, wearing a superb blue close-fitting coat with dark fur trim and a matching hat that set off her pale skin and rich auburn hair to perfection. Even from twenty feet away her piercing blue eyes caught the light as she looked at the three of us and then back at me. Our eyes met, and I felt my heart pound with excitement.

All this in a moment, and then Lord Bridport was walking down the steps and speaking to her. Mrs Welling and I followed.

'My dear Annetta, how lovely to see you again.'

'And you, cousin,' replied the countess, smiling and leaning forward a little so he could kiss her cheek. 'It is so nice to be back at Bancroft. It brings back such happy memories.'

Somewhere in my head I noted that she had ignored his disfigurement, which presumably meant she had seen it before, and that her English was excellent, but primarily my mind was reeling. They were related. Cousins, in fact. And she had clearly been here before. How had Hector not known? Or maybe he had concealed it from me? Above all, what did this mean for the fate of the mysterious portfolio? So many questions flowed from one small remark.

But then suddenly she was before me, and Mrs Welling was making the introductions.

'May I present Mary Felix, my lady. She is to be your temporary maid after the unfortunate incident at the hotel. She was sent by the agency in London and is not a local girl.'

I curtseyed a little and said, 'Good evening, my lady.' And then I shut up, as I could feel the housekeeper's eyes boring into me, as though daring me to make another gauche error.

Up close, the countess's eyes were quite wonderful, blue as blue can be, and they remained fixed on me as she nodded slowly and replied without smiling. 'I am fatigued after a long day, Mrs Welling, and will retire early. Please arrange for a cold supper to be served in my room. Felix, you will attend on me there and unpack.' She broke eye contact with me and turned to the housekeeper. 'My man Lindemann is here also. I presume arrangements are in place for him?'

'Of course, Countess. Mr Lindemann will eat with us below stairs, and he has a room in the male servants' quarters on the third floor.'

She nodded her approval at this and, taking Lord Bridport's arm, they mounted the steps and walked into the hall. I found myself alone in her bedroom some fifteen minutes later. Her three suitcases had been brought upstairs, and I was unpacking and hanging her dresses in the wardrobe when she entered. Without exception they were of the finest quality I had ever seen.

'Good evening, my lady,' I said and curtseyed. She didn't reply but walked purposefully across the room to stand right in front of me and stared directly into my eyes. It was like bathing in the radiance of an angel. She examined me for some time, then finally spoke quietly.

'I see I have a rival. You are remarkably beautiful. Flawless, in fact. I am surprised that your looks have not provided you with an alternative to the life of a lady's maid.' It was clearly a question and not completely unexpected. Hector and I had discussed and agreed on a simple refurbishing of the story which Georgina and I had created for the benefit of the Earl of Culligan, and I had it ready.

'I have had some setbacks in life, my lady, and because of them, this is where I find myself.'

'Setbacks?' she queried, her eyes still on me. She was standing closer than necessary, I realised.

'I was a foundling child, raised by the city of Exeter in Devon. As I grew older, I fell into bad company.' I lowered my eyes. 'I ended up being taken to work in a house of ill repute in London. A place for rich gentlemen to take their pleasure. I was rescued by a clergyman, who suggested domestic service would be a way to earn a respectable wage and give me a chance to mend my immoral character.'

She smiled thinly at this for a moment, then replied. 'Yes, that sounds like a man of God. Well, your honesty is a good start. I will call you Mary. I am not sure how long our association will last, but I expect to be here at

Bancroft for two weeks. The next few days will decide if we are suited.'

'Yes, my lady.'

'Complete the unpacking and then go and fetch my supper from the kitchen. I will bathe after eating and then have an early night. In the morning I will rise at eight, so attend on me then.'

'Yes, my lady.'

'And introduce yourself to Max Lindemann. He is my man and something of a confidant. You may consult him on matters you are not sure about with regard to my habits.'

'Yes, my lady.'

'Very well. Carry on.'

*

Alaric Ransome arrived at the Highwayman Inn in Bradstock later that evening on the premise that he 'had a fancy to have a break from London and do some walking in the countryside'.

He dined simply but well on a thick beef sandwich and an excellent pint of beer, which Jeremiah Whithers, the rotund and genial landlord, proudly announced had been brewed by his wife in the cellar, and then retired to his room. Before doing so, he casually let slip that he was a poor sleeper and much given to nocturnal rambles when insomnia overtook him. 'Don't worry if you hear me up and about during the night, Mr Whithers. I'll just quietly come and go by the back door, if that's all right with you.'

Therefore it was no surprise when Mrs Whithers, a poor sleeper herself, heard the back door latch open just before half past eleven. She nudged her husband and said, 'There he goes,' but her only reward was a disinterested snore from the large form beside her. Uttering a little sigh, she closed her eyes and shortly afterwards drifted off herself, her speculative dreams populated by their curiously attractive visitor who gave off such a reassuring air.

Dressed in a dark tweed suit and cap, Ransome walked silently up one side of the main street, keeping to the shadows. An observer might have marked the feline quality of his movements, but the village was deserted at such a late hour, as the rural community rose at first light and retired early.

As he reached the end of the buildings, he slowed and looked to his right before uttering a quiet grunt of satisfaction. A small gate showed in the hedgerow, and he slipped through the narrow gap to enter a large field recently mown of its final crop of hay. Keeping the hedge on his left, he set off walking briskly in the dim starlight, at first in the same direction as the road before reaching another hedge that marked the field corner. Here he turned right and continued across country, nothing more than a silent shadow in the night for ten minutes, passing through two more gates until he arrived at a stone wall some six feet high. The boundary to the Bancroft Hall park.

A dense wood of mature broadleaf trees stood on the other side, and he scaled the wall easily with the aid of two large stones laid crossways through it to provide footholds. Even in the faint light below the trees, a clear path led straight away from the wall, and he guessed he was following the daily road for the villagers who worked for the estate.

Ignoring the path, he moved along the wall and disappeared into the trees for some minutes before returning and setting off along it. Alert to the chance of a gamekeeper being on patrol, he moved with caution for another five minutes before coming to the edge of the wood. Below him a quarter of a mile away Bancroft Hall nestled in the rich parkland, its long Georgian frontage and two wings clearly visible.

'Is that you, Captain Ransome?' A quiet voice to his left momentarily startled him.

'Yes. Mary?' he whispered.

There was a rustle and she appeared from behind a tree. The starlight caught her anxious face, and he was again struck by her beauty. 'I'm here,' she said.

'Is everything all right?'

'Yes. She's arrived, and I am accepted as her maid for now.'

'Well done. Did you have any trouble getting away?'

'The back door key hangs on a hook in the corridor. I took it and locked the door behind me. They all seem to be in bed, but if anyone wants to go outside …'

He could hear the tension in her voice. 'I understand. Come with me, quickly then.' With that, he turned and retraced his steps to the wall and then into the trees. They walked for ten yards and then he stopped and pointed at the wall. 'Look here, Mary. There's a loose stone. Pull it out.'

Shadowy in the starlight, she did so. In the space behind it there was a gap, and she saw the faint gleam of a tobacco tin. 'Is this it?' she asked.

'Yes. I removed the stone behind it, so we have a fine hidey hole. As we discussed in London, if you have anything to impart, write a note and leave it in the tin when you can. Do not address it or sign it. Just write the message. I will check it two times a day as a minimum. Equally, if I need to inform you of anything, I will do the same, so try and come here once a day yourself. Now replace the stone and mark it well in your mind. See, it is opposite this broken branch.' He pointed.

She nodded silently, then spoke. 'I have news already. About the timing of the thing. Two more guests are expected on Friday week, so the auction cannot be before then.'

Ransome gave a quiet whistle. 'Sir Hector's faith in you was well founded. That is excellent, Mary. Do you know who they are?'

'No.'

'Nevertheless, a fine start to your espionage career.' He smiled. They walked back to the steps in the wall, and with a gesture, Ransome pointed along the path through the woods. 'It's fine in the trees, but when you come up here again, I suggest you avoid taking the path across the open parkland. And tonight, follow the edge of the wood to get back down to the rear of the house. Keep an eye open for gamekeepers.'

She nodded. 'Goodbye, then.'

'Goodbye and good luck, Mary. Remember you are not alone.' He stood and watched until her outline faded into the darkness. *Gutsy girl*, he thought, then turned and slipped over the wall and away into the night.

*

The next day was busy for me and the weather held fair. The countess breakfasted in her room and then went down to meet Lord Bridport. I watched them stroll away from the hall across the parkland arm in arm, going in the opposite direction from my own route the previous evening. It seemed to me, even from a distance, that my lady was being most charming to her cousin, her head leaning into him as she nodded and laughed at his conversational sallies.

She is going to work straight away, I thought. *And as I am not required until lunch time, so must I.*

My first priority was to learn the geography of the house better and familiarise myself with the routine. With that in mind, I spend most of the morning wandering alone along the many corridors and empty rooms, most of which were filled with sheeted furniture. Both wings had four bedrooms on the top floor, which faced each other across the formal parterre behind the hall's Georgian frontage. As far as I could establish, there were only attics above these, as there was no obvious access from anywhere. Below, on the ground floor, there was a ballroom on the right-hand side and, on the left, three reception rooms of differing sizes.

In the main frontage, Lord Bridport's first-floor bedroom was at the end of the corridor. I had a quick peek inside. It was a fine double-aspect room with a window looking to the front and one to the side, both of which gave an excellent view of the path across the parkland and into the woods. Captain Ransome's advice last night had been well observed, I thought.

My lord's study was on the ground floor directly below his bedroom. A corridor ran from the domed entrance hall and passed doors to a sitting room and music room to reach it. On the opposite side, a similar passageway gave access to the dining room, library, and finally a billiards room redolent with the lingering smell of cigars.

Outside, to the left of the hall when facing the main entrance, there was a large, cobbled yard. The stables, head gardener's office, and various other buildings lay around it, and a pair of tall wooden gates meant the whole area could be made secure at night. A door from the servants' quarters gave entry to the yard and was the back door for the hall and the one through which I had passed on my arrival.

I made my way through it again and begged a cup of tea from Miss Wolstenholme in the kitchen. We chatted about this and that as she and the kitchen maid prepared the midday meal, which was to be a large and rather tasty-looking minced beef pie. She hailed from Bridport and was a cheerful type, plain looking, unmarried – and happy with that state, apparently, considering that she had a good place at Bancroft. I fielded her questions about myself easily enough, and after twenty minutes I took my leave, realising that I had only half an hour to continue my explorations before I was due to attend on the countess in her room when she got changed for lunch.

As I reached the back stairs that led to the entrance hall, an arm suddenly reached around my neck from behind and I was pulled into the buttery. I heard the door slam shut behind me and turned to see Mrs Welling with her face contorted in fury. There was no preamble, just a finger in my face and a vicious diatribe, delivered in an impassioned whisper.

'Now listen, you little tart. I saw you presenting your charms to His Lordship. Don't you think I didn't notice.

Well, I'm here to tell you that he's mine. More than a year I've been working on him, and we have a fine understanding. If you think you're going sneak in and take him away from me, you're very much mistaken.'

My shock at this verbal assault turned to horror as she held up a knife and pressed it against my cheek. I recoiled, but she pressed me back against the cool wall of the buttery and held me firm. An image flashed through my mind of a spray of bright crimson blood dripping down the white tiles as I fell to the floor.

'You fucking little bitch. I'll cut you. See if I don't. I'll take away those pretty looks for good. No more flashing your eyes and tits at another woman's man.' Through my fear I saw a glimpse of madness in her eyes, a true distortion of character, as she ranted on. 'It would be a kindness anyway. To stop you being pestered. I'm a kind woman at heart, Mary Felix. Yes, maybe I'll do it now. Yes, it'll be a kindness.'

She leered wildly at me, and I felt the blade press against my cheek.

'No, Mrs Welling, don't. Please, I beg you,' I cried, my voice loud with panic. Even in the moment, I had enough sense to realise that denial would only invite further vehemence as I gabbled on. 'I'm sorry. It was all my fault. You are right, I was tempting him, but I've learnt my lesson. Lord Bridport is yours. I promise. And when the countess leaves, I will go with her and never ever come back. I swear on my honour.'

'Honour? You have no honour,' she spat at me.

'No, you're right, Mrs Welling. I'm just a dirty little tart. I am so. But I promise, I swear to you I will not pursue your man.'

Tears were rolling down my cheeks, and in that moment I genuinely meant it. To be honest, it had occurred to me that Lord Bridport might be tempted into an indiscretion if I caught him at a weak moment, but with this deranged witch watching my every move, that was no longer a consideration.

She stepped back and dropped her hand from my face, eyes still wild, and then pointed her knife hand at me. 'Just remember. I'll cut you,' she said breathlessly. Then, with incredible speed, she swung her other hand and gave me a vicious slap across the cheek. The impact was like an explosion in my head. With a little laugh, she turned and left the room.

Heart pulsing with fear and fury, I ran all the way up to my room, flung myself face down onto the bed, and howled into the pillow for five minutes.

Quite how I managed to gather myself and help the countess some twenty minutes later I don't know, but somehow it was done. And when, with some trepidation, I joined the others in the servants' kitchen for the aforementioned pie, Mrs W was all sweetness and light, enquiring after my morning and solicitous in her desire to ensure that I was 'settled and happy in my duties at Bancroft'.

She met my eye and we smiled kindly at each other. It was a simple enough understanding. We were enemies now, and in time there would a reckoning and a winner. I was determined to ensure it would be me.

*

It was in the afternoon of the following day that the intimate and delicious events described right at the beginning of this account took place. You may care to re-read them, but I will not repeat them at this point. Suffice to say that when I went to bed that evening, my head was full of confusing feelings.

The countess's combination of beauty, desirability, and power had had a profound effect on me, and, as I lay there unsleeping, I seriously considered throwing my mission completely, helping her to obtain the portfolio, and fleeing back to Germany as her maid, her confidante, and, most deliciously, her lover.

Perhaps it was the incident with the housekeeper in the buttery which had cast a long shadow and upset my reason, for I was certainly still troubled by it. I had never been threatened before, never mind struck, and my fear had turned into a deep and slow-burning anger. I reluctantly conceded that this was partly directed at Hector for putting me in such a position.

Or maybe I was just teasing myself, trying out the thoughts inside my head to see how they felt. I do not know. But staring at the ceiling in the dim light, my arms crossed behind my head, I felt a rare indecision, a deep anxiety that seemed to possess me entirely. When it was least expected I had suddenly come to a fork in the road, and I did not know where my best path lay.

At last I slept, albeit fitfully, but repose must have achieved something, because when I awoke, my mind was clear and filled with a firm resolve to continue my task. I could see that the countess was used to manipulating people – as was I to some extent, but she was accomplished way beyond my experience. The likelihood was that I would be nothing more than an amusement until she tired of me, I told myself firmly, whilst my dear Georgina and Jimmy and Hector were more akin to a family. And they were all relying on me in different ways. As for Mrs Welling, if I could do her a disservice, then I would; if not, then I would forget her.

So with these resolutions made, my long night of the soul passed. I had been tested, and in all honesty I had wavered, but in the end, I made the right choices for the right reasons.

And, of course, the countess was a German. There was no getting away from that.

Saturday began quietly. My lady made no mention of our intimacy the preceding afternoon and it was not my place so to do, so remarkably we continued as though nothing had happened, although her mere proximity continued to throw me into a confusion at times. When I stood behind her and brushed her hair as she sat at the dressing table, her eyes met mine in the mirror and I found myself blushing deeply. This elicited a cool and measured smile on her part but no remark. It was a measure of her power and presence that I, by then an experienced seductress in my own right, should be so thrown by her charisma, I reflected later.

My duties were not onerous and centred on assisting her when she got up in the morning, changed for lunch, got ready for dinner, and when she retired to bed. Beyond this, I found I had plenty of spare time to continue my explorations of the house, and so I spent the morning doing just that. The midday meal in the servants' kitchen was spiced up somewhat by Mrs Welling's announcement that the two additional visitors due the following Friday were foreign gentlemen. It was not really a surprise to me, but that did not stop my heart racing as she spoke.

'Lord Bancroft has informed me this morning that a Monsieur Henri Dubois from Paris and Señor Javier Lopez from Madrid will be visiting Bancroft from Friday next.' Mrs Welling addressed the table. 'I understand they will both be staying two nights and departing on the Sunday. So we shall have a proper house party for the weekend. William, you will pick them up from the station once we have their itineraries.'

There was a buzz of excitement around the table at this news.

'Are they friends of Lord Bridport?' asked Lizzie.

'I really couldn't say, and as you know, it is not our place to speculate, Lizzie,' replied the housekeeper. 'However, given that they have been invited to Bancroft for the weekend, that is a reasonable assumption,' she added.

Well, it might be, Mrs W, but it is the wrong one, I thought as I sat quietly and sipped my tea, distinctly pleased to know something that she did not.

After lunch I wrote a short note to Captain Ransome, folded it tightly in my pocket, and set off via a roundabout route for the cache in the wall. The weather had cooled somewhat, and as I made my way along the path through the woods, a stiffish breeze was moving the tree tops vigorously as they shed their leaves. I was glad I had put on my coat.

At the wall, I glanced casually back the way I had come and, observing no one, slipped into the trees and quickly found myself by the broken branch. I removed the stone and pulled the tin out of its place of concealment. It was empty, which disappointed me considerably. Somehow I had expected something, even if it was only a note saying there was nothing to report. However, a moment's thought made me realise how ridiculous that notion was, and so I quickly tucked my own missive into the tin and replaced it and the stone.

'At least someone is doing some work, Captain,' I whispered to myself as I tracked back to the path, quite delighted with my espionage skills.

Back at the house, I spent some time sitting in my room thinking. My perambulations had made me realise the house was very large and, whilst it was well maintained, it was also largely empty. Over the time I had been exploring, I had only chanced upon other staff on two occasions, both times a daily from the village brought in to clean and dust. It was clear to me that one person could not search the place in any useful way, and furthermore, creeping about and listening at doors was unlikely to produce a useful result whilst being fraught with the risk of getting caught.

I shuddered to think of the consequences of being dragged before a fulminating Mrs W, intent on dishing out retribution 'as a kindness'. Clearly some other strategy was needed, but what? I tried to think about the problem logically. The portfolio would be located in the most secure place in the hall. That, surely, would be a safe. And the safe was most likely to be either in Lord Bancroft's study or his bedroom. Finding the safe would be a further piece of information to impart to the disappointingly silent Captain Ransome.

So that was my plan. It was simple enough. Somehow I must gain entry to both rooms and search them.

Chapter Fifteen

The downfall and punishment of Herr Lindemann.

Crouched by the wall in the dark shadow of the trees, Alaric Ransome removed the loose stone from the wall, slipped his hand inside, and grasped the tin. He gave a grunt of frustration as he opened it to reveal nothing but the dull gleam of its interior.

'Come on, Mary, there must be something,' he muttered before quickly replacing both tin and stone and heading back to the Highwayman at his best pace. The church clock chimed one o'clock in the morning with a single flat clang as he slipped through the back door and quietly climbed the stairs to his room.

A minute later, that same hour was also marked by a single and more melodic chime from the small bell that crowned the clock tower above the stables at Bancroft Hall. In one of the rooms of the dark and silent house, a shadowed figure picked up a piece of paper, heavily creased from its tight folding, and held it up to a candle to read it.

It was short and to the point, with no salutation or signature.

Henri Dubois from Paris and Havier Lopez from Madrid arrive Friday. Leave Sunday.

*

Secure in the knowledge that Captain Ransome now knew the names of the other bidders and confident that he and Hector would be acting on this intelligence, I was free to concentrate on the serious business of being a sneak.

If challenged, my plan was to say that the countess had misplaced an earring and had charged me with finding it, which would seem reasonable to most people but not, I feared, to the roaming and ever-dangerous Mrs W. In any event, the day being Sunday, we were all expected to go to church in the morning. I briefly considered feigning illness, as it would have presented an ideal opportunity for a little snooping, but decided it was better to comply with what was clearly an expectation on the part of the entire household.

I have never had much time for God, and absolutely none for the clergy. Like Lucy, I had fallen foul of the local vicar in my teens and been subjected to far too many unwelcome squeezes and touches, all disguised as 'Christian friendship', the randy git.

At least I have always been honest with myself about what I did and what I thought about it. It seemed to me that to the three great tenets of faith, hope, and charity could be added a fourth – hypocrisy. In all my years, I never met a bishop who would not have had me given the chance. Some preferred to bugger their choirboys, of course, but even they looked interested.

Nevertheless, I went along and sang the hymns, listened to a smug little homily from the pulpit, and then shook the vicar's hand as we filed out, confident that my mortal soul had been redeemed for another week. I loitered by the church door for some minutes hoping that

Captain Ransome might be in the congregation, but alas, he did not appear.

It seemed that Lord Bridport and the countess had accepted an invitation to lunch at the vicarage, and I heard him instruct William to collect them from there at half past two. The chauffeur confirmed that he would and then fell into step with me as I walked towards the lychgate. Waiting in the road beyond it I could see the big open carriage and two draught horses that had brought the staff from the hall.

'Fancy another run in the motor, Mary?' he asked quietly. 'We can go for a spin and I'll drop you at the hall before I come back here to collect His Lordship and the countess.'

I hesitated. There was something his tone of voice that alerted my female instincts, and not in a good way. He was a handsome fellow all right, and well used to attention from acquiescing ladies I imagine, but that does not always breed good behaviour in a man. On top of that, I knew that I had given a poor account of myself on the journey from Bridport station to the hall, and further inquisitive conversation was not an attractive proposition.

Accordingly, after a brief moment's thought, I opted for safety in numbers and chose to disappoint him. 'Thank you, but I think perhaps I'll travel back with the others in the carriage and take the opportunity to have a rest after lunch. I am rather tired.'

He did not like it. Not one bit. I saw him struggle to conceal a shadow much like real anger that crossed his face as we stopped and looked at each other.

'Are you sure? It's no trouble.'

'Perhaps another time,' I replied in that way we ladies do when we wish to make it clear further requests will be equally unsuccessful. With that, I climbed up into the back of the carriage and squeezed in.

'You may give me a ride back to the hall, William.'

Mrs Welling had heard the exchange and clearly decided that her station in life merited such consideration if the motor car was available. Within a short time it had departed, leaving a dust trail behind on the quiet village street.

'Right then, all aboard,' Mr Ellerman called, and with a shake of the reins and a cry to the horses we trundled off. The journey back took getting on for half an hour, and when we trooped into the kitchen for lunch, it was clear something had happened. Herr Lindemann was sitting at the large table looking uneasy, whilst Mrs W was at the other end of the room by the range, a furious expression on her face.

As an outsider myself, it took some time and discreet enquiries throughout the rest of the afternoon to get to the bottom of what had happened. But I finally winkled it out of Lizzie after I had bribed her with a large chunk of my secret but very necessary supply of Fry's chocolate cream.

It was sensational news. The German had been missing from the church outing, ostensibly because he was a Catholic. In reality, it was now apparent the countess had had exactly the same thoughts as me regarding the opportunities the empty house presented. Unlike me, however, she had acted upon them, and her henchman had clearly been instructed to remain behind to have a good rummage through Lord Bridport's private chambers.

And he had been caught in flagrante.

Of course, he would have been tipped the wink by the countess that she and Lord Bridport were going on to lunch so would not be back directly after church. But it was the housekeeper's decision to insist on a having a lift in the car which had thrown him. She had arrived back well before the rest of us and had gone directly to the study on an innocent errand of her own.

There she had found the hopelessly inept German seated at Lord Bridport's desk busying himself with an examination of the contents of the drawers. Bang to rights, as they say. I must confess, I felt a little sorry for him, as the wrath of Mrs W had apparently been biblical. The countess had been consulted and flatly denied any knowledge of the thing.

Lindemann's insistence that he had been 'looking for some writing paper' was some way below the quality of my earring tale, I felt. In private, it was viewed with derision around the servants' quarters. Although, of course, the natural politeness and diplomacy of the English when dealing with foreigners did mean that on the surface, at least, it was all treated as a misunderstanding, meaning Herr Lindemann continued to eat at our table and to be received in company below stairs, as it were.

There was also considerable speculation amongst the staff about Herr Lindemann's purpose in rifling His Lordship's desk, which in turn prompted me to wonder if Mrs Welling was aware of the portfolio and impending auction. Had Lord Bridport brought her into his confidence? And if so, what were the implications of that?

Not for the first time I felt out of my depth as I tried to work out what it all meant.

Monday morning brought further news. Mrs Welling and Lord Bancroft had discussed the matter and it had been agreed that whilst Lindemann's explanation was to be publicly accepted, his behaviour in entering His Lordship's private study without permission was unacceptable. Even for a German.

He would, therefore, be punished in the traditional manor for Bancroft Hall, and afterwards the matter would be considered closed. The countess had agreed to this course of action, and the thing would take place that same evening.

I felt brave enough to mention the matter to her just before luncheon, when I was helping her to change from her outdoor walking clothes into a day dress.

'It's a shame about Herr Lindemann. It all seems to have been a misunderstanding, my lady. There is writing paper available in the library if only he had realised,' I said innocently as I tackled the eighteen mother-of-pearl buttons that ran down her spine.

She was admiring herself in the long freestanding mirror, lifting her chin and turning her head to the left and right as I spoke. She paused and clicked her tongue in irritation, then met my eye in the reflection. 'Stupidity and incompetence bring their own reward, Mary, and now he will pay the price,' she replied dismissively and then returned to her languid contemplations.

I was well satisfied with her response. If ever confirmation was needed that he had been acting under the countess's bidding, then she had just supplied it.

At lunch time, as we tucked into chicken stew in the servants' kitchen, Mrs W made an announcement regarding the arrangements for Herr Lindemann's censure.

'It will take place this evening at nine o'clock in the red bedroom above the ballroom. In accordance with the practice agreed with Lord Bridport, some members of staff will witness the event. You will be advised this afternoon if you are on the list.' I still had no idea what his punishment would involve, but the unholy gleam in the housekeeper's eyes did not bode well for Herr L as he sat opposite me, gloomily staring at the table.

As directed by my lady, I had taken the opportunity to introduce myself the morning after their arrival, running him to ground in the stable yard. He seemed a pleasant fellow, and his English was good enough to explain that he was the bloodstock manager for the countess and normally ran the stables at her estates in Bavaria. I sensed that he was more than an admirer of hers and wondered if they were lovers but, strongly built though he certainly was, I suspected her tastes would run a little more sophisticated than his seemingly uncomplicated character.

There was also the fact that he suffered from severe alopecia. The poor fellow didn't have a hair on his head, and although he had a ready smile and rather cute dimples, his blue eyes denuded of eyebrows and eyelashes peered out of his shiny pale skull in a rather fishlike way that left a lingering feeling of unease in me.

I could imagine his expression changing from benignity to intimidation at the flick of a switch. Or at the command of a countess, perhaps.

I finished my stew and put my knife and fork on the plate. As I raised my glass to take a sip of water, he lifted his head and looked across the table and our eyes met. His face was expressionless for a moment, then he gave me a wry smile. A guilty man resigned to his fate, I thought.

After lunch, Mrs Welling informed me that Lord B and the countess were dining in Bridport that evening and were expected back around eleven o'clock. More interestingly, I was to be one of the witnesses to the punishment, and so, at five to nine, I paraded outside the red bedroom on the first floor of the unused wing above the ballroom.

Julia Wolstenholme the cook and Lizzie the maid were already there as I came to a halt. This was the official party then and, as the clock above the stables chimed nine, the door to the bedroom opened to reveal Mrs W standing in the dimly lit doorway.

'Come in,' she said, and we moved forward obediently. Lizzie was in front of me, and she give a little gasp and hesitated momentarily as she crossed the threshold. A second later, as the interior came into view, I realised why.

Herr Lindemann was standing to one side of a large four poster bed, and a row of three plain wooden chairs faced him some six feet way, their backs to the curtained window. But what caught the eye was the fact that he was naked apart from a white towel wrapped around his waist and that his head was covered with what appeared to be a pillowcase, rendering him blind. His hands were clasped behind his head in a position that had clearly been dictated to him.

I saw him turn his head and listen to our footsteps on the wooden floor as we entered, as though he was trying to identify us by sound alone.

'Remain silent and sit down on the chairs, please,' said Mrs W quietly. We did so. I sat at the far end, then Lizzie next to me, and then the cook. 'You will notice that Herr Lindemann is blindfolded. Although he has been told that his punishment will be witnessed by some members of staff, he is not be aware who they are. It is a protection for you all.'

Also a further punishment for the culprit, I thought, not knowing which of his fellow servants had witnessed his humiliation.

Without further ado, she reached forward and pulled the towel off him. I heard Lizzie take a deep breath as his full nakedness was revealed to us. And mighty impressive it was too. He was wide, stocky, and muscular, making up for a lack of height with a pair of powerful arms and shoulders and a flat stomach. His thighs were brawny and bulging, and the overall impression was of an immensely powerful and fit man, even though he must have been well into his forties.

But I suspect we three ladies in the audience were not expending too much time on his torso. Frankly, it was his long, fat cock and heavy balls that caught the eye. Denuded of hair as they were, the man looked like an absolute bull. I saw Mrs Welling take a very obvious look at it before she turned and picked up a tawse from the bed. The leather blade was about eighteen inches long and an inch and a half wide, its polished surface shining faintly in the dim light from the single bedside lamp that lit the room.

So that was to be it. A rite of beating.

She spoke again, her quiet voice quite distinct and curiously energised in the silence of the room, and I realised that she was aroused by the prospect of what was to come.

'You are granted a kindness, Herr Lindemann. It is to be the tawse and not the horsewhip, so you will not be scarred. As you know, there are people watching, so I suggest that you maintain your dignity in the face of the pain to come. And stand still. Do not move. Each observer will deliver five strokes, and then I will continue until I decide enough retribution has been delivered.' Smiling, she leaned forward and whispered into his ear, 'Take your punishment like a man, sir.'

With that, she looked at me and held out the tawse.

I had not expected this, but there was no avoiding it. I stood and walked over to her and took the thing into my hand. The handle was warm after her touch, and I swung it experimentally a couple of times, although to be fair, it was not an unfamiliar device.

'Full strokes. On the buttocks. Say nothing,' she instructed. The excitement in her voice was barely contained as she stood to one side to give me room.

Oh well, I thought, sorry and all that but, as the countess had said, 'incompetence and stupidity bring their own reward'. I swung the tawse. It connected with a flat, loud crack on his backside and he grunted. Rather enjoying myself, I swung again to the same effect. On the third stroke he gasped quietly, and I saw the material of the pillowcase suck inwards as he inhaled. Two further crisp blows and my work was done. I was a little disappointed it was over but looked across to Lizzie and held out the tawse to her.

She took a moment to return my gaze, her eyes seemingly fixed on his groin, and as I moved from behind him, I could see why. His cock had thickened and lengthened and, though still hanging slack, was noticeably larger than when it had been first revealed to us.

I took my seat as pretty, luscious young Lizzie assumed her position behind him, all curly hair, rosy lips, and freckles. Her face was a picture of alarm and indecision but also something else – oh yes, there was definitely something else. They start them early in the country, and, looking as she did, I did not doubt that she had been tumbled behind a haystack a time or two and that our German friend wasn't the first naked man that she had seen.

'Full strokes. On the buttocks. Say nothing,' our head girl repeated.

She obeyed, swinging the tawse five times, the fifth noticeably harder than the first. By the time she had finished, Lindemann's shaft was at half stand, and I was starting to speculate where all this might lead.

She passed the tawse to the cook and resumed her seat.

I noticed Miss Wolstenholme passed close by the German as she assumed her position. Close enough, in fact, to let her dress brush the end of his cock, leaving it stiffening visibly. *That was no accident, you naughty lady*, I thought. She delivered her ration of blows, swinging strongly as her heavy breasts moved freely under her dress. Then she handed the tawse to the housekeeper and returned to her seat, managing to catch him again, I noticed.

It would be fair to say the atmosphere in the room was hotting up at this point. Our naked and muscular German was now fully aroused, his thick white shaft pointed upwards and balls high and tight below. I was feeling distinctly tingly down there myself, and when Mrs W stepped forward, her erect nipples were clearly visible through the thin dress she wore. She did not appear to be wearing anything underneath it. But then again, neither was I. Not a thing.

'What a disgusting display, Herr Lindemann,' she said disdainfully and, leaning forward, she flicked his cockhead with the tawse.

He groaned, more in humiliation than pain, I think, and then gasped as she repeated the movement, this time a little harder. His cock bounced and he moved a little on his feet. 'Stand still, sir. Do not move,' she cautioned. 'I will now continue with the punishment. As some perversion seems to have aroused you, it may take some time before I consider it to be complete.

With that, she set to work, swinging the tawse with enthusiasm and application as a steady series of flat cracks echoed around the bedroom. The pain must have been considerable and, stoic though he was, an occasional gasp emerged from underneath the pillowcase. More obviously, as the strokes found their mark, he naturally pulled his buttocks inwards and away from the impact, which had the effect of thrusting his hips and therefore his straining cock in our direction in a gratuitous priapic display. I saw a trickle of sweat run down his chest and squeezed my thighs together.

Glancing to my left, I saw Lizzie staring, seemingly transfixed by the image in front of her. I took her hand and gave it a squeeze. She squeezed back but did not take her eyes off him. Beyond her, Miss Wolstenholme was leaning forward, grinning openly, her eyes narrowed and focused. She was clearly enjoying herself.

As the punishment continued, it became clear that Herr Lindemann was in danger of disgracing himself further. His cockhead was now glossy and wet and fully skinned back. And he was starting to moan with every blow. To add to his discomfort, Mrs Welling, who seemed to have completely forgotten our presence, was alternating her attentions between beating his buttocks and flicking at his groin. After one particularly enthusiastic series of blows, she finally reached over and grasped the shaft with her hand and pumped it a dozen times whilst whispering audibly in his ear.

'Whose hand is that, Herr Lindemann? Is it me or someone else? Someone round the breakfast table in the morning, for sure. But who, sir? Who? We will know and you will not.'

This produced a stream of muttered German under the pillowcase and then another groan as she returned to his backside. She repeated this treatment three times, each time stroking his cock for longer. I heard Lizzie give a little sigh as she watched intently.

The fourth time brought matters to a conclusion. Eyes narrowed and a thin smile on her face, Mrs Welling began to concentrate on his painfully swollen and slick cockhead, rubbing it slowly between her looped index finger and thumb as he pleaded with her.

'Nein, Frau Welling, bitte nein,' he gasped, the pillowcase moving under his panting breath as her merciless stimulation led him towards its unavoidable conclusion. At last, in desperation, he emitted an anguished moan of surrender and his thighs shuddered as his resistance crumbled and he crossed the point of no return.

Timing it to a nicety, Mrs Welling released him and started to beat his buttocks again as his freestanding cock jerked and bounced, and he spent powerfully, four strong spurts rising high into the air in front of us before falling towards the polished wooden floor at our feet.

I saw a line of silver pearls appear on Lizzie's black boot, and her hand squeezed mine tightly as I felt her shaking and realised that she was coming spontaneously, carried away with the scene being played out in front of her. I must confess, I was not far behind, and doubtless a few well-placed strokes of my fingers would had have the same effect.

At the end of the line Miss Wolstenholme, clearly lost in her own world like Mrs Welling, was leaning back in the chair, her legs apart and her hand at her groin and openly working through her skirt. She spent quietly as I watched, gasping with pleasure as a deep red flush spread across her throat and neck.

Distinctly wild eyed and with the tawse hanging loosely from her hand, the housekeeper addressed us. 'You may leave.'

We filed out. As we stood outside, I heard the door click shut and the lock engage. It appeared that Herr Lindemann's ordeal was not yet over.

As the cook tripped off down the corridor at high speed, I glanced at Lizzie, who was standing loosely next to me. She was managing to look aroused, delicious, and vulnerable at the same time, her mouth open and face and neck flushed red.

I just could not help myself. She looked so ripe and ready.

Stepping forward, I wordlessly took her hand and led her towards the first door I could see. We went in and I shut and locked it. She looked at me with hot eyes. *Oh, yes please, you little beauty*, I thought and, pressing her up against the wall, kissed her hard and full on the lips.

She stiffened in shock and for a moment I felt her hesitate, but by then my tongue was at her mouth and within a second she was opening her lips to me and responding. My head swam as I lifted her dress, intent on keeping the momentum of the moment going. And then suddenly my hand was on her cunny and she uttered a gasp and then a long, low, and almost despairing moan of pleasure as my fingers stroked and probed her.

'No, Mary, you mustn't. It's wrong,' she managed to whisper, but her words were in vain. The poor girl was dripping wet and overrun with passion. Clearly her earlier spend had been an hors d'oeuvre rather than a main course. As she pressed her hips forward and wrapped her arms around my neck, another sound penetrated the room. A regular, rhythmic moaning that rapidly grew in intensity and was coming from the other side of the wall against which Lizzie was braced.

‘Listen to that, Lizzie. He’s fucking Mrs Welling,’ I said in a low voice into her ear. ‘Just next door. She’s getting that big white German cock deep inside her. Can you hear it? You’d like that too, wouldn’t you? A long stiff cock fucking you hard.’

Her only reply was a gasp that turned into a sob. Pushing her raised dress into her hands and whispering, ‘Hold it tight,’ I sank to my knees. Her soft curls parted as I sucked her clitty into my mouth and went to work, my hands firmly clasping her delicious bum. Completely overwhelmed, she came almost at once with a series of hoarse grunts, her hips thrusting involuntarily as she released a flood of delicious juice into my mouth. I lapped and licked and gurgled away as further spasms followed, until she eventually calmed and removed her hand from my head, which she had inadvertently grasped in the throes of passion. At the same time a scream of joy from Mrs Welling and a guttural roar from her German beau sounded clearly through the wall, indicating that matters had reached a very satisfactory conclusion next door.

Which just left me. Oh, goody.

With a knowing smile, I climbed up from my knees and held Lizzie’s face in my hands, then kissed her again gently. ‘Nice?’ I whispered as a precursor to inviting her to explore my own body as a matter of some urgency. But instead of a little giggle and a hand-in-hand procession to the large bed I had noticed to my right, an expression of shock and distress suddenly appeared on her face.

‘Oh, Mary, what have we done?’ She held her hand up to her mouth, pushing mine away. ‘Oh, dear Lord, what have we done?' With that, she burst into tears and ran for the door, unlocking it and disappearing before I even had a chance to say anything.

'Lizzie, come back,' I cried as I reached the corridor, but all I got was a wave of her hand over her shoulder as she sped away from me and around the corner. I groaned with irritation and frustration. Especially the latter. The silly girl. The silly, delicious, lovely girl.

Slowly, I followed her, walking along the corridor to where the wing joined the main frontage, and turned into the passageway that ran behind the first-floor rooms, passing Lord Bridport's bedroom on the corner. A grandfather clock showed the time to be just after half past nine, so the whole event had taken just half an hour.

Thinking I might find Lizzie in the kitchen, and keen to alleviate her distress, I walked down the main stairs to the hallway and turned back on myself to find the back stairs and descended those in turn. But everywhere was deserted down below. I wandered through the kitchen and past Mrs Welling's sitting room and bedroom. Well, I knew where she was – trying to tempt one more round from our robust Bavarian, no doubt. But everyone else seemed to have disappeared, and a deep silence pervaded the rooms. I followed the corridor that led to the back door and the stable yard, thinking to have a breath of air, but as I passed the short passageway that led to the dairy, I heard a noise.

It was a muted groan of the sort I had heard a fair amount of in the past half hour or so. It was also the kind of noise that merited investigation.

Silently I tiptoed the few yards to the dairy door, which stood eighteen inches or so ajar. Further quiet sounds of the same nature reached my ears, and I risked a quick peek. I must say, my immediate reaction to the sight that greeted me was further frustration. For heaven's sake, was every servant except me enjoying a lascivious night?

Sideways on to me and quite naked, Miss Wolstenholme was lying on her back across the end of the narrow dairy table. Standing between her legs, John Ellerman, the head gardener, was fucking her, his hands holding her knees high and wide as he thrust forwards. The sensible lady had reached down and gripped the edge of the table, enabling her to push back against him, and they were going at it hard and fast. Her large breasts and plump belly were rippling and rolling with the impact of his thrusts, and she was uttering muted animal-like grunts as his cock did its work. As I watched, he grinned at her, released one knee, and reached forwards to squeeze her breasts. She lowered her leg, and I had a fine view of her being deeply penetrated. What a lucky girl.

And they were not alone. Standing on the far side of the table, Thomas the footman was also naked, with his stiff cock in his hand. He stepped forward and I heard him mutter, 'Suck it.' She obliged silently and without hesitation, bending her neck fully backwards so her head reached down over the edge of the table, her hair cascading towards the floor. He slid it into her open mouth, placed his hands on the table, and started to move his hips.

'That's it, Thomas, fuck her throat,' muttered Mr Ellerman breathlessly. A loud moan of submission filled the room as Miss Wolstenholme submitted completely to the attentions of the two dominant men.

How long has this been going on? I wondered as I watched them. It was no surprise that the cook had told me she was 'well satisfied' with her position at Bancroft. Three meals a day and comprehensive fucking when you needed it. Also, Mr Ellerman was supposed to be happily married and living in a cottage on the estate. No wonder he popped in for his tea three times a week. However, fully engaged though they were, I knew my own position was precarious. A single glance from any of the three of them and I would be spotted, so reluctantly I withdrew and slipped back along the corridor and out into the yard.

A light burned in the room above the stables that was occupied by the chauffeur, and I briefly contemplated going to see him with a view to having my tensions eased a little. But reason prevailed as I remembered his ill-concealed anger the previous day outside the church. My instincts had told me to avoid him, and I would obey them.

After all, I had had the foresight to bring a certain Dr Bone as my confidential travelling companion. With this happy thought uppermost, I retired for the night.

Chapter Sixteen

Blackmail and its consequences.

At breakfast time the following morning Lizzie caught my eye a couple of times, and I made a point of smiling warmly at her, but she blushed furiously on both occasions and said nothing. I hoped that I would be able to have a quiet word with her at some point, as the previous night's events were clearly preying on her mind.

Herr Lindemann was cheerful enough and, although I caught him looking at his fellow servants once or twice, an obvious question in his mind, he seemed to be happy that matters were behind him, and he was officially forgiven. I wondered what next steps the countess had planned, as to be caught again would be inexcusable. I also wondered if he had found anything useful in the study. A safe or a key, for example.

Everyone else seemed to have a spring in their step. What a surprise.

After breakfast I ambled openly across the parkland as though I was going for a walk and deposited another brief note in the tin advising of the events regarding Herr Lindemann. Well, up to a point anyway – you will understand my discretion.

To my great frustration, there was no reply to my previous missive to Captain Ransome, and I must confess to feeling very much alone and a little tearful as I stood by the wall. On impulse, I decided to force the issue and opened the tin again to add a brief postscript in pencil on the reverse of the note.

'Need to see you. Meet me tonight by the stable yard gate at midnight.'

With that, I headed back through the woods and across the park to the hall.

I spent much of my remaining free time before lunch loitering uselessly on the ground and first floors of the main section of the building, trying to summon up my courage. I knew I was being rather foolhardy, given the punishment I had witnessed, but nevertheless, I was resolved to search both Lord B's study and bedroom if possible, and that meant picking my time. He and the countess had gone for a walk, but for once the corridors seemed unaccountably busy with the 'dailies' from the village about their business. And, of course, there was the ever-present threat of Mrs W, who seemed to patrol the building like a stealthy tigress. And she had her eye on me.

After our midday meal, I finally got my chance. The housekeeper announced that she was going to walk into the village, and, having watched her cross the park and enter the woods from an upstairs window, I scuttled off to Lord Bridport's study. Thankfully the door was not locked, and I opened it quietly and peered in.

Silence and emptiness greeted me. I stepped inside and shut the door, then, after a moment's thought, turned the key in the lock. It engaged with a heavy and positive click, and I turned to face the room.

It was large and gracious in a quietly masculine way. The polished wooden floor was dotted with lovely antique Turkey rugs, an old-fashioned desk sat before the window facing into the room, and two worn Chesterfield red leather settees were positioned either side of a low table. A plain marble fireplace dominated one wall, and another was hung with fine pictures of rural landscapes. To my left the wall was covered with shelves of books, and in the corner a collection of bottles and decanters stood on a wooden table with an attractive inlaid surface. A faint aroma of cigars permeated the air, and the rhythmic tick of a large carriage clock somehow added a timeless sense of permanence to the scene.

It was a room for reflection and serious thought. A room to hatch a plan to bring down an empire, even.

There were some photographs on the desk, and I walked over and examined them. Two were of what I assumed were his parents and the remainder featured men in uniform, often with himself included. One showed Lord Bridport, much younger and unscarred, standing with another man. They were both grinning at the camera. In the background was a high conical hill with a narrow scar running up it almost to the top. Was that the infamous defile, I wondered? As I stared at it, I realised that the man standing next to His Lordship was John Ellerman. In contrast to the previous evening, he was fully clothed in a khaki uniform bearing the three stripes of a sergeant's rank.

Enough. Time to search.

I sifted through the contents of the desk without finding anything interesting and moved on to the chest of drawers to the right of the fireplace. Again I drew a blank and stood thinking for a moment. Those were the only obvious places to keep rather than hide a portfolio, but the more likely option was a safe. A concealed safe, in fact.

I walked over to the paintings and worked my way along the ones I could reach, gently lifting each one and putting my eye to the wall to peer behind it. Nothing.

Tapping my foot gently on the wooden floor and ever conscious of the need to keep listening for movement outside, I eyed the books. They stretched the full length of one wall, seven shelves high, and were broken into sections a yard wide by vertical wooden spines. A short stepladder stood in front of them. I reasoned that if the safe was concealed behind them, then, for convenience, it would be above waist height and below shoulder height. Two shelves, then – the third and fourth. I began at one end and worked my way steadily along, removing every fifth book. As I approached the drinks table, the book I selected refused to move. I pulled harder and a section of them moved together. Heart racing, I brought my other hand into play and lifted a line of about ten false books out in one complete section.

I hissed in triumph. Behind, sitting snugly in the wall, was a wide, low safe door with a handle on the left and a large keyhole front and centre. 'That's the ticket,' I whispered to myself. More in hope than expectation, I pulled the handle downwards, but it did not move.

Nevertheless, a step forward and more progress to report. If ever Captain Ransome deigned to get in touch, I thought with a touch of bitterness. Hopefully I would see him later. I replaced the books and checked the time on the clock. Five to three. I had been in there twenty minutes, and all was quiet outside.

Now for the key. I ran my eyes around the room and let my brain do some work. It was very likely that the key would be secreted in the study. Locating it in another room might be more secure, but it would also be inconvenient to a fault. No, the thing was here somewhere, no more than twenty feet from where I was standing.

Trying to see the room from Lord B's point of view, I crossed to the desk and, after a cautious look outside, sat down in his chair. As with many grand houses, the steps up to the main entrance meant the ground floor was raised above the ground outside, so I was quite well concealed from anyone walking past.

I studied the room carefully. The hiding place could be small, but it would need to be accessible. I did not imagine His Lordship would want the rigmarole of moving three or four things each time he wanted to open the safe. Perhaps a hook on the back of the chest of drawers? I went over and put my face against the wall to peer into the gap. It did not appear so, although I would need a torch to be sure.

On the mantlepiece above the fire there were three beautiful Chinese porcelain vases. Heart beating, I examined each one hopefully. They were empty.

I pursed my lips gently. It was starting to look as though there was only one option left, and it was the one I wanted to avoid. I looked back at the books. The most likely hiding place for the key was in another false book, as I had realised straight away. And there were seven shelves, each about twenty feet long. Over fifteen hundred books, I estimated, and each one would have to be picked out, opened, and replaced. It would take hours.

Perhaps there was a better way, though. It did not look as though most of the books had been moved for years. Might a close study of the shelves reveal one that had been handled more often? A lack of dust, for example?

I stiffened in alarm as I heard a female voice outside the door, soft with the Dorset brogue.

'Oi'll do 'is Lordships study now then, Mavis,' it called, obviously addressing someone else further along the corridor. I heard a muted reply and then a laugh followed by 'Oi reckon so too,' from just outside.

I looked wildly round the room. There was nowhere to hide. Nowhere. And in any event, if the blasted woman was going to clean, she'd certainly find me. Should I bluff it out? The door handle turned, and I stood there slack faced and utterly devoid of ideas.

'E's locked it, Mavis.'

In my panic, I had forgotten. Relief flooded through me as I heard more muted voices from far off.

'Olright, then,' my persecutor replied. Then silence.

Heart pounding, I waited stock still for five minutes, then decided I had had enough for one day. However, just as I prepared to unlock the door and tiptoe away, a thought occurred. Walking over to the desk, I slipped behind it. There were four tall sash windows arranged in parallel within a slight bay. Each lower pane had a catch on the top, and I reached up and pushed the one in the left-hand corner so that it disengaged. The window was now free to open from either side. I stepped back and admired my handiwork. It really was not obvious unless you were looking for it.

Glancing out across the parkland, I received another shock. Fifty yards away and in full view, the housekeeper was approaching the hall, moving at a brisk pace, her eyes seemingly fixed on little me. She had turned back for some reason.

My nerve failed me. Uttering a little whimper, I dashed across the study, unlocked the door, and put my head around it. The coast was clear. With a sigh of relief, I slipped out. Enough thrills for one day. And it was only ten past three.

Later, when I was helping the countess change for dinner, I noticed her mood had changed. Normally with me she was aloof, serene, and a little cold, even, but not unkind. A woman in charge of her life and those around her. But that evening she was tetchy and irritable, castigating me for dropping a hair pin and then getting out the wrong dress for the evening. And she moved constantly, pacing around the bedroom as though unable to settle.

Finally I summoned my courage up and said something. 'Are you quite well, my lady? If you will forgive me, you seem a little out of sorts this evening. Is there anything I can do to assist?' *Like taking you to bed to ease your tension and mine*, I added silently.

She glared at me, imperious and beautiful in her immaculate green silk gown, and snapped, 'Don't be impertinent, child. And mind your place.'

I lowered my eyes. 'Yes, my lady. I am sorry.'

But in my head I wondered if perhaps things were not going according to plan. After a few days of softening him up, had she put her proposal to Lord B and been rejected? Was he intent on holding the full auction? Now

Lindemann had been caught searching his study, perhaps my lord had put two and two together and made four. And in consequence given his cousin a flea in her ear.

No wonder she was cross. She would not be used to being rejected, and certainly not by a mere man. Unconsciously, I smiled to myself at the thought of it.

Unfortunately, she saw it and pounced. 'Is something amusing you, Mary?'

'Oh no, my lady.' I replied. There was a short silence as she studied me, her face expressionless. Then she spoke again.

'I wonder what's going on in that beautiful head of yours. Perhaps I should keep a better eye on you. What do you think?'

How cunning she was. It was a trap, conjured up out of nothing, for her own amusement.

If I answered yes, I was admitting that she did need to keep a better eye on me, inviting the assumption that I had something to hide. And yet a no invited her to believe that I did not want her to, the implication again being that I had something to hide. Both yes and no would condemn me equally. I sighed silently inside my head. Life was much easier when I was simply being paid to seduce men and women.

'I would welcome your attention any time, countess. I really would.' I said this quietly and gave her a look, letting my meaning sink in.

She smiled, wolf-like, at me. 'And perhaps that will happen, Mary. And soon. Now run along, and attend on me at ten o'clock when I retire.'

'Thank you, my lady.' Another hurdle cleared. I bobbed a goodbye and fled the room.

*

The evening passed quietly enough. After our tea I did manage to corner Lizzie, and, over a stroll around the gardens in the twilight, I hope I put her mind at ease about our intimacy. I was a very good girl and did not try to kiss her once, even though I was tempted and did sense that an advance might not be rejected now that she had had time to think about things. I think she was embarrassed more than anything, and partly about her own reaction.

'Some people think intimacy between two women is an unnatural sin,' I concluded, 'but it comes as naturally to me as intimacy with a man. If you wish to explore your feelings any more, then let me know. I am very discreet. Otherwise, we shall speak no more about it.'

As we headed back to the house, she did tell me one thing I was not expecting, which was that she had a baby boy who was being looked after by her parents in her home village. The father had fled on hearing she was with child, and she had had no choice but to go into service to support him. She was only able to see the little fellow for one afternoon every month and clearly missed him very much.

Life is hard sometimes. I did feel very sorry for her and did my best to cheer her up, with the result that we were on friendly terms by the time we arrived back at the door in the stable yard and went inside for a cup of tea.

At ten I assisted the countess with her retirement routine and by a quarter to eleven I was sitting on my bed in my room. I read for an hour and then made my way quietly down the three separate flights of stairs to the servants' quarters and thence to the back door.

Outside, the mellow light from the quarter moon was catching the brass headlights of the Mercedes Simplex as it slumbered in its doorless garage. No lights showed in the line of windows above, where the chauffeur slept. As expected, the big double doors to the yard were closed tight, but there was a wicket gate near the hinges on the left-hand side and it was the work of moments to cross over and reach for the bolt. To my surprise, it was open, suggesting whoever had closed up for the night had been less than diligent in their duties.

I slipped through and quietly pulled it to, eyes already scanning the front of the house for any sign of Captain Ransome. But down the long frontage and across the shadowed parkland, nothing stirred. *Come on, man*, I thought. I really needed to talk to him and feel his reassuring presence, if only for a few minutes.

A quiet footstep on the gravel sounded to my right, and I spun around and looked across the gates. Relief flooded through me. He was here already. Of course he was. A man like him would be well used to these night-time excursions. I saw movement in the shadow of the stable block and set off, walking as quietly as I could.

'Captain Ransome?' I whispered, although who else would be loitering outside the gates at that time of night I could not think. But perhaps I should have thought a little harder because, as I came up to the man, with a shocking disappointment I recognised William Stone.

'Hello, Mary,' he said quietly. 'Are you meeting someone too?'

'Er …' I waffled hopelessly. Where was the infernal Ransome? Was he watching us even now but not coming out because the blasted chauffeur was waiting on some eager village girl? Being a government agent really is very trying at times.

He felt in his pocket, pulled out some paper, and said, 'You see, I am merely responding to an invitation.' He peered at his hand. 'Yes, here we are: *"Need to see you. Meet me tonight by the stable yard gate at midnight."* But it is unsigned, so I am not sure if it is you I am to meet or some other mysterious being. Exciting, isn't it, Mary? Why are you here, anyway? You mentioned a Captain Ransome just now. Is he your beau? How romantic.'

I felt sick. Oh, his voice. Just listening to it I knew I was in terrible trouble.

The connections in my mind went *click, click, whir*, and everything fell into place. By accident or design, Stone must have seen me hide the note to Ransome in the tin and had removed it before it could be collected. Actually, the word was stolen. He had stolen it, I corrected myself.

If the note had merely proposed a meeting, I might have passed it off as an invitation to some lusty rural fellow for a little night-time frolicking, but, as I well knew, the reverse contained a brief but pithy summary of Herr Lindemann's adventures.

In fact, it was worse than that.

'And here is another from Saturday last,' he continued, holding the paper up to the moonlight and reading out loud. '*"Henri Dubois from Paris and Havier Lopez from Madrid arrive Friday. Leave Sunday."* Yes – in passing, I think you spell Javier with a J, Mary, but perhaps you didn't meet many Spaniards in Devon.'

He was sneering now, and I was crushed. Utterly crushed. My eyes were wet. So Ransome knew nothing of events at Bancroft. As far as he was concerned, there had been no notes. I had told Hector that I would not be any good and I had been proved right. And still he had not finished, the smug bastard.

'And one final one, also on Saturday and in a different hand, although again there is no salutation or signature. Here we are: *"Concerned no news. Are you all right?"* your correspondent enquires. Well, tell me, Mary, are you all right? Because I would say that you are not.'

Unable to think of anything to say, I said nothing. A good policy normally, although less so if born of desperation

'You see, I had my suspicions about you from the start, Mary Felix, and followed you on Saturday. A maid more used to sitting in the back of a motor car? And expecting polite conversation with a lord of the realm? No, you are not who you say you are at all. When I asked to come for a drive on Sunday, I was going to have a nice chat and see if we couldn't come to some friendly arrangement.'

Oh, dear God, I could see where this was going now. My face was wet with tears, and I stood silent as he continued.

'But no, little Miss Mary Felix was far too high and mighty to go with a chauffeur. Aiming for the gentry, aren't you? But what I cannot work out is why you are spying on the household and what your interest is in a dago and a frog.' He was hissing now, his voice low and vicious. My instincts had been right: there was real cruelty there, and not far below the surface.

‘What is your price?’ I asked quietly. Although, sadly, I already knew it. ‘For your silence, William. What do you want?’

He stuffed the notes back into his pocket and smirked unpleasantly at me. ‘Well, a little consideration would be a good start. Consideration and co-operation. I am not an unkind man.’

Play to your strengths, Mary. He is undeniably handsome. It will not be too bad. This is what Georgina and Jimmy were warning me about, I thought miserably, though standing there in the darkness, the safety and warmth of Arundel Court felt a world away.

‘Where and when?’ I said.

‘Why, now, of course. And I have an idea of where, too. Quietly now.’ He stepped forward, grasped me tightly by the upper arm, and steered me back through the wicket gate and across the yard to the garage. ‘Get in the back of the motor car. That’s where you like to be, isn’t it? In the back.’

I got in and sat down on the heavily padded leather seat. He followed and sat next to me. It was surprisingly roomy. I fixed his eye in the gloom, summoned my courage, and addressed him.

‘Understand me, William Stone. I do not welcome this, nor do I invite your attentions, but if it is the price of your silence, then I will comply. Do I have your word on that?’

‘You do.’

Thus the bargain was sealed.

I will not expand upon the next half hour. It was neither pleasurable nor was it dreadful. As I had suspected, he was an experienced man and took his time, and he was not rough with me. Suffice to say that.

When it was over, I left him sitting in just his shirt on the back seat of the car and climbed slowly to my room. Although it was late, I had a hot bath and afterwards lay in bed for some time, staring at the ceiling and thinking hard.

Resilience is a desirable quality in a government agent, and I was honest with myself in acknowledging that I was no trembling love-struck virgin. Indeed, where my work was concerned, I was always the predator, not the prey, and people had suffered greatly because of my expertise in the bedroom. Yet two things kept me awake. The first was the idea that I had been trapped and outmanoeuvred, that Stone had known for some days about me and had bided his time watching and waiting as I had acted my part unaware. That irked me considerably and was a lesson hard learned.

The second thing was that, sooner or later, Mr Stone would realise that there was nothing to stop him acting like Mr Dickens's Oliver and wanting more. And there would be nothing I could do to stop him.

I sighed in the darkness. Sometimes His Majesty's soldiers are wounded in action, but they must still fight on.

*

All hell broke loose the following evening.

The countess went into Bridport in the Mercedes in the afternoon and returned about five o'clock. She rang for me and I attended on her immediately. When I entered the bedroom, the first thing I saw was her coat thrown onto the floor. She was standing at the window with her back to me, staring out across the parkland. And she had a riding crop in her hand.

Sometimes you can tell when people are angry just from their stance. My instincts proved correct, as when she finally turned to look at me, her face was tense with fury.

'Come here.'

I crossed the room and stood in front of her. From the way she was looking at me, it seemed I was the target of her rage. But why?

'My lady, have I angered you? What have I done?' I asked, my alarm growing by the second. Had she somehow learned of my explorations in the study, I wondered?

'What indeed, Miss Felix? What indeed?' She smiled thinly and continued. 'Remember when I agreed to take you on as my permanent maid there were three things I required of you?'

'Yes, I do. Honesty, discretion, and –'

'Complete obedience,' she interrupted. 'That is the final one. And do you also remember that I warned you that to transgress would be to invite punishment and pain?'

This was not going well. 'Yes, I do remember. But I haven't –' But again she spoke over me.

'As you have such a fine memory, you will also recall that I told you that your pleasure is mine to give and mine alone. You were instructed to never spend without my permission. Is that not so?'

'Yes, my lady, but I haven't. Truly, I have been faithful to your instructions.' There was no need to introduce the estimable Doctor Bone to our discussion at this point, I thought.

But she seemed not to have heard my answer. Her eyes were suddenly far away as she started to speak. 'I remember a maid in Bavaria when my husband was alive. She was a good girl, attentive and quiet. But it turned out she was also a thief. Only small things from my room, but nevertheless. My husband gave me permission to punish her myself, so I took a riding crop to her. This crop, in fact.'

She held it up to me and I eyed it nervously as she continued.

'Max Lindemann stripped her and held her down, and I whipped her on the buttocks until she was bleeding. The noise was dreadful. Then he gripped her hair and I put a single deep stroke onto each side of her face, scarring her for life. Afterwards she was thrown out onto the street.' She smiled with the memory of it and met my eye.

'Truly, my lady, I have been obedient. I swear it,' I stammered, panicking now.

'Then explain this.'

She held out her left hand. It was clenched, but she slowly unfurled it. Sitting in her palm was a single blue button, a short length of broken thread still attached. I looked at it uncomprehendingly for a moment.

'A button, my lady?'

'See if you can find a match to it.'

'A match, my lady?'

She snorted in angry frustration and brought the crop down hard on the window ledge with a vicious crack, causing me to jump in alarm. 'Yes, you foolish girl, a match. I suggest you try your cuff.'

I glanced down and my heart sank. Unusually for a maid's dress, mine had double buttons on each cuff. On my left wrist there was only one. The one behind was missing, and I simply had not noticed. I looked at her. Suddenly I knew what was coming.

'This afternoon when I was sitting in the motor car coming back from Bridport, I found this on the seat next to me. How do you think it got there?'

It must have shown in my face. I could not take my eyes off the thin black crop.

'Well? Why was your cuff button in the back seat of the car?' Her voice was ominously quiet now. 'At least tell the truth, Mary. Have the courage to do that.'

I started to cry. Well, if all else fails … 'I was in the car with William Stone, my lady. Late last night.'

'Did you let him have you?'

'Yes, my lady.' I saw her face tighten and hastened on. 'I didn't want him to. He made me.'

She laughed sardonically at this. 'Oh, really? A likely story. A handsome fellow like that. I'll bet you led him there by the hand, like an alley cat on heat.'

'No, my lady. Please. It wasn't like that.' I bawled and trembled and shook my head. And with my desperation came inspiration. 'He blackmailed me,' I blurted out.

She raised her head in surprise at this. 'He what?'

Encouraged, I babbled on. 'He blackmailed me, my lady. Somehow he found out about my …' I hesitated for dramatic effect, 'past. My work in the house of ill repute in London. He said he'd tell all the other servants if I didn't go with him.'

She looked at me, narrow eyed. 'Blackmail? He blackmailed someone under my protection?'

'Yes, my lady, he did.' I blubbed away merrily and added a few despairing hand gestures for good measure. 'I was forced into co-operating with him to protect my reputation below stairs. And yours too, of course. I am so sorry, countess, but I had no choice. The button must have come off whilst he was having his way with me.' I lowered my eyes. 'He was not gentle.'

Well, why not? She had not been there.

She looked at me for a long moment and then said quietly, 'Go and find Max. Bring him here.'

He was in the kitchen enjoying a rather lovey-dovey cup of tea with Mrs Welling when I ran him to ground, and we returned to the countess's bedroom together. There was a conversation in German between the pair of them. Nowadays I could have followed it, but at the time they might have been speaking ancient Greek for all the sense it made to me.

After he had left again, the countess addressed me with a remarkably kind smile given her mood twenty minutes earlier.

'Your story is accepted, Mary, and you are reprieved. The matter will be dealt with and he will not bother you again. You may leave now. Attend on me at ten o'clock as usual.' I nodded and turned towards the door, but she stopped me. 'And Mary …'

'Yes, my lady?'

She held out her hand. 'Sew it back on again.'

Chapter Seventeen

I meet Lopez and Dubois and am unmasked.

After the shenanigans of the preceding two days, it was a relief that Thursday morning was relatively quiet. Preparations were finalised for the arrival of Messrs Lopez and Dubois the following day, and when telegrams arrived from both of them advising their arrival times at Bridport station, it became clear that they were both coming on the same train from London at half past four in the afternoon.

Mrs Welling sought out William to give him his instructions, dispatching Lizzie to his room to collect him. But she returned empty handed and with curious news. The room was empty, the bed had been made, and all traces of William had disappeared, including his suitcase. In short, it appeared he had left Bancroft unannounced.

I was relieved, of course, and assumed he had been confronted by Herr Lindemann in an uncompromising mood. For Mrs W, the reasons for his abrupt decision were less of a concern than the need to collect our esteemed guests from the station the following day. Fortunately the German came to the rescue, announcing that he was able to drive the Mercedes and would undertake the task. This delighted Mrs W, and from the way she beamed at him, I imagined she would be showing him just how pleased she was later.

As for myself, I spent the morning wandering around the house and the garden killing time whilst I waited for a chance to examine the books in Lord Bridport's study. But all to no avail; he was present all morning and did not go out with the countess, which added weight to my speculations about her being warned off.

The weather remained fine, so after lunch I asked the countess if I could have permission to walk into Bradstock. She agreed to this, so I set off, intending to confront Ransome in his lair at the Highwayman. True, he did not know his note had been intercepted, but even so, it seemed to me that he had shown precious little interest in my welfare, and I meant to have it out with him. Walking briskly along the path through the woods, I got crosser by the minute.

On my way I checked the tin and infuriatingly found nothing yet again and was a muttering and tightly wound ball of tension and ire as I climbed the steps to enter the field. To my surprise, the man himself was fifty yards away, striding towards me across the grass, and it was the work of moments to duck back down and conceal myself behind a handy bush close to the tin's hiding place.

Along he came and cursed quietly to himself as he discovered it was empty. As he stood irresolute, I said, 'Ere, what be you doin' with His Lordship's wall?' in my gruffest voice. Which was not very gruff, to be truthful. But it produced a most pleasing start in the man as he spun round and stared at the talking shrub.

'Mary? Is that you?'

I emerged into view and smiled, all my anger dissipating with the relief of seeing a friendly and reassuring face at last.

'It's me,' I said. And then, embarrassingly, I burst into tears as the tension of the last few days caught up with me. He said nothing but simply stepped forward, wrapped his strong and oh-so-capable arms around me, and held me tight as he whispered quiet and reassuring words into my ear.

His chest was wide and his neck smelt faintly of a delicious cologne, and I think it was as he whispered for the third time what a 'strong and talented and brave girl' I was that I stopped blubbing and raised my mouth to him. Moments later we were kissing passionately, and moments after that, we were twenty feet deeper into the woods and he was laying me down on a mossy bank, raising my dress and taking me, with my wholehearted encouragement.

I came strongly, bucking my hips as he possessed me. It felt utterly wonderful to surrender myself to his fine cock, secure in the knowledge that at last I had a protector and was no longer alone. Afterwards we lay together in the warm glow and talked, his hand gently stroking my hair. He redeemed himself by telling me that he had been coming to the hall with the intention of checking up on me, if necessary by the straightforward expedient of knocking on the front door and begging, 'a cup of tea for a lost and tired bird-watcher.'

Then he listened and occasionally commented as I ran through the events of each day.

I told him about Dubois and Lopez and their impending arrival, and my exploration of the study, and the finding of the safe and the unlatching of the window. Then about Mrs Welling and her jealousy, and William Stone and the price of his silence, at which he whistled quietly through his teeth and held me closer, and finally my theory about the countess's failure to win over Lord Bridport.

When I had finished he told me how wonderful I was, and then I cried again, and he held me tight and said small intimate things. And then suddenly we were kissing again (I confess I started it) and off for a second round of delirious life-affirming pleasure. It was much more prolonged this time, and gloriously if quietly concluded, and witnessed only by the ancient and impassive trees.

Then we made a plan. As plans go, ours was not complicated. The captain would wait until the house was asleep, enter the study through the window, and search the books for the key. I would do nothing, which suited me fine. Then, with another rather nice kiss, we parted.

We met up again the following afternoon as arranged, and after a further and rather urgent interlude on the mossy bank – which we had both been thinking about all day, I suspect – he rather breathlessly reported back.

'I didn't find it. I was in that study from midnight until dawn and checked every damn book on the shelves and it wasn't there.'

'So where is it, do you think?' I asked.

'Well, either he carries it around with him all the time or it is secreted in his bedroom somewhere.'

'Will you search in there tonight?' I asked, deliberately leaving myself out of the action.

'Hardly.' He snorted. 'He'll be in bed, won't he? I mean, I just don't think that's on, Mary.' He paused for a moment, glanced at me a little too meaningfully, then added, 'Of course, he's unlikely to be in there during the day.'

We argued a little. I felt I had done enough. He felt I needed to do more. He won. It was agreed that the following day, Saturday – which was presumably the day of the auction – I would do my best to search his bedroom as early as possible. But there was no denying our shared tension. Time was now very tight. Even if I found the key, it was a moot point as to whether there would be an opportunity to enter the study and remove the portfolio prior to the auction.

Having made arrangements to meet again, we parted gloomily, both well aware that there was a very real chance that we were about to fail in our mission.

Monsieur Dubois and Señor Lopez arrived as scheduled, but I did not meet them until it was almost time to retire that evening. I had attended to the countess and popped back down to the kitchen to make a cup of tea when the billiards room bell went. Mrs Welling, who had just walked in, cursed to herself and set off, directing me to 'make enough for two' as she departed.

She returned shortly afterwards and went through to the wine safe, unlocked it, and collected a bottle of brandy. She put it down on the table in front of me. 'Our continental guests have emptied the decanter; take that up to them, would you?'

I nodded and made my way to the billiards room.

The two gentlemen were chalk and cheese. Dubois was a tall, angular, and bland-looking fellow, clean shaven and aged in his late thirties. He had receding and prematurely grey hair. Lopez the Spaniard was slightly built, dark haired, moustachioed, and at least twenty years older. Both men had removed their jackets and were in shirt sleeves and open collars. The room smelt strongly of cigar smoke and I sensed that the men, if not fully drunk, were well on the way. Both were holding cues, and it was clear a game was under way.

They turned and looked at me as I knocked and entered, and both reacted. The Frenchman raised his eyebrows in surprise and said, 'Quelle très belle femme de chambre.'

Lopez spoke in English. 'My dear, Mrs Welling is an attractive woman, but you are quite exceptional. As my French friend points out.'

'Thank you, sir. The brandy,' I replied neutrally and held up the bottle as somewhere in my head an alarm bell started to ring.

'The decanter is over there.' Lopez pointed to a table in the far corner. I crossed towards it and, as I removed the cap from the bottle, I heard the unwelcome sound of the key being turned in the lock.

My heart sank. *Oh, Mary, you foolish girl*, I thought. You should have known better. You should have been more alert. Knowing the men were drunk and the other servants had retired, Mrs W had seen an opportunity to do me harm and pursued it.

I completed the refilling and turned to face them, keeping the empty bottle in my hand.

'What is your name? Will you join us for a drink?' Lopez asked, smiling at me with all the warmth and charm of a peckish cobra eyeing a mouse.

‘Oh, sir, I don’t think so. It’s not my place,’ I answered, setting off briskly across the suddenly enormous room. It was at least thirty feet to the door, but thank heavens, I could see the key was still in the lock. Schoolboy error, Mr Lopez, I thought.

But the Frenchman cut me off before I had got more than ten feet and put his hand on my arm. ‘Just one drink. To allow us to celebrate your beauty,’ he said in heavily accented English.

‘No, sir. Really. Mrs Welling wouldn’t allow it,’ I replied, shrugging him off and veering towards the billiards table whilst taking the opportunity to switch my grip on the bottle to its neck. Lopez was also on manoeuvres, though, and within moments they had trapped me with my bum against the table as they stood six feet away staring at me hungrily.

Lopez said something in French to Dubois and glanced at him quickly.

‘Oui, bien sûr,’ the Frenchman replied, smiling lecherously at me.

Well, one did not need to be Goethe to work out that exchange, and frankly I had had enough. I had already succumbed to blackmail and was not about to be coerced again. And certainly not by a garlic-chewing Frenchman and a Spaniard who looked like an amorous lizard. I took a firm grip on the bottle and, as they advanced on their prize, I smashed it against the edge of the billiards table.

The noise of shattering glass was remarkably loud and discordant in the big room and stopped both men in their tracks. In the silence, I held up the jagged end towards them and whispered viciously, my face contorted with fear and anger.

'Fuck off. Fuck off, the both of you.'

As they stood frozen with shock, I pushed between them and walked briskly to the door, unlocked it, and took the key into my hand. Standing in the doorway, I turned and threw the bottle at the men, then left the room and slammed the door shut. I relocked it from the outside, hauled up a sash window, and chucked the key into the garden. A tidy piece of work, although I say it myself.

It was only later when I lay in bed that the shivers started, and I wept myself to sleep.

*

The following morning, my attempts to search for the safe key in Lord Bridport's bedroom came to nothing. First of all, the countess found a slight tear in her day dress and insisted that I review all her dresses in case any others needed repairs. Then Mrs Welling, who had not mentioned anything about the previous evening, asked me to assist her with various chores, which I was scarcely able to refuse.

The long and the short of it was that I simply did not have any time until the middle of the afternoon to even try a reconnaissance along the first-floor corridor. As I loitered outside his bedroom, one of the dailies approached.

'Don't go in there, my love, 'e's having a nap,' she said as she passed.

Thus I was thwarted, and as the afternoon drifted frustratingly into evening I found myself reflecting bitterly on the failure of my mission. It seemed now that nothing would stop the auction taking place and the portfolio being spirited away.

After tea I managed to slip out and found the captain sitting in cover not far from where the path through the trees entered the woods. I explained my failure, and I saw a shadow of disappointment and anxiety cross his face.

'So be it, Mary. I must go into Bridport and telegraph Sir Hector. If you can at least find out who wins the auction, the day may not yet be lost. Although extreme measures will now be called for.'

The same thought had crossed my mind. 'Captain Ransome, could you not just take some soldiers and demand that Lord Bridport hand over the portfolio?'

He smiled grimly at me. 'A frontal assault with no quarter, eh? The problem is that we do not know for sure that all the photographs and the original film are together in the safe. He could just deny everything, In which case we will probably never recover the goods.' He shrugged.

'So it's photographs we're after?' I asked, thinking, *well, that is a coincidence*.

He nodded. 'And the film. Someone of very high rank. Embarrassing photographs. To say there would be a scandal is an understatement. We must strain every sinew until we have won or truly lost, Mary.'

There was something about the way the captain asked you to do things that made it very easy to say yes, even if inside a voice was screaming no.

'All right. I will do my best to find out who wins the auction. That is all I can do. I'll come here as soon as I know. You must be here, though.'

He nodded firmly. 'It's a night in the woods for me. I'll be here from six o'clock onwards.'

That at least was reassuring. 'If I find out, I will come and tell you, and then I will simply not go back to the hall. If not, the countess has told me that we shall be departing tomorrow for London, so I will go with her then and find an opportunity to slip away when we reach the capital,' I said.

And good riddance to it all, I thought to myself.

*

I was sitting in the servants' kitchen at half past nine in the evening when Mrs Welling came in.

'That is dinner over. They have gone into His Lordship's study and left instructions that they are not to be disturbed until the bell. Then we are to take some champagne up.'

It is happening, I thought. *It is happening now.* I racked my brains as to how I could establish who had won. I guessed that if the countess had been successful, or more to the point had not been, then it would be obvious from her mood when she retired. But if she had failed, then how could I work out which of the others had placed the winning bid? My deliberations were unanswered, but, as fate rolled the dice, they became irrelevant as well.

The bell rang and Thomas duly disappeared with a bottle of Bollinger. He returned shortly afterwards and nodded at me.

'She wants you. And she ain't happy. In the study.' I stood up and brushed the front of my dress. Perhaps the first question of the evening had been answered.

I climbed the service stairs, crossed the domed entrance hall, and made my way along the corridor to the study. As I knocked and entered, Lord Bridport was sitting behind his desk and speaking.

'… and, of course, following your unexpectedly late arrival. Nevertheless, congratulations to you, sir. I propose that the package remains secure in the safe overnight, and in the morning we can complete the financial formalities and conclude our business. Then you may take possession.' He smiled.

The two Chesterfields had been pushed back and matching chairs placed in front of the desk. They were high backed, and I could see Lopez, Dubois, and the countess all staring grimly at His Lordship as he spoke. But he was not addressing them.

To my surprise, there was a fourth chair. Its back was facing me, and the top of a balding pate belonging to its occupant was just visible. And it seemed his had been the winning bid, judging by what I was witnessing. I looked at the countess and she beckoned me over with a gesture. Her face was grim.

'I will retire immediately. Bring a whisky and soda to the room.'

'Yes, my lady.' I gave a little curtsey and turned, anxious to get a look at the successful bidder.

Our eyes met. I stared in appalled horror. He cried out in shock and half rose in his seat, astonishment quickly giving way to anger, then furious rage. Pulling himself to his feet, he pointed an accusing arm at me and cried out.

'What is that little bitch doing here, Bridport?'

Clearly shocked at the man's reaction, Lord Bridport had also risen. 'What do you mean, sir? She is a servant. The countess's maid.'

'No, sir, she is not. She is an agent of the Crown. She works directly for the government's head of espionage in Whitehall, you bloody fool.'

There was a collective intake of breath. They all stared at me. I felt my cheeks starting to burn and tears welling up.

'Hello, Lord Culligan,' I said miserably.

*

Well, if the others were unhappy before, things had not improved for them twenty minutes later. Unable to think of anything to say in my defence, I stood in the centre of a circle of hatred with tears slowly trickling down my face and listened to the discussion about what to do with me.

Culligan's reaction had been so compelling that no one in the room thought to question it. That I was a fox in the hen house was accepted by them all without question. The only points at issue were firstly what to do with me, and secondly the fact that the government was aware, at least to some extent, of the events taking place at Bancroft.

On realising this, both Dubois and Lopez fled. They had lost the auction, and the revelation that there was an enemy spy in the camp had been enough to panic them into action. They had demanded a horse each from Lord Bridport and departed without packing.

Mrs Welling joined us at Lord Bridport's request, his brief explanation of 'she is aware' to the others answering my question about whether she was in his confidence or not. At one point I caught the countess's eye. I mouthed a tearful 'sorry' to her, but her stony face gave nothing away, and it was clear that I could expect no reprieve from that quarter.

Culligan questioned me, demanding to know how the plot had become known in London. I stonewalled him, saying I did not know. So he hit me. It was a smashing sideways blow on the face that knocked me over and made my nose bleed and caused Mrs Welling to clap her hands and cry out in delight.

'Steady on, Culligan,' muttered Lord Bridport. It really had come to something when the leader of a plot to bring down the empire was my only friend in a room full of enemies. Well done, Mary, I thought to myself bitterly.

I hauled myself to my feet, a slow-burning anger igniting deep within me as blood from my nose dripped onto my dress. I assumed that Culligan was representing the Fenians in the auction and could see how they would want to have a dog in any fight that might bring the British into disrepute. Well, I was a patriot and was not going to add to our fine nation's troubles. They would get nothing.

It is an extraordinary thing to stand, bleeding and in pain, and listen to others decide your fate. I had realised where it was going to go, of course. We all knew that I could not be left to tell tales. And if I simply disappeared, then so what? Captain Ransome would eventually institute a search, but Mrs Welling and Lord Bridport would concoct a story and gag the staff, and our foreign friends would be long gone by then anyway. And the portfolio would be in the hands of our mortal enemies in Ireland.

Finally Culligan just came out and said it. 'She will have to be killed. I will do it. Bridport, you will need to bury her on the estate.' My heart went cold as he withdrew a small gun from his pocket and looked at me.

'You ruined my life. Now I will end yours. Truly, fate is a strange beast at times.' He smiled at me and added, 'Having regrets now, Mary?'

Oh, well. If it was over … I smiled back and spoke clearly, so everyone heard.

'You weren't much of a fuck, my lord. One of my poorer clients, to be honest. Distinctly under-gunned if you know what I mean. And you liked it up the bum, didn't you? Oh yes, you loved that …'

He snarled and swung again, and down I went, feeling as though a loud explosion had gone off in my head. Dizzy and only vaguely aware of what was happening, I was dragged along the corridor and across the library to a pair of double doors that led outside. Darkness enclosed us as we went out into the night, down the steps, and through the formal gardens at the back of the house. Vaguely I realised that Lindemann had also arrived, and it was he and Culligan who had my arms. Mrs Welling strode in front, and I sensed the countess bringing up the rear.

An execution party of five, including the guest of honour.

When our dismal little procession reached the shadowy shrubs and trees of the pleasure grounds, Mrs Welling led the way down a narrow cobbled path between enormous rhododendron bushes that towered over us on both sides. It twisted and turned for fifty yards before opening out into a clearing.

'What is this place?' asked the countess as we all looked at the curious domed structure visible in the gloom.

'An ice house,' the housekeeper replied. 'It will serve our purposes for now, until Lord Bridport and I can make other arrangements. Bring her.'

She crossed to the building, then opened a door and I heard the click of a light switch. A pool of light appeared on the floor of the clearing, and inside I glimpsed an open, brick-lined space.

'Go on,' said Culligan, giving me a hefty shove, and I staggered, regained my balance, and walked over to the housekeeper. I felt numb. I was going to die, and no one would ever know what had happened to me. My eyes started to well up again, but I furiously controlled them. If this was indeed the end, then I would face it like a proper Englishwoman.

I lifted my chin and glared at Mrs Welling.

'Stand in the doorway,' she said. In the light, I could see her eyes were gleaming with excitement and arousal. I obeyed. In spite of everything, I was oddly curious to look inside. We are used to our refrigerators these days, of course, but before their invention, ice houses such as this were once used to store ice collected from estate lakes in the winter.

The interior was like a huge hollowed-out egg buried in the ground with only the top third showing. Within its thick brick-lined walls, the ice would last all year and could be used for the creation of all manner of exotic desserts. I glanced downwards, wondering if there might still be water in the bottom. Twenty feet below me, barely visible in the gloom, the face of William Stone was staring sightlessly upwards, the ligature that had been used to strangle him still wrapped around his neck. His suitcase lay next to him.

I screamed and fell backwards to everyone's general consternation.

'What the devil is it now?' said Culligan, striding forward. He and Mrs Welling arrived at the doorway at the same time, and both peered down into the gloom. 'Ye gods, who is that?' he exclaimed.

'William Stone, His Lordship's chauffeur,' I said. I saw the countess give Herr Lindemann a quick glance, and he moved his eyebrows a fraction in reply. Hell's bells, he had not been persuaded to leave; the German had killed him. Because of me. But there was no time for further reflection as Culligan's voice sounded again in the clearing.

'Let's get on with it. Lindemann, get Mary into the doorway. It appears you will be having some company for a day or two.' He smiled as he addressed this last remark to me and removed the gun from his pocket.

I was crying silently as the German manoeuvred me into position above the drop and stood back. I thought of Georgina, the adorable love of my life, and Jimmy and my parents living in blissful ignorance in Exmouth. It was so desperately sad that I would never see them again. And then I locked my eyes on Culligan and drew myself up.

'Do your worst then, you fucker,' I said loudly. I would keep my eyes open, I decided.

He laughed. 'Gutsy to the end, I see. Very well, Mary, it will be quick. A head shot. I promise you will not feel a thing.' And then he raised the gun and extended his arm.

'Wait.' The countess stepped forward and smiled with empty eyes at me. 'It is me she has deceived in this affair. I claim the right to take the shot.'

I heard Mrs Welling sigh with pleasure. There was no doubt the woman belonged in a lunatic asylum. Culligan looked at her for a moment and then shrugged. 'As you wish. You have fired a pistol before, I take it?' he asked as he passed it into her outstretched hand.

'Yes, my lord. Many times.'

And with that she took a single pace backwards, raised her arm, and shot him in the middle of the forehead at point blank range. As he fell, she turned and shot Mrs Welling, who was standing ten feet away, also in the middle of the forehead, and then stood still, her gun arm slack at her side, her face expressionless. The violent noise of the two shots seemed to linger in the clearing.

'What?' I managed to exclaim, then started to shake and shiver uncontrollably. I was not even crying any more, just vibrating like a plucked rubber band.

I heard the countess say something in German to Lindemann, and he grunted and nodded, then lifted the earl's body up, carried him over his shoulder to the ice house door, pushed past me, and tipped him in without ceremony. Mrs Welling followed immediately afterwards. Then he flicked off the light and closed the door.

The countess looked at me. 'And that is that, as they say. Come here, child.'

Barely able to walk, I crossed to her and she embraced me, holding me tightly and silently for a long time until at last the shaking started to ease and she addressed me quietly. 'I think you have had a trying day, Mary. You are inexperienced to be playing such powerful games.'

'I know.' I snuffled into her neck. 'I told the man who sent me that I wouldn't be any good. But he sent me anyway.'

'Men.' She sighed in judgement. Out of the corner of my eye I saw Herr Lindemann disappear silently down the path.

'Why did you save me?' I asked in a small voice, holding on tightly. I liked it. She smelt lovely and I felt safe.

Her voice was low and warm in my ear. 'Because you are simply too beautiful to die young. It would be easy to love you, Mary Felix, and I think perhaps we have a future together.' She placed her hands on my shoulders and pushed me gently back, then kissed me. A long and lingering kiss that made my head swim and my heart race.

At length we parted, and she continued. 'I will deal with my cousin. Don't worry; it won't take long. I shall tell him that you wrestled the pistol off Culligan, then shot him and Mrs Welling before disappearing into the woods. He will realise that we can do nothing tonight, and I will tell him that in the morning I will pay a fair price for the portfolio. By ten o'clock the matter will have been resolved and it will be in my possession. And then we will leave for Berlin together.'

She smiled with real warmth and her eyes creased deliciously. I suddenly felt a curious ambivalence about who got the damn portfolio as the old temptations of a life in Germany with this utterly alluring woman flooded back. Did it really matter to me? A glorious future full of adventure and romance with the most dangerous and beautiful woman in Europe as my lover was being placed in front of me. All I had to do was let it happen.

'All right, then,' I said.

'You will go stealthily up to my room, and when you get there, you will run a bath. I will be no more than five minutes with Lord Bridport, and when I arrive, we will bathe together, and then you will come into my bed. I think we both need a little kindness tonight.'

'Oh, yes please, my lady,' I said breathlessly, my eyes fixed adoringly on her face.

'Go, then, Mary. I will see you shortly.' Then she kissed me again.

As I slipped back down the narrow, dark path, my mind was fizzing with excitement. At last the countess was going to give herself to me in every way, and the thought was intoxicating. I could hardly wait. But there was something else. In that never-ending moment when Culligan had raised the gun and aimed at me, I had suddenly realised something. It had just popped into my mind.

I knew where the safe key was hidden.

Chapter Eighteen

A night of passion and the safe is opened.

I loved Georgina more than anyone else in my life. I still do. She was my soulmate, my trusted confidante, and my best friend for many years. But that single night with the countess at Bancroft Hall was the most intense and aroused lovemaking I have ever experienced.

True to her word, we bathed together, undressing each other and squeezing into the scented water with much giggling and splashing. And then I stood, and she gently soaped me all over with a soft sponge, her hands and fingers exploring me in a delectable precursor to the events to come as I gasped and trembled at her touch. When she had rinsed me, I did the same thing to her, taking my time with her lovely body and feeling her shiver with anticipation.

And then we went to bed.

If lust can ever transcend love, it was surely that night. She had delivered me from certain death, and, oh my dear Lord, did I want her. From the first moment that her tongue slipped into my mouth and her fingers pulled on my long nipples, I felt as though I had been rolled over by a powerful wave. Unable to resist, I simply surrendered completely to her.

We both came quickly as we sucked and licked and kissed and stroked ourselves into a raging passion, but our mutual hunger was not satisfied and we kept at it, crying and laughing together with the sheer joy of the pleasure we gave and received. Finally we paused and lay together, breathless and damp with perspiration, and twisted our fingers in each other's hands, momentarily silenced by the sheer wonder of it.

Then, hungry for more of her sweet domination, I whispered to her.

'Will you spank my bottom, my lady?'

She stirred and I saw she was smiling in the faint light of the bedside lamp. 'Do you deserve it, Mary?'

'Well, I did trick you into making me your maid.' I gently scratched her nipple.

'That is true. Very well, I will spank you. On your knees, please.'

'Yes, my lady,' I said obediently and rolled onto my front, then drew my legs up and spread my knees wide, so my bum was unprotected and vulnerable. 'And then it will be your turn,' I whispered. So quietly that I do not think she even heard me. Kneeling behind me, she went to work, planting brisk firm slaps onto my buttocks, which rapidly warmed up and started to sting quite deliciously.

'I am so sorry for my behaviour, my lady,' I said as the sensations began to reach my cunny.

'It is a mistress's onerous duty to maintain discipline amongst the servants. I will do this as often as is necessary to ensure your obedience.'

'Yes, my lady,' I said again. Oh, goody. Then I slipped my hand between my legs and started to touch myself as she continued to spank me. My cunny was completely exposed to her gaze, so I knew that she would be able to see what I was doing, and sure enough, after a moment she stopped.

'This is not supposed to be a pleasurable experience for you, a mere maid.'

'I'm sorry, but it just feels so nice. I can't stop myself.' I felt her hand remove mine, or rather replace it. I wriggled my bum gently. 'Oh, yes please, my lady.'

'You should consider yourself highly indulged,' she said as her expert fingers started to probe and stroke quite delightfully.

'Yes, thank you,' I gasped and then shut up as I felt a finger slide inside me, then withdraw, then slide in again.

'Ein,' she said quietly and continued in the same vein a minute or so before quietly saying, 'und zwei,' and a second finger joined its busy little friend. 'Drei' and 'vier' followed. I splayed and relaxed, groaning and dropping my head onto the pillow. 'Do you want more, Mary?' she asked quietly as each thrust took her hand deeper and deeper inside me.

'Yes, please,' I whimpered, pushing back hungrily onto her. I was going to come again soon.

'All of it?'

I answered by pushing back hard. She held her arm steady and I felt her whole hand enter me. Then she started to fist me slowly and deeply, gently turning her clenched hand as she did so. I heard myself crying out as the most extraordinary sensations pulsed through me in waves. Any moment now. She shifted position and I felt her warm mouth close over my bum hole, her stiff tongue licking and tickling as her hand continued to pump inside me.

The sensation was electrifying. I screamed and frantically thrust backwards as wave after wave of intense orgasmic pleasure pulsed through me. On and on she went, mercilessly driving me to climax after climax until finally in desperation I reached behind and grasped her wrist.

'Please, countess,' I managed to gasp.

She slowly slid her hand out and I rolled over onto my back, legs apart, and held out my arms to her as she slid on top of me, her open mouth reaching for mine.

Some time later, with the countess feigning reluctance, which only served to arouse us both even more, we reversed our positions. Declaring myself unhappy with her behaviour as a mistress, I insisted she assume the same submissive position and spanked her flawless white buttocks until a fine rosy pink glow appeared. Then I fisted her ruthlessly to powerful multiple spends as my tongue wriggled away in her bum hole.

'What is good for the maid is good for the madam,' I whispered to her as we drifted off to sleep.

I woke in the middle of the night. She was asleep with her back to me, breathing quietly and rhythmically. To my surprise I was wide awake, and I lay there for some time with my hands behind my head wondering what to do. Because, be in no doubt, I told myself, it is finally, definitely, decision time.

Roll over, put your arm around the most dazzling and erotic woman in Europe, and you will be tucked up in a Bavarian castle with her and the portfolio before you can say pumpernickel. As an idea, it was not without its charms.

On the other hand, you could sneak out of bed, go to the study and get the safe key, pinch the portfolio, and never see the goddess again. *Well, Mary*, I thought, *what is it to be?*

I pondered, I agonised, I dithered. And then I went. Of course I did. For king and country and all that.

I tiptoed into the corridor quite naked, carrying my dress and shoes, and put them on when I was round the corner. The grandfather clock showed a quarter past four, and through the window the night sky was half covered with clouds. In the parkland the individual specimen trees were standing tall, and beyond them I could see the dark line of the wood. *You had better be there, Captain, because I am going to be in a hurry*, I thought.

The study was unlocked and the curtains were not drawn, meaning the muted light from outside created shadows by the big chairs that had been brought in for the auction.

I reached down and took the key out of the door lock. Oh yes, I was fairly sure that was the one, hiding in plain sight. When I had locked the door to secure our two randy continentals in the billiards room, the whole mechanism had felt flimsy by comparison to this one. Further discreet tests on other door keys had confirmed this. The study door key was completely different from all the other keys in the house. And the lock itself was much more robust. It had to be the one. So convenient, so unnoticeable, so clever, my lord.

I removed the set of books and, with a beating heart, fitted the key into the lock. It turned with a smooth positive click and I reached for the handle, pressed it down, and pulled. The safe door swung silently open.

Inside was a dark cave. I took two short paces to the drinks table and switched on a lamp. Although the interior was shadowed, I could now see the contents. A dark leather folder with a buckle was sitting on a pile of other papers and documents. There was also a bundle of cash. I hesitated. Was I a thief? Not normally, but Bridport was a traitor to the realm and therefore not worthy of proper behaviour. I quickly slipped it into my dress pocket, then reached for the portfolio, unbuckled it, and walked back to the light to examine the photographs it contained.

Oh, dear.

There were plenty of them, and Jimmy would have been proud of every single one. They showed a stark-naked Prince Albert, as he would have been when they were taken, frolicking on a double bed with a handsome, well-hung, and very excited lad in his late teens. An older woman, also naked, seemed to be directing operations whilst helping out with an occasional hand or tongue, and the two men were going at it hammer and tongs.

No wonder Hector was panicking. If these were published, the ridicule would destroy the royal family's credibility and threaten Britain's ability to rule across the empire. Even rumours of their existence could do terrible damage.

Wholly absorbed, I worked my way through them and had just discovered the original film at the bottom of the pile when the main light went on and the countess's voice rang out clearly in the silent room. I almost dropped the lot.

'Are you enjoying yourself, Mary?' she asked. Lindemann was with her. He walked forward, smiled sadly at me, and gently took the folder from my reluctant hands. 'As a precaution, Max was positioned down the corridor. When he saw you enter the study, he came and got me,' she added.

Hell and damnation. I actually stamped my foot with frustration. So near and yet so far. I gathered myself and tried one more time. Perhaps our extraordinary lovemaking had given me some influence over her. It did with most normal people.

'Please, Countess. I beg you to release the portfolio to me. Blackmail is a terrible crime.' (I crossed my fingers as I said this, for obvious reasons.) 'Would you condemn a man to ridicule and ruin because of a single night of weakness?'

'Certainly not,' she replied, shaking her head.

'I mean, have you no sympathy? Have we not all made foolish mistakes at some time? Is it fair that we should be punished for them?' I continued, getting into my stride.

No, I don't think so,' she replied, smiling at me.

'And furthermore …' I sailed on majestically, then paused and looked at her. 'Sorry, what?'

'I agree with you, Mary.' Both she and Lindemann were smiling at me now. A little voice in my head told me they knew something I did not.

'Do you know something I do not?' I asked.

'I do think that, perhaps, I have a surprise for you. It appears that whilst we are not quite on the same side, we do have the same objective. Which is to prevent these photographs of your noble king and a randy youth buggering each other from ever reaching the public domain.'

Astonished, I stared at her. Surely she was the enemy, albeit someone I was just a teeny bit in love with. 'I don't understand,' I said. 'I was told that they would be used as a lever by foreign powers to embarrass and control Great Britain.'

She nodded. 'Quite possibly if Lopez or Dubois had obtained them. Those French.' She rolled her eyes and sneered disdainfully before continuing. 'I work directly for the Kaiser, Mary. He is a close and very personal friend, but he is also Queen Victoria's grandson and your king's nephew. They may have had their ups and downs during the yachting races at Cowes, but he would never allow Uncle Bertie to be humiliated like that. For him it is a question of family honour, you see. So yes, my mission is to obtain the pictures, but only in order that they may be destroyed.'

'What about the photographs that Lord Bridport sent out with his letters?' I asked.

'All the samples were returned to the portfolio last night by the four of us. It was a condition of bidding. So, you see, once you were unmasked as a British agent and Lopez and Dubois had fled, I knew Culligan was my only rival for the complete set. One way or another, he would not have lasted the night, I can assure you.' She glanced at Lindemann.

I slumped down into a convenient chair and thought about the three cold, pale bodies in the ice house and shivered. 'Did you suspect me?'

She smiled. 'Oh yes, I did, Mary, right from the start. You really are too beautiful to be a lady's maid. Next time may I suggest a better cover story?'

So she had just been playing with me. You can go off people sometimes.

'It was Sir Hector's idea,' I said. It just came out. Maybe it was the relief or the tiredness or the fact that she really was not the enemy after all. She pounced, her eyes lighting up like a cat that has seen a mouse.

'Ah, yes. Thank you, Mary. So he does exist. We have heard rumours of Sir Hector in Berlin. And of William Munroe. There is considerable interest in their activities.'

'I'll tell him. When I give him the portfolio.' Well, it was worth a try.

She laughed delightedly and looked at Herr Lindemann. 'What do you think, Max? Shall we take it to Berlin or send it to Sir Hector with our compliments?'

Their eyes met and he smiled and walked over to me. Drawing himself up to his full height, which was not much, he clicked his heels, leant forward, and placed the portfolio in my hands.

Got it. At last.

'Thank you, countess.'

'And thank you, Mary Felix. I must say it has been a most amusing and invigorating two weeks, and I have found your company quite delightful. Both clothed and unclothed. You must come and visit me in Bavaria. I am sure we will find much to entertain us.'

Just hearing her say it made me tingle, and I knew I would go.

And right at that moment, Lord Bridport stuck his head round the door.

'I thought I heard voices. My bedroom is directly upstairs, you know. What is going on? Annetta? What is this?' There was a dramatic pause as we all took a breath, then the countess spoke, her imperious manner back instantaneously.

'Oh, it's quite simple, cousin. Max discovered Mary stealing the portfolio from the safe. We have only just managed to apprehend her in time.'

I was already moving as she started to speak, and by the time she had finished her sentence, I had reached the sash window. The catch was still unlocked. Hauling the pane up, I sat on the ledge, swung my legs over, and pushed off without looking. I did not even know how far the drop was.

Shouts pursued me as I hit the ground with a thump and fell to one side. I sprang to my feet and took stock for a brief moment. Thankfully my ankles seemed all right, so, with one hand grimly clutching the infernal portfolio, I hauled the front of my dress above my knees and set off at a canter straight across the gravel circle in front of the house. I cleared the ha-ha in a single bound and sped onwards into the shadowy open parkland, head up and going like a classy hunter in a point to point.

A gunshot rang out, and I heard the whine of a bullet high over my head and more shouting. And then even more shouting, but this time from in front of me, not behind.

'Here, Mary, here!' Captain Ransome was running towards me from the woods, beckoning frantically. Less than a quarter furlong to the steeple. I put on a sprint, and together we dashed into the welcoming darkness of the narrow path through the trees.

We paused and stood facing each other.

'Is that it?' he enquired calmly, but I could feel the tension in his question.

'Yes, in its entirety, film and all,' I panted.

The relief in his voice was palpable. He almost sobbed. 'Well done, Mary. That really is a superb effort. One more heave and we'll be home and dry.'

He led me straight across the fields at a trot to a powerful closed car that he had waiting outside the Highwayman in Bradstock.

'Best stay off the railway from Bridport today, Mary,' he said firmly as he announced his intention of driving to London. 'You get in the back.' He handed me in, still clutching the portfolio, and covered me with a pair of lovely thick rugs. 'Get some rest. I'll take it from here.'

I had one last sleepy thought as I lay back on the soft leather and felt us surge off into the night. Look at me now, in the back, William Stone, you bastard.

*

It was late morning when I wearily rang the doorbell at Arundel Court and surrendered myself to the clucking concerns of my darling Georgina and lovely Jimmy. I was so very, very happy to see them.

I was kissed, hugged, bathed, fed, kissed again, given a very large whisky and soda, and then put firmly to bed. And when Georgina quietly wriggled in next to me and I instinctively turned to her, she whispered, 'No, no, dear Mary, it's sleep time for you. I'll just hold you.' I drifted off, remembering a similar scene when she had returned from Paris all those months ago.

I was quite ill for a couple of days and stayed in bed. Nervous exhaustion, the doctor called it, which was hardly surprising. Poor Georgina was bursting with curiosity and kept appearing with a cup of tea and asking me if there was anything I wanted to 'get off my chest'. An offer which I politely declined on each occasion.

On the third day I heard footsteps on the stairs, and she put her head round the door.

'Are you decent?' There are two visitors for you.'

I sat up and answered in the affirmative, and moments later, Sir Hector and Captain Ransome came into my room. The latter was carrying my suitcase from Bancroft, I noticed. Georgina bustled about, arranging chairs, including one for herself, I was amused to observe.

When he saw this, Sir Hector frowned and said, 'Georgina, we are planning to have a discussion about recent events. I think Mary deserves to be brought up to date.'

Perched innocently, she nodded her head vigorously. 'Oh yes, I am sure that's true. Carry on, Hector.'

'So perhaps you could give us a few minutes?' he persevered.

'I beg your pardon?' She gave him a look that would have felled a horse, but he smiled and soldiered on.

'I mean, dear lady, that you must leave the room.' There was touch of Scottish granite in his voice and she stood and walked slowly to the door, then turned. When she spoke, her eyes and her voice were dripping liquid honey and molten steel in equal measure.

'I'll get it all out of her when you're gone. In the end. You know I will.'

He looked at her for a long moment and then sighed. 'Oh, for heaven's sake, Georgina, sit down, then.' Grinning delightedly, she scuttled back to her seat and looked at me in triumph. I smiled back. I loved her so much.

Then Hector talked. The portfolio had been destroyed. The captain had taken it straight to the office after dropping me at Arundel Court on the morning of our return to London. Then he and Sir Hector had set off back to Bancroft to 'clear up the loose ends', as he put it.

He continued. 'When we arrived, the countess and Herr Lindemann had left, taking the Mercedes with them. It was subsequently found parked in a side street in Weymouth. I believe they made private arrangements for an immediate passage across the Channel with a fisherman or some such.'

He paused and cleared his throat. 'The news regarding Lord Bridport is not good. We had a private conversation in his study, and I told him that I believed that he had a legitimate grievance against the government. However, I also told him that his actions could not be forgiven or forgotten. I am sorry to say that he was unrepentant. When I went to inspect the ice house, I heard a single shot and returned to the house to find he had taken his own life.'

I stared at him, a suspicion forming in my mind. 'Was Captain Ransome with you when you went outside?'

He looked at me with his grey flinty eyes. 'Oh yes. He was with me.'

'It's just that you said when "I" went to the ice house.'

He made a dismissive gesture. 'A slip of the tongue, Mary. At all events, it is better this way. A clean finish with no loose ends.'

'Did he explain how he obtained the photographs of the king?'

'He did. They were fakes – as we knew, of course.' He met my eyes with a long, even stare before continuing. 'It seems that when he returned from South Africa, he spent six months recuperating in a sanitorium in a remote part of the French Pyrenees. He noticed that a man who worked in the gardens bore a remarkable resemblance to Prince Albert, and the scheme developed in his mind from there. The fellow was a simpleton but amenable to money, and when Bridport had recovered, he made the arrangements for the posed photographs to be taken. When he saw them, he realised that his scheme would be all the more potent when Bertie had acceded to the throne, hence the delay.'

What a convenient explanation, I thought. 'So that is to be the official line, Sir Hector? Lord Bridport killed himself and the photographs were fakes.'

'There is no official line because nothing happened, Mary. But it is the truth, and I strongly urge you to remember that.' He said it flatly, his eyes on mine.

'I am sure she will,' said Georgina hastily, 'when she has fully recovered her strength.'

I looked at Captain Ransome, who pointed to my case and spoke. 'I've brought your things from the hall. I've got everything, I think.' He looked at me evenly. I blushed. The case had been empty, apart from Dr Bone. When he opened it to pack my clothes, it would have been the first thing he saw.

'I'm glad to hear that, Alaric.' Our eyes met and he smiled gently. I did not. Changing the subject, I addressed Hector again. 'Did Lord Bridport mention how the Fenians managed to outbid the others?

He nodded. 'It seems they did not. However, they were backed by sufficient funds from an American sympathiser to offer a significant sum. Bridport apparently decided that the Republicans would cause the most trouble with the pictures and chose them over the other bidders.'

No wonder the atmosphere was so tense when I walked into the study, I thought.

When they had gone, I spent a long time lying staring out of the window at the distant cupola of St Paul's Cathedral and turning the affair over in my mind. Lord Bridport's life had been ruined by powerful people intent on protecting another whose value they set higher. It was a salutary lesson for me. When I finally drifted off to sleep, my dreams were full of that dismal procession through the night-time gardens at Bancroft and the ice house and the moment I thought I was going to die.

*

In the morning I was much recovered. St Paul's was still there, I was alive and safe at home, and, more to the point, I had one more thing to do. For a lovely girl with a sad tale to tell.

It was just before nine o'clock as I let myself out of the silent house. I hailed a cab and instructed him to take me to Farthings Bank on Leadenhall Street. It had barely opened when I arrived, but my request to see the manager was processed with due efficiency, and shortly afterwards I was sitting in front of him.

'It is very nice to see you again, Miss Connors.' He smiled. 'How may I assist you today?'

I placed the bundle of cash that I had taken from the safe at Bancroft on his desk. 'I wish to open an account, Mr Openshaw. Here is five hundred pounds.'

He beamed in that way bank managers do when they are pleased with your behaviour. 'A very significant sum, Miss Connors. But do you not have a very satisfactory account here at present? Surely we can credit your deposit into that one?'

'You may deposit half of the money there, but the remainder is not for me. The new account is to be in the name of Miss Elizabeth Baker, and credit is to be made available to her at Farthings Bank in Bridport. You can do that, I take it?'

He raised his eyebrows in surprise but nodded. 'Yes, that is quite possible.'

'Then please do so, and then I'd be obliged if you would write to Miss Baker, care of Bancroft Hall, Bradstock, Dorsetshire, informing her that an anonymous benefactor has opened the account on her behalf and advising her as to how she may access the funds in Bridport. Then perhaps a separate letter to the manager of Farthings down there asking him to assist her. She is not experienced in financial matters at all.'

He jotted a note, then nodded and said, 'Yes, Miss Connors. All that will be put in place.'

'Then our business is concluded for today, Mr Openshaw, and I'll wish you good day.'

When I got back to Arundel Court, the mouth-watering smell of frying bacon was permeating the hall. Suddenly starving hungry, I made my way down the corridor to the kitchen in search of jentacular delights.

They both turned to look at me as I entered.

'Good morning, Mary,' said Jimmy formally. 'Bacon and eggs?'

'Yes please, you life saver,' I replied. 'And coffee.'

Georgina was reading a copy of the *London Times*. She beamed at me and patted the chair next to hers at the kitchen table.

'You'll never believe what's happened, Mary, darling. Listen to this,' she said, giving me the most delicious eye-rolling look of intrigue and excitement. There was a chink as Jimmy placed the coffee cup in front of me. Our eyes met in a smile of mutual recognition.

'No, I am sure I won't, Georgina. Tell me all about it.'

I was home.

Epilogue

By royal appointment.

Lights from the Christmas decorations strung along the Mall reflected in the sides of the highly polished motor car as it headed slowly towards Buckingham Palace. It stopped outside the main gates and an attendant checked the occupants before allowing them through.

I was in the car along with Georgina. A month before, she had been thrown into an orgy of eye-rolling ecstasy when an expensive envelope marked 'On His Majesty's Service' had been hand delivered to Arundel Court. It was addressed to me, which was entirely incidental as far as she was concerned, and contained a short letter, which I have in front of me as I write.

Dear Miss Felix,

It has come to His Royal Highness's attention that you have performed a notable service on his behalf. He wishes to acknowledge this and place his gratitude on record with the award of an Order of Merit.

This will be conferred upon you at a private ceremony at Buckingham Palace at four o'clock on the 22nd December 1902. Following the award, you will be entitled to use the letters OM after your name.

I look forward to hearing your confirmation that this is in order.

Yours sincerely,

Sir Oliver De Vere Brown

Private secretary to His Majesty King Edward VII

The car rolled slowly under the arch in the centre of the rather austere palace frontage and came to a halt. A uniformed footman opened the door and stood to attention as we emerged in all our glory.

And believe me, we had dressed up; oh my word, had we dressed up.

The very distinguished and rather handsome Sir Oliver was there to greet us, and we followed him down a thickly carpeted corridor and up a flight of stairs to a beautifully furnished anteroom. He then opened a door and disappeared.

Even Georgina was silenced by the thought that the man in command of the greatest empire the world had ever seen was in the room next door. But we did not have long to wait, as Sir Oliver reappeared quite quickly and smiled at me.

'Would you both like to come in?'

We crossed to the door and followed him through it. I heard him say, 'Miss Mary Felix and Mrs Georgina Beaufort,' and then suddenly the king was walking forwards, a twinkling smile on his face. We curtseyed as he came to a halt. Slightly to my surprise, he was wearing a suit. I had been expecting him in coronation robes and carrying an orb. *Foolish girl*, I thought.

'Miss Felix and Mrs Beaufort, it is great pleasure to meet you, and I am most pleased that you are able to attend our modest ceremony,' said the king.

'Thank you, Your Highness,' I replied before he continued.

'The Order of Merit is a new decoration which I have established. It rewards distinguished service in various fields and is in my personal gift. I am deeply grateful to you for your activities on my behalf and in the defence of our great country.' He nodded to Sir Oliver, who stepped forward with an open box and placed it in the king's hand. He, in turn, placed the box in my hand.

As he did so, he met my eyes and said, 'I know what you did, and I thank you for it. Congratulations to you, Mary Felix OM.'

I glanced down and saw a gold cross sitting on a maroon-and-blue ribbon. My hands shook. I could hardly believe it, and to my horror, my eyes welled up. My perennial weakness, curse it. He noticed, the lovely man, and said, 'Well, now that the formalities are concluded, I recommend a glass of champagne.'

'Oh yes, Your Majesty. That would be lovely,' Georgina replied, and she must have given him her eyes at full wattage, because I saw him do a brief double take and smile broadly.

As Sir Oliver departed, the king turned to the footman standing rigidly by the door and said, 'Open two bottles and then leave us.'

Within a minute, Georgina and I were alone with His Majesty King Edward the Seventh.

He smiled. 'It is a great shame my dear Alexandria is so far away at Osborne House, as she would have enjoyed meeting you both, I think. Anyway, come with me and bring your glasses,' he added over his shoulder as he picked up the bottle from the ice bucket and led the way into a much smaller and more intimate salon. It was richly decorated with thick pile rugs and a pair of crimson settees on either side of a fire. Three lamps gave the room an intimate glow.

'Please sit down.' He filled our glasses and took a cigar from a box on a side table, lit it, and puffed away for a moment, then sat down opposite us. 'Now then,' he said. 'Tell me a little more about your work for Sir Hector, Miss Felix.'

So I did. I pulled no punches, and Georgina chipped in from time to time, giving him a clear idea of our line of work and the services we provided in the defence of the realm.

Through all this he smoked quietly and sipped his drink and said very little. Finally he addressed Georgina directly. 'Mrs Beaufort, I surmise that you too have performed and continue to perform essential and noble work on behalf of the empire. It seems fitting that you too should receive the Order of Merit, and I will ensure those arrangements are put in place.'

I looked at her and smiled as she gasped, and her eyes brimmed over with delight. 'Thank you, Your Majesty. I am always happy to serve,' she paused and added, 'in any capacity',

They looked at each other. He looked delighted as well, I thought.

Greatly daring, I asked him a question. 'Your Highness, might I enquire as to how you became aware of those events in the autumn? Sir Hector tells me he mentioned them to no one.'

'Ah.' He puffed and smiled and puffed some more. I knew Georgina was working him over with her eyes just by the way he kept looking at her, and I gave her a gentle nudge. He was not a client, for heaven's sake.

After a moment's further thought, he answered. 'My nephew Wilhelm sent me a private letter from Berlin. In it he told me about a personal mission that his close friend the Countess von Straum had undertaken for him in Dorsetshire. Your name was mentioned – very creditably, I might say. He wished me to be aware of the fact that you had done me a great service.'

Well, well. Thank you, Countess. 'But how did you find me?' I asked.

He smiled at this. 'My dear Miss Felix, I am the king. One does have,' he gestured vaguely with his cigar, 'resources.'

There was a silence in the room as he looked at us. Then he continued. 'You know, I cannot recall ever seeing two quite so beautiful ladies in one room before. You are both utterly exquisite.'

'Thank you, Your Majesty,' we cooed at him in unison.

'My nephew mentioned that you, Miss Felix, have a most remarkable tattoo. A concealed tattoo.' His eyes twinkled charmingly. 'The countess recommended that I should ask you to show it to me.'

I heard Georgina unsuccessfully attempt to muffle a giggle.

We were on familiar ground now.

'I do, sir. The countess did not lie.' I thought it might be time for a smoulder, so I gave him a long look full of promise. 'And Georgina has one too,' I added.

He spluttered a little at this and stared. 'Good heavens. Both of you?'

'Oh yes,' I said.

He put his glass down on a table at his elbow. 'I must admit that I would be most interested to see them.'

I stood up and Georgina followed suit, her eyes alive with delight and naughtiness. She reached for the top button at the front of my dress and undid it. As she moved on to the next one, I smiled at the most powerful man in the world and gave him his answer.

'Of course, Your Majesty.'

The End

Printed in Great Britain
by Amazon